The Plug 2: The Power of Choice

By CELLINI

Dedication

To Ray-Ray Varner – Rest in Peace Cuzz!

Acknowledgements

As always, I have to first thank those who mean the most to me, my better half, Mrs. Jana McDaniel, my dear mama Mrs. Emma Hodoh, my step father Doc, my kids Suave Corleone (DYS) and Martinique (Pretty Bosses), my grandparents Charles and Katherine Housel (R.I.P.), my grandfather Samuel Reynolds (R.I.P.), and Dr. Henry C. Kinley, my father Terry Reed (Emperor of the North), my brothers Terry Jr., Richard, Kenny, Marcus, Lorenzo, and my sister Charniece, and my uncles Bunky, Michael, Charles, Brucie, Brudgie (R.I.P.), and Mikey (R.I.P.) my cousins Big Walt, Tonya, Elton, Quashane, O.J., Quiana, and the entire McDaniel, Reed, Higgins, Hodoh, and Varner families.

The legends – Barry Mack, Leo Caldwell, Stan Hamilton, Chaddie Frazier, Tommy Fortson, Donald Leathers (Hollywood), Emery Lee (Mulehead), Michael Starks, Bruce Caldwell (Sleepy), and Jimmy Coppinger (R.I.P.).

Much love to North Akron (Non-Stop Growth) – Mama Charles, Calvin Wells, Sancole Wilson (Flyboy), Lil' Keno, Mike Murda, L. Dawson (my best man), Joe Bushner, Timothy Rogers, Shawn Gray, Wayne Rosser, Roc, Mike J., Yavetta Brockman, Fawn Gatling, Rex Oliver (R.I.P.) Bahati Griffin (R.I.P.), and Tony Secession (R.I.P.).

My Real Figgas – T. LaRocc, Dominque Wilkes, Auntie Margaret, Home Alone, Mary J, Phat Baby (Blue Sky), To Tha Left, Sing G (Addict), L.T. (Tyler Made), Carmika Williams, Tia Hampton, Luchi, Twin, Levi, Sir James, Ziggy (Tru Capaliss), Rachelle Burley, Laylo (Loudpak), Collion, Little (R.I.P.), DoDo (R.I.P.), Chard (R.I.P.), and FREE BEEF!

My Eastside Family – my lil' cousin Bam, T.J. Anderson, Mike Higg, Ed Fetti, Craig Johnstone (Baby Jesus), King Locust (Red Sky), D-Nell, and Randy Cooper.

The 216 – Lil' John Gardner, Mike Vinney, Shoboat (Ballhogg), Mike Davis (10th Ward), Al Richardson (E.C.), Greg Gresham (St. Clair), P.A. (93rd), and Big JoJo (Tarkington).

Special shout out to Norma and Debbie at 2 Live Music in Akron, Nikki's (Cleveland), 7th Heaven (Kansas City), Marcus Bookstore (Oakland), and all the venders nationwide that support Stand Up Media.

My graphic Designer Jon Scott (you are the best in the biz!).

Last, but not least, I would like to thank YOU, the reader for partaking in my vision.

If life teaches us anything, it's that there's nothing that men and women won't do to get power. **Bob Dylan**

Chapter 1

War Games

For Lil' Billy, it was the best of times and the worst of times. He was experiencing the highs and lows of life at the same time. It seemed like on one hand he had laid the foundation for an empire, but on the other hand he felt like death was right around the corner.

Lil' Billy had just gotten back to Akron after spending three months in Atlanta, but so much had happened it felt like three years had passed. Lil' Billy's record label, Stay Solid Records, was on the rise in the underground rap scene and the trip to Atlanta had only increased their momentum.

Stay Solid Records had formed an alliance with the hottest rap label in Atlanta; Black Cartel Entertainment. What began as a partnership in the rap game, now extended to the dope game in a major way. Lil' Billy had made an agreement with Sincere, the leader of the Black Cartel, to accept fifty kilos of cocaine on consignment and that was just the beginning. Sincere had made it clear to Lil' Billy that the load would increase whenever Lil' Billy was ready. In other words, Lil' Billy now had access to hundreds of kilos.

Also while he was in Atlanta Lil' Billy had knocked off a stripper named Molly. Molly was what old players called a million dollar ho. She was a redbone, short, and thick with light brown eyes and long black hair. When it came to tricks she had a catch hand that extended from street tycoons to NBA stars. Molly chose Lil' Billy and followed him back to Akron ready to do whatever was necessary to expand his empire.

Lil' Billy was about halfway back to Akron when the calls started coming in that all hell had broken loose.

Somebody had shot up Lil' Billy's mama's house while his mama and his little brothers and sisters were inside. Luckily no one was hurt, but that was only the beginning. Lil' Billy's entire team was catching hell.

Rick who was the C.E.O. of Stay Solid Records and the legit businessman of the click had also received a call that his mama's house had been shot up. Rick had never played in the streets, so somebody shooting up his house didn't make any sense. On top of that, it was idiotic considering the fact that Rick's uncle was a Summit County Deputy Sheriff.

Lucky, the team's killer, had just been arrested and charged with murder. He was sitting in the county jail on a million dollar cash bond.

T-Man, the fist fighter and ladies' man of the click, had been ambushed coming out of the Delia Market. The gunmen fired off nine shots, but only two hit T-Man, one in the arm and one in the shoulder. T-Man was able to get back inside the store before he was seriously hit.

Unfortunately Cash, the bonafied hustler of the click, wasn't so lucky. He was the victim of a successful ambush. He died on Peckham behind the wheel of his car, his body riddled with fifteen bullets.

When Lil' Billy got the news about Cash, he pulled to the side of the highway and broke down in tears. Too much was happening too fast and Lil' Billy's mind couldn't process it all. Lil' Billy had never had to deal with death before, that was Lucky's line of the work, but now death seemed to be the biggest issue in his life.

Since Lil' Billy didn't know who or what was the source of all the drama, he figured he 'd better move around Akron with caution . To make sure his family was safe, he put them in rooms at the Radisson Hotel downtown. Next he had his gangsta bitch Dasha get out in traffic to see what the word on the street was. Lil' Billy knew if anybody could get info it was Dasha and as usual she didn't disappoint.

"Well where do you want me to begin?" Dasha asked as soon as she entered Lil' Billy's room at the Radisson. Lil' Billy, Rick, T-Man, and Molly had been sitting in the room for hours watching movies. Each one lost in their own thoughts.

"With Cash," Lil' Billy answered.

"Well, it wasn't a robbery," Dasha began, "Cash still had a couple thousand dollars, a track of coke, and his Stay Solid chain on him when he died. It was a hit and the biggest rumor is that it came from the Eastside."

"The Eastside? Cash ain't never had no issue with niggas over there," Lil' Billy said.

"This ain't about just Cash, it's about all of y'all," Dasha paused before continuing, "Niggas over there was feeling a certain way when Stevie and Dre got killed. Now Lucky done got arrested for killing Bulldog. The Eastside niggas supposedly felt like it was time to bite back."

"Okay, but which Eastside niggas? The Eastside ain't

just one unit. They just like the Westside with different sections and different teams."

"The name that keeps coming up is a nigga named Kat. He a money getter from the Wilbeth that just got out the joint. Bulldog was his little cousin and word is that when Bulldog first got killed Kat spoke about retaliation."

"Bulldog was a crack head, do you really think them niggas would go to war over that nigga?"

"Baby I don't know, I'm only telling you what's being said in the streets."

Lil' Billy did the math on what Dasha told him. While it was certainly possible that the Eastside was bringing the drama, they had to be getting some type of help from niggas on the Hill. All the gunplay was taking place on the Hill and there was no way some Eastside niggas could be operating in the hood like that without inside help.

Another thing that weighed on Lil' Billy's mind was where Cash was killed; on Peckham between Wildwood and Madison. That block was controlled by the Gorillaz. The Gorillaz were a street gang that specialized in murder for hire, but the only way they would take a hit on Cash was if their leader, Fat Chad, signed off on it. On top of that, Cash had four and a half ounces of coke on him when he was killed, so he was obviously on his way to make a drop .Cash never rode dirty unless he was in the middle of a drop. If Lil' Billy could find out who called Cash for that work he knew he might be able to solve the whole mystery.

"Dasha, I need you to go to the Eastside and track down Stan," Lil' Billy said, "I need to know what's being said over there."

"Okay," Dasha said.

"You think we can trust Stan?" Rick asked.

"Yeah, Stan wouldn't cross Lucky like that," Lil' Billy replied.

"Stan is all the way solid," T-Man added, "That nigga probably already looking for us."

Stan was from Baird Hill, but he and Lucky had a bond that went back to the days of doing time in juvenile. If anybody knew what was going on the Eastside, it was Stan. He was a major factor over there.

In the midst of all the drama Lil' Billy also had to keep in mind that in a few weeks he would be in possession of fifty kilos that he would need to distribute. Akron was a battlefield, so Lil' Billy figured it was time to relocate to Cleveland until the smoke cleared. Lil' Billy had lived in Cleveland until the age of fourteen and most of his family was still there. He had a cousin his age named Ace from 134th and Kinsman, who was making a few dollars, so Lil' Billy knew it wouldn't be hard for him to set up shop.

Lil' Billy also decided it was time to do what he had been meaning to do for a long time; buy his mama a bigger and nicer house somewhere deep in the suburbs of Cleveland. It was time for his family to experience life outside the hood without having to worry about bullets flying through the windows.

Lil' Billy knew he was at war with somebody, but until he knew who that somebody was he needed to move in the shadows. Once he learned who his opponent was, Lil' Billy planned on using every resource he had to destroy them and everything they loved.

"Damn baby, here it come!" Fat Chad yelled as his legs began to shake. He was receiving the best head he had ever had courtesy of Peaches, the baddest bitch he had ever had.

As soon as Peaches felt Fat Chad's body tense up, she took his dick out of her mouth and stroked it with her hand. Fat Chad immediately shot his seed in Peaches face.

This bitch a boss freak, Fat Chad thought while he looked at the hot and sticky cream running down Peaches' face. Having sex with Peaches was mind blowing for Fat Chad. There was no limit to what she would do in bed. Fat Chad didn't realize it yet, but he was pussy whipped.

While Peaches went to the bathroom to wash her face, Fat Chad sat on the couch plotting his next move. He was playing with fire and he knew it. Sooner or later word would get out that he was behind Cash's murder and all the rest of the drama the Stay Solid Boys were dealing with. Once that happened he would no longer be the hunter, he would become the hunted. But then again, Fat Chad figured if he really thought things out, he could make it where no one ever knew he was the unseen hand.

First and foremost Fat Chad knew he had to continue pushing the blame on the Eastside. To make it more real he would make Kat the sacrifice since he was the main suspect anyway. The Eastside niggas would definitely go to war about Kat and the Stay Solid Boys would be their target. The Stay Solid Boys would be so caught up warring with the Eastside that they wouldn't have time to investigate Cash's murder.

Fat Chad's second issue was Lil' Man. Besides Peaches and Big Mike, Lil' Man was the only one who knew the truth. Fat Chad had used some niggas from Youngstown to pull the trigger, but Lil' Man had helped put all the pieces in place. Fat Chad knew Lil' Man couldn't be trusted, so he needed to keep an eye on him. After things settled down, killing Lil' Man would be the first issue on Fat Chad's agenda.

Meanwhile Peaches was in the bathroom thinking about her own agenda. She knew the easiest way to control a nigga was to make the nigga think he's in control and that's what she was doing.

Her man, Big Mike, who was doing a dime in the joint, thought he was controlling Fat Chad and Fat Chad thought he was controlling his Gorilla movement. In reality, Peaches was controlling the whole show.

It was Peaches who took the five bricks of coke out of Big Mike's stash house and gave them to Lil' Billy, her first love. It was Peaches who after being scorned by Lil' Billy, retaliated by telling Big Mike that Lil' Billy and the Stay Solid Boys had robbed her for the five bricks and a $100,000. Peaches had even orchestrated the breakup between Lil' Billy and his fiancé' Sandy by sending Lil' Billy a copy of a sex tape involving Sandy and Big Mike.

Peaches was a master manipulator. Even though Peaches' lies had led to the death of an innocent man, she felt no remorse. As far as she was concerned, Cash was just collateral damage.

Her real target was Lil' Billy and she wouldn't be satisfied until he was in a casket.

Peaches planned on using the power of pussy to continue manipulating Fat Chad until he did her dirty work; killing Lil' Billy. Afterwards Peaches planned on kicking Fat Chad to the curb. Peaches could tell that Fat Chad was getting attached to her, but she couldn't care less. To Peaches, Fat Chad was just an actor reading a script she had written and eventually all movies have to end.

"Marshall!" The voice shouted through the cell's intercom.

"Yeah," Lucky replied, jarred awake from a nap.

"Attorney visit. Get ready."

Lucky quickly got up and brushed his teeth. When he heard the cell door click, he grabbed the manila envelope containing his legal work and stepped out of his cell. A deputy was standing at the pod's main door to escort Lucky to his attorney visit.

Waiting in one of the attorney conference rooms was Angelo Pellini; the most powerful lawyer in Akron. Pellini was the lawyer of choice for street bosses and the Stay Solid Boys kept him on a retainer.

"Hey Lucky. How ya holding up buddy?" Pellini said, shaking Lucky's hand.

"I'm good, I just hope you got some good news," Lucky replied.

"Well I got some good news and some bad news. What you want first?"

"Gimme the bad news."

"The judge is not gonna budge on your bond."

"Damn, them muthafuckas act like I'm in here for killing the President!"

"My sources downtown tell me you're a suspect in at least six other homicides, so the police are demanding that your bond is kept high."

They tryna take me out the game forever, Lucky thought. He felt like he was fighting for both his physical and mental survival. When he found out Cash had been killed, he did something he hadn't done since he was a kid.

He cried.

The fact that he was in the county jail fighting a murder case was secondary in Lucky's mind. The only thing that mattered to him was killing any and everybody that played a part in Cash 's death, but first he had to shake this case. "Okay, so what's the good news?" he asked.

"Well they only got one witness," Pellini smiled.

"That's it? Who is it?"

"Lucious Thomas. Ya know him?"

Lucky shook his head no.

"I didn't think you would," Pellini said, "he's an elderly guy. He claims that he was looking out of his window and saw you commit the murder."

"In other words, no Lucious Thomas, no case," Lucky said, getting to the heart of the matter.

"Bingo! By the way, stay off the phone as much as possible. They're paying extremely close attention to your phone conversations."

"Okay."

The visit with Pellini ended and Lucky headed back to his cell feeling better about his prospects. There was no doubt in Lucky's mind that Pellini would let Lil' Billy know that the whole case hinged on one man and Lil' Billy would make sure things got handled. Lucious Thomas probably wouldn't make it to court and if he did he would be singing a different tune.

Big Mike walked into the visiting room at Mansfield Correctional feeling like a million bucks. No longer did he feel powerless like a typical nigga in jail. He was making shit on the streets happen in a major way. Thanks to Fat

Chad, he was moving kilos and taking niggas to war when he had to.

Even though he would never admit it, 90% of what Big Mike was doing was driven by fear; fear of losing Peaches.

Every hustler in the city wanted Peaches, from the block bleeders to the bosses. Desired by all the men and envied by all the women, Peaches was hands down the cream of the crop.

Big Mike was a six figure nigga, so he had the resources to keep Peaches living the life of luxury while he was in the joint. Nevertheless, when Peaches told him that the Stay Solid Boys had not only robbed his stash house, but also pistol whipped her, Big Mike knew he had to retaliate. If he didn't bite back, Peaches would think he was weak and leave him for another boss.

With that in mind Big Mike gave Fat Chad the order; kill all the Stay Solid Boys.

Big Mike had been hearing rumors on the rec' yard about the gunplay that had been going down on the Hill, but now that Peaches was here to visit him he would be able to get the real story.

"Hey Baby, what's going on?" Big Mike greeted Peaches with a hug and a kiss.

"Hi Daddy," Peaches replied.

"Is Fat Chad taking care of my business?" Big Mike asked, getting right down to business.

"Well I'm sure you heard about Cash," Peaches began, "T-Man got shot at the Delia Market, but he survived, Lucky in the county fighting a murder case, and Lil' Billy and Rick in Atlanta, so Fat Chad had their mamas' houses shot up."

"Everybody in here think the Eastside is behind everything."

"That's what people think on the street too. You don't want people to know you behind it do you?

"Hell naw!" Big Mike replied, but in reality he did want the streets to know he was calling the shots. He couldn't help it, he had the typical dopeman ego.

"Well anyway," Peaches continued, "Fat Chad said that shit is hot right now and that he'll finish the job when things cool off."

"Okay, tell that nigga, don't shoot up no more houses. That's young boy shit. This is grown man business. But enough about all that, I got some good news baby."

"You coming home!"

"Naw, not yet, but the lawyer looking for a loophole. The good news is that I should have a jack in a few days."

"A jack?" Peaches had no idea what Big Mike was talking about.

"That's a cellphone Baby."

"For real!" Peaches tried to sound excited, but honestly she was unhappy with the news. With a cellphone Big Mike would be able to keep tabs on her 24/7. *I'll never be able to do my thang with this nigga calling all day and night,* Peaches thought.

"By the way, when you leave here stop by the BMW dealership on East Market. They got some car keys waiting on you," Big Mike said.

"Daddy you got my truck!" Peaches exclaimed before leaning over to kiss Big Mike.

"Okay baby be cool, you know we can't kiss until the end of the visit," Big Mike replied. He had been promising Peaches a new truck for the longest, but now that he was back flipping bricks he was ready to splurge. *Wait to them niggas out there hear about this,* he thought. Big Mike knew when the word got out that he had bought Peaches a Beemer truck from the joint he would be the talk of the town.

Big Mike was obsessed with keeping up appearances. Because of that, while he had moved millions of dollars' worth of cocaine through the years, he didn't even have a half a million dollars put up. Everybody thought Big Mike was a millionaire and to him that was more important than actually being a millionaire. Add Peaches to the equation and the stakes were even higher.

Big Mike didn't care what it cost, he planned on holding on to Peaches by any means necessary.

———————

I need to get a new spot, Lil' Man thought while he sat looking out the living room window of his dope house on Peckham. It was from the same dope house that Lil' Man lured Cash to his death.

A makeshift memorial was in place at the spot where Cash was killed, so everyday Lil' Man was reminded of his treachery.

Lil' Man was seventeen years old and a child of the streets. He didn't know who his daddy was and his mama was a crackhead. Lil' Man had, for the most part, been on his own since he was eleven.

It was Cash who first recognized the hustler's spirit in Lil' Man and took him under his wing. Cash had big plans for Lil' Man but with Fat Chad's release from prison there had been a change of plans, at least from Lil' Man's perspective. Lil' Man got down with the Gorillaz.

Fat Chad and his Gorilla' movement were taking over the hood. They had a lot of coke and a rising body count. Cash on the other hand was losing momentum in the hood. He wasn't as visible as he used to be and a few times when Lil' Man needed to re-up, Cash didn't have any coke.

When Fat Chad first approached Lil' Man about setting Cash up for a robbery, he presented Lil' Man with a choice; be true to his oath as a Gorilla or lose his life. When given a choice between life and death most men choose life and that's what Lil' Man did.

Once the play unfolded Lil' Man realized that Fat Chad had tricked him. This wasn't a robbery, it was a murder from the jump and Cash's blood was on Lil' Man's hands.

Lil' Man was in too deep and he knew it. The best he could hope for was that the truth about Cash's death never came out. Meanwhile he had to watch his back in case Fat Chad tried to cross him.

As soon as Fat Chad's Grand National hit the block Lil' Man could hear the growl of the dual exhaust. Lil' Man took his .45 off safety and went outside to meet Fat Chad.

Lil' Man opened the passenger door and glanced in the back seat before he got in the car. "What's good big homie?" he said once he was in the car. "Here hit this Purp," Fat Chad said and passed Lil' Man a lit blunt.

Lil' Man inhaled the potent weed smoke and started coughing.

"Be careful my nigga, that's the real Purp," Fat Chad laughed.

Once Lil' Man regained his composure, Fat Chad got into the real reason he had picked up Lil' Man. "How you feeling?" he asked.

"Shit, I'm cool I guess," Lil' Man replied.

"You guess?"

"I mean what's done is done. I just thought it was supposed to be a robbery."

"It was a robbery, but instead of taking money and dope they took his life."

Fat Chad's remark left Lil' Man speechless, but happy that he had his .45 with him.

"Lil' bruh you made the right decision," Fat Chad continued, "Cash was a cool nigga, but he didn't give a fuck about the hood for real. All he cared about was his niggas. All the work them Stay Solid niggas be playing with, why Cash ain't never throw you a brick?" Fat Chad paused to let what he was saying sink into Lil' Man 's young mind. "I'll tell you why," he continued, "Cause he didn't want you to come up for real. Grab that bag out the backseat."

Lil' Man reached in the backseat and grabbed a black duffle bag. "Open it up," Fat Chad instructed him.

Lil' Man unzipped the duffle bag and pulled out a half-a-brick. He looked at Fat Chad and said "What I owe you for this?"

"You don't owe me shit," Fat Chad replied, "If I'm eating my nigga, you gon eat. That's how Real Gorillaz get down."

I guess I did make the right decision, Lil' Man thought as he stared at the half-a-brick. "You a real ass nigga big homie," he said as he gave Fat Chad some dap.

"Bullshit ain't nothing lil' bruh," Fat Chad said. "You a solid nigga, the type of nigga I want close by my side." *Close enough to kill you when the time is right*, Fat Chad thought.

Meanwhile Lil' Man sat comfortably in the passenger seat, oblivious to the sinister thoughts swirling around next to him. Any guilt he felt about Cash's death, had been wiped away by eighteen ounces of cocaine.

Chapter 2

Down - But Not Out

Cash's funeral service was a gut wrenching affair to say the least.

Paramedics had to be called for Cash's mother. She had a mild heart attack upon seeing her son in a casket. Tionna, Cash's girlfriend had even tried to get in the casket with him.

Throughout the service Lil' Billy had kept a poker face. He knew that someone in attendance at the funeral probably knew what really happened to Cash, so he was searching everyone's eyes for signs of guilt.

There was a heavy police presence at the funeral home and at the cemetery.

While the local police were visible, the feds were there incognito. Some of the biggest factors in Akron's underworld were on the scene, so the feds weren't about to pass up a chance to take their pictures.

Peaches made an appearance at the funeral also. She could see the pain in Lil' Billy's face and it filled her with joy, so much joy that she had to fight back the urge to smile.

Don't worry nigga, you gon see Cash again a lot sooner than you think, she thought bitterly as she stared at Lil' Billy from afar.

After the burial service Lil' Billy slowly made his way towards the limo. He was physically and mentally drained. He hadn't slept in three days and the stress of the situation was wearing on him. He was tired of all the hugs and "call me if you need anything" remarks. Nevertheless, when he saw Fat Chad approach he stopped to hear what he had to say.

Fat Chad hugged Lil' Billy and whispered in his ear "Niggas gon pay for what happened to Cash. I promise you that bruh."

Lil' Billy didn't respond, he just nodded. He wasn't giving anybody any clues to what he was thinking.

Next Stan walked up and Lil' Billy smiled for the first time in days. "I need to talk to you in private," Stan said.

"Yeah I been meaning to link up with you, shit just been hectic," Lil' Billy said.

"I already know my nigga. It's some shady shit going on in this city."

"Yeah I'm hip, but check this out. I'm staying at the Radisson downtown. Meet me there in about two hours. I'll be waiting in the lobby for you."

"Okay, we'll holler then," Stan gave Lil' Billy some dap and a hug.

Lil' Billy was looking forward to hearing what Stan had to say. He knew without a doubt that Stan would give him the raw and uncut, no matter how painful it was.

———————————

If Lucky didn't know how to do anything else, he

knew how to do time. While the typical inmate whined and complained about the conditions of the county jail, Lucky took it all in stride. Lucky's focus was on getting out of jail, not being comfortable while he was there.

Lucky did all his communicating with Lil' Billy through Dasha. She came to see him every week and filled him in on everything he needed to know.

After a visit, Lucky would go back to his cell and mentally dissect everything Dasha had said.
If the rumors about the Eastside's involvement in Cash 's death were true, then in Lucky's eyes he was responsible for Cash 's death since he had not only killed Bulldog, but Stevie and Dre also.

Just like Lil' Billy, Lucky also suspected that the Eastside had got some help from somebody on Hill and that filled him with even more rage. The whole situation was foul and thinking about it gave Lucky headaches.

Lucky was on the county jail's super max pod, 1-C. Most of the inmates in 1-C were facing serious time, so the tension stayed thick. Lucky kept to himself. He spent most of his time in his cell reading. Most of the niggas on the pod were familiar with Lucky's reputation, so everyone gave him his space.

It was the day of Cash's funeral, so Lucky decided to step outside and get some fresh air in hopes of clearing his mind. There were a couple of young niggas already outside talking amongst each other. Lucky took a seat off in the corner by himself and stared up at the sky.

"I'm telling you bruh, them Hill niggas so scared right now, Madison is like a ghost town," one of the young niggas said.

Lucky heard the remark, but kept staring up at the

sky. The young nigga doing the talking was named Lamar . He was from Joy Park projects on the Eastside. Lamar was a typical "in the way" nigga that liked to run off at the mouth about niggas he didn't know .He had no idea that the man sitting quietly in the corner was the infamous killer Lucky. If Lamar had known, he probably would have thought twice about continuing the conversation he was having.

"The Beastside ain't playing no games," Lamar continued, "They hit that nigga Cash like fifteen times!"

Upon hearing this Lucky looked to see who the speaker was. Next he calmly got up and went back inside the pod, while Lamar, oblivious to the danger he was in, continued running his mouth.

Lucky walked to the main door of the pod to see where the deputy was. The deputy was across the hall from the pod, talking to some other deputies with his back turned. Next Lucky looked under the sink where the cleaning supplies were kept and grabbed some rubber gloves. His next stop was the mop closet, where he grabbed a mop wringer.

With mop wringer in hand Lucky quietly stepped back outside. Lamar was so caught up in conversation, he didn't notice Lucky. One of the niggas Lamar was talking to saw the mop wringer in Lucky's hand but by then it was too late. Lucky swung the mop wringer like Barry Bonds swinging a baseball bat and hit Lamar in the back of the head. Lamar fell forward on one knee, when he turned around he was greeted with another blow .This one to the face.

The second blow broke Lamar's nose and knocked him out. While Lamar laid there defenseless, Lucky continued to beat on him. Lucky had snapped and the beating he gave Lamar was brutal.

Amazingly the deputies never turned around, so Lucky beat Lamar until he got tired. Afterwards he put the mop wringer back in the mop closet and rinsed it off. By the time the deputy discovered Lamar laying outside unconscious, Lucky was chillin' in his cell eating a bag of chocolate chip cookies.

When Lil' Billy stepped off the elevator, Stan was already sitting in the lobby waiting on him. They immediately headed up to Lil' Billy's suite.

"You want a drink?" Lil' Billy asked as he held up a bottle of Hennessy, Cash's favorite drink.

"Hell yeah, that's right on time," Stan replied.

Lil' Billy poured two shots of Hennessy. After handing Stan his glass Lil' Billy suggested a toast. "To Cash," they said in unison before downing their shots.

"What's the deal my nigga?" Lil' Billy asked. Whatever Stan had to say he was ready to hear it.

"I had a conversation with Kat," Stan replied, "He saying he ain't behind what happened to Cash."

"I guess he would say that my nigga. Only a fool would take credit for a murder," Lil' Billy said.

"No doubt," Stan continued, "But the things he told me make a lot of sense."

"Like what?"

"Well cousin or no cousin Bulldog, was a crackhead and he did his family bad chasing that shit. He broke in Kat's mama's house while Kat was in the joint, so there ain't no way Kat would put his life on the line for Bulldog."

What Stan said made sense, but Lil' Billy was still

skeptical. "That nigga might just be feeding you that story cause he know you fuck with us," Lil' Billy said.

"Yeah anything is possible, but that ain't Kat's style. Kat is a no nonsense type of guy. He wouldn't have hunted me down just to tell me a lie."

Lil' Billy thought about what Stan was saying. He knew Stan knew the Eastside like the back of his hand. On top of that Stan was solid all across the board. If he thought Kat had anything to do with Cash's murder, that's what he would say. Nevertheless the questioned remained, if Kat didn't put the play down on Cash, who did?

"If you want my honest opinion," Stan began, "I think this was a Hill play."

Lil' Billy was thinking the same thing, but the question of who, still remained. The drama was bigger than Cash. Somebody was coming at all of the Stay Solid Boys. Lil' Billy knew the worst thing he could do was react off of emotion. He had to think strategically. Patience was the key. Eventually everything would come out, he just had to let it come naturally. On top of that, Lil' Billy knew his limitations; he wasn't a killer.

Murder was Lucky's game and with Lucky in jail Lil' Billy wasn't in a position to go to war. With that in mind Lil' Billy decided that he needed to focus first on relocating to Cleveland and then getting Lucky out of jail. Once Lucky was back on the streets, then they could get down to the nitty-gritty of avenging Cash's death.

———————

With all the drama surrounding the Stay Solid Boys, Peaches' new truck didn't receive all the attention she would have liked, so in an attempt to get the streets talking, Peaches decided to be more visible for a few days. She was an attention whore. She had to have it.

The hand car wash on Copley Road was the go to spot for the West Akron hustlers who wanted to put their rides on public display. When Peaches pulled up in her royal blue BMW truck, she was immediately the star of the show.

Every hustler in attendance at the car wash had on his game face, in hopes of catching Peaches' eye.

Meanwhile, Peaches basked in the attention she was receiving. She was always at her best when she was at the center of things. While she strutted around switching her voluptuous ass and being flirtatious, a few niggas got on the phone to put the word out that Peaches was on the set.

"Make sure y'all do a good job on the rims. Y'all know how much I like shiny things," Peaches said to everyone's amusement.

"Baby when I get through, you gon be able to see the reflection of yo pretty face in these rims," one of the workers replied.

Peaches spent the next few minutes trading one-liners with the various players on the scene. Even though none of them had a chance of scoring, Peaches enjoyed listening to niggas shoot their shot.

"Damn, two Beemer trucks in one day!" A younger worker exclaimed, causing everyone to take notice of another BMW X5 truck that was now on the scene.

This Beemer truck was cocaine white and while Peaches' truck was sitting on twenty-inch rims, this truck was sitting on 22's.

Everyone at the car wash stood in awe as Dasha and Molly got out of the truck, dressed head to toe in designer clothing. Dasha was wearing a Dereon blouse and jeans with a Gucci handbag and Christian Louboutin pumps. Meanwhile Molly was wearing Louie Vuitton, carrying a $10,000 Hermes handbag and had Jimmy Choo's on her feet.

Peaches stood there staring like everyone else was. She was at a loss of words. Since they were kids, Peaches had always felt above Dasha, but today was different. Peaches had never seen Dasha shining so bright and the glare was hurting her eyes.

Most of the niggas at the car wash knew Dasha, so they all made their way over to her to say hello. Dasha could hold her own, but it was Molly who stole the show. Molly was a redbone, with the thickness that southern women are known for. Her whole demeanor was sexual. Molly was used to dealing with millionaires, so hustlers at the car wash were no match for her.

"Damn Dasha, I guess you been too busy to call yo sister since you been back huh?" Peaches said in an attempt to shift some of the attention back to herself.

"Ah girl, don't take it like that. I just been caught up in what happened to Cash," Dasha replied.

"Yeah, that was some fucked up shit."

"It sho was, but one thing I know for sure, is that whatever is done in the dark eventually comes to the light."

Dasha's remark unsettled Peaches, so Peaches quickly changed the subject. "Well how was Atlanta?" she asked.

"It was beautiful. I can't wait to go back," Dasha said, "By the way, this is my girlfriend Molly. Molly this is Peaches."

Peaches nodded and gave Molly a fake smile, while looking her up and down. *This bitch toting a Hermes bag!* Peaches thought, as usual looking at life through a materialistic lens.

Meanwhile, Molly stood there staring at Peaches like she wanted to eat her alive. The sexual energy coming from Molly was overwhelming. Peaches couldn't tell if she was irritated or aroused. Because of that, she made a mental note to stay away from Molly.

Dasha could see how uncomfortable Peaches was and even though she enjoyed watching her squirm, she cut the show short, so she could pick Peaches brain for information.

"Molly, Baby could you grab me a cranberry juice from that store across the street?" Dasha asked.

"Is that all you want?" Molly replied.

"Yeah, that's it."

Molly gave Dasha a passionate kiss before heading to the store. The kiss drew whistles and applause from the men at the car wash, while Peaches shook her head. "I guess you all out with it now, huh?" she asked.

"Shit girl, don't knock it till you try it," Dasha replied, "But anyway, who killed Cash?"
The abruptness of Dasha's question caught Peaches off guard. "They say the Eastside did it," Peaches answered .

"Yeah but they had to have some help from somebody on the Hill."

"You really think somebody from the Hill would cross Cash like that?"

"Why wouldn't they? That Hill shit don't mean nothing no more, it's every man for himself," Dasha paused then added, "The truth gon eventually come out and when it do shit gon get real in the city."

Dasha's remark bothered Peaches somewhat because it brought her back to the reality of what she was caught up in. Peaches was playing the most dangerous game there was. She was playing the game of death. If all the scheming she was doing in the dark ever came to the light she would lose her life.

For Peaches, the key was keeping up with Lil' Billy. She knew she would never be able to get close to him herself, but maybe through Dasha she could get close enough to at least know where he was laying his head at.

"How is Lil' Billy holding up?" Peaches asked.

"He dealing with the situation like any solid nigga would. He ain't about to let nothing or nobody stop him," Dasha replied.

"Well I know we ain't on the best of terms, but let him know that I'm praying for him."

"I'll sure do that."

Peaches looked at her watch. "Girl, I gotta get outta here. I got a nail appointment and I'm running late," she said. "Make sure you call me, so we can get together. I wanna hear all about Atlanta."

"Okay, maybe we can hookup next week," Dasha said.

Molly walked up right as Peaches was leaving, "I want that bitch," she said referring to Peaches.

"I know you do, but Baby right now we gotta stay focused," Dasha said while waving goodbye to Peaches.

Lil' Billy had given Dasha and Molly an important and Dasha wasn't going to let anything or anybody get in the way of completing that mission.

———————

"Damn Baby, why you ain't wake me up?" Kat asked while yawning and stretching.

"I thought you was gon spend the night," Tiny replied as she rubbed on Kat's chest.

"Baby you know it's too much bullshit going on right now. I can't be fucking around on this Westside like that," Kat said. He was extremely paranoid. His name was ringing heavy in the streets for all the wrong reasons.

Kat hadn't been out of the joint for a year yet and all of a sudden he was being accused of a murder he had nothing to do with. Kat knew eventually the truth would come out, but in the meanwhile he was moving with extra caution.

Shit it's four in the morning! Kat thought as he looked at his watch. Pretty soon it would be daylight and Kat knew it would be dangerous to be seen on the Westside in the daytime.

Tiny was Kat's stripper of choice. He usually fucked her three or four times a week. Their usual routine was to get a hotel room, pop a few pills, and have porno style sex for the rest of the night.

Ever since Cash's murder, Kat hadn't been able to hook up with Tiny like he wanted to. He had been too occupied with clearing his name. Kat was feeling a lot of stress and figured sex with Tiny would be the perfect way to unwind.

Kat picked Tiny up at Summit Mall and drove to Montrose to get a hotel room. When Kat walked into the manager's office to pay for the room, he ran into a nigga named Dean. Dean wasn't a Stay Solid Boy, but he was a Hill nigga from Wildwood and seeing him made Kat even more paranoid.

After being spotted by Dean, Kat wasn't about to get a room in Montrose, so Tiny suggested that they just go to her house. She lived on Hartford, a quiet residential street on the Westside. Tiny assured Kat that nobody was there or would be coming by, so it was a safe place to chill.

Kat went to Tiny's house with the intention to bust a couple of nuts and slide back to the Eastside, but ended up falling asleep from exhaustion.

"Baby, why don't you just chill for a few more hours and I'll cook you breakfast. You safe here, I told you that," Tiny said.

"I understand what you saying, but now ain't the time to be taking chances," Kat replied, "When all this shit blow over, we'll be able to spend more time together. I promise you that." Kat leaned over and gave Tiny a kiss, then quickly got dressed.

Tiny walked Kat to the front door and gave him another kiss before opening the door. Before stepping outside, Kat looked both ways up and down the street. Confident that the coast was clear, Kat took his own gun off safety and walked to his car, which was parked on the street.

Once Kat was in his car he sat his gun on the passenger seat and plugged his cell phone into the car charger. After checking his missed calls, Kat started up the car. He heard a car coming down the street behind him so he checked the driver's side mirror but was blinded by the bright headlights.

By the time Kat regained his focus, a minivan had pulled up beside his car with an AK-47 hanging out of the passenger window.

Kat was left dusted and disgusted. The bullets from the assault rifle tore his body to shreds. Meanwhile, Tiny shut her front door without a shred of remorse for what she had just done.

Chapter 3

Making Moves

Since moving to Akron at the age of fourteen, Lil'
Billy had only been back to Cleveland a hand full of times.
Nevertheless, whenever he did visit Cleveland, he always
made sure he linked up with his favorite cousin Ace. When
they were kids Lil' Billy and Ace would spend the night over
each other's house every chance they got.

Ace was from an area of Cleveland known as Up
The Way. His block was 134th and Kinsman to be exact.
Ace was a certified street nigga. From gangsta' shit to
getting money, he had done it all.

Lil' Billy's Aunt Helen, Ace's mom, lived on Abell,
a side street off of Kinsman. Lil' Billy and Ace met over
there to get caught up on things.

"Damn cuzz, I didn't know it be going down like that
in Akron," Ace said after listening to Lil' Billy tell him
about all the drama that was going on.

"Yeah it's a little city, but it's dangerous," Lil' Billy
replied.

"Well just so you know, I got killers on the payroll

that don't mind making road trips."

Lil' Billy shook his head and said, "It ain't time for that yet, but it will be one day." Lil' Billy paused then continued, "How you doing on the hustle side?" he asked.

"I got damn near eighty bands in the stash and I been copping two bricks at a time," Ace replied, "I'm the go-to-guy for all the young niggas on 134th and Kinsman, plus I got a lil' Puerto Rican bitch that dance at this strip club on 93rd and Nelson. She been turning a whole lotta paper for me lately."

"Well how you feel about expanding yo operation?"

"Talk to me Cuz. You know I'm down for whatever."

"Good, cause I got a major league plug and soon as I give the green light they gon deliver fifty bricks."

"Damn family!" Ace exclaimed, "I knew you could hoop, but you ballin' for real."

"Shit nigga you bout to ball with me," Lil' Billy said, "I need you to play point guard for me. I'm tryna be low key and keep building my rap label, so while I'm in the Land I wanna stay behind the scenes."

"Okay, gimme the numbers on the fifty bricks."

"My plug want fifteen a brick, so we can let 'em go for twenty and split the extra $250,000.I'm gon shoot ten bricks to my people in Akron, but the other forty is yours to move. I can increase the order to a hundred bricks or more whenever we ready."

Ace did the math in his head before saying, "I got niggas up and down Kinsman, plus over on Buckeye and Harvard, so I ain't gon have no trouble moving that shit."

"What about stash houses?" Lil' Billy asked.

"I got a nice low key spot out in University

Heights," Ace replied.

"Good, so once I find a place to lay my head, we'll be ready to roll."

"I thought you copped a house in Pepper Pike?"

"I did, but that was a gift to Mama, I need to find a nice bachelor spot."

"You might wanna check out the Qua55."

"What's that?"

"Some luxury apartments downtown on the Lake."

"They let niggas live there?"

"Hell yeah, if the nigga's paper is right. A lot of Browns and Cavs players live there, so they used to dealing with niggas with money."

Niggas with money.

The statement resonated in Lil' Billy's mind as the realization hit him that he was now a nigga with money. Being back in Cleveland meant that he was going to make even more money and it was going to come even faster. Nevertheless, he needed to be prepared for everything cause like Biggie said; *Mo money usually means Mo problems.*

———————

There was a capacity crowd at the strip club, but when Dasha and Molly walked in, all eyes were on them. Even some of the strippers stopped shaking their ass momentarily to take a look at the dynamic duo. Word was all over the Westside that Dasha was sliding thru the town in a Beemer truck with a bad bitch from Atlanta riding shotgun. The fact that the bad bitch in question was Molly created even more buzz. Most niggas that had been to Atlanta were familiar with Molly. She was a stripper legend.

Besides all the attention her and Molly were

receiving, Dasha could also feel the high level of tension in the air. Kat had just got killed on the Westside, which everyone assumed to be retaliation for Cash's murder. Now the underworld was expecting the pendulum to swing the other way. Kat was a factor, so street politics dictated that someone would have to answer for his murder.

As Dasha and Molly approached the bar, Jack the owner of the strip club approached them with a big smile on his face, "Chocolate City!" he exclaimed referring to Dasha. "Welcome home baby," Jack gave Dasha a hug.

"Jack this is Molly. Molly this is Jack," Dasha said.

"Molly from Sin City in Atlanta?" Jack asked.

"The one and only," Molly smiled.

"Well let me say it's an honor and a pleasure to have a legend such as yourself in my establishment," Jack said.

"Thank you." Molly replied.

"Jack you think we can talk in private?" Dasha asked.

"We sho can baby," Jack replied then looked at his barmaid Lexus, "Lexus baby if anybody ask, I'm in a important meeting and don't want to be disturbed."

"Okay boss," Lexus said.

Jack led Dasha and Molly to his office, "Have a seat," he said as he sat down behind his desk. Jack bit the tip off a cigar, lit it up, and then asked Dasha, "What's on yo mind?"

"Cash is on my mind, all day every day," Dasha replied.

Jack got up and walked to the door of his office and locked it. "Dasha I hope you understand, I wanna die from old age," he said.

"Jack I promise I won't repeat anything you tell me,

except to Lil' Billy of course," Dasha assured him.

"I don't think the Eastside killed Cash."

"What makes you say that?"

"Over fifty years of street knowledge makes me say that." Jack went on to tell Dasha about some of the things that had been going on at the strip club.

Before going to Atlanta, Lil' Billy had controlled the drug traffic at the strip club, but right before he left he put Lucky in charge. According to Jack, Fat Chad and his Gorillaz had begun making their presence felt at the club and that had led to tension between them and Lucky. Fat Chad had even been trying to backdoor the Stay Solid Boys and buy the strip club from Jack.

"So what you telling me is that Fat Chad ain't as cool with Stay Solid as he tries to portray?" Dasha asked after hearing Jack's story.

"I don't think so, but the plot thickens," Jack paused, "Earlier today I overheard a discussion between one of my dancers, Tiny and Lil' Man."

"Cash's young nigga Lil' Man?"

"Yep."

"About what?"

"Well I only got bits and pieces, but I heard Tiny say, tell Fat Chad I want my money."

"Didn't Kat get killed outside Tiny's house?"

Jack nodded yes.

While Dasha reflected on what Jack had just said there was a loud knock at the door.

"I'm in a meeting!" Jack yelled.

"We got a problem, you need to come out here!" Lexus hollered back from the other side of the door.

When Jack stepped out of the office he saw a crowd

gathered in the VIP area, so he headed that way. As usual, it was the Gorillaz who were at the center of the drama.

"Bitch I told you I ain't want no dance from yo crackhead ass!" Lil' Man barked as he smacked Jazzy viciously in her face, knocking her to the floor. Jazzy used to be one of Jack's top dancers but the powder and pills had taken a toll on her. The death of her baby's daddy Joe had only accelerated her decline and now she was rumored to be smoking crack.

While Jazzy was curled up in a ball on the floor, Lil' Man stood over her. "Man I'm bout to piss on this stanking ass bitch!" he said while unbuckling his belt.

"Yeah make it rain on that ho for real!" One of the Gorillaz chimed in. Jack had seen enough. "You can piss in the toilet, not on my dancers," he said as he helped Jazzy to her feet.

"Nigga I'm a Gorilla. I can piss wherever I want to!" Lil' Man fired back.

Jack paused and weighed the pros and cons of punching Lil' Man in his face. He knew the odds weren't in his favor, so he had no choice but to swallow his pride. *You'll bark up the wrong tree eventually lil' nigga*, Jack thought as he retreated to his office with Jazzy.

Meanwhile, Dasha sat back in the cut quietly analyzing everything she had just seen and heard.

———————

Detective Bryant's usual style of investigating homicides was to focus on the freshest murders first. He believed that ninety percent of the information needed to solve a murder case came within the first 48 hours after the murder occurred.

Under normal circumstances Detective Bryant would be focused on Kat's murder, but besides interviewing a few people who lived near the murder scene, he hadn't actively pursued any new leads.

Detective Bryant was obsessed with the Stay Solid Boys, Lucky in particular. Because of that he had put everything else on the backburner. He had been able to arrest Lucky on one murder, but for Detective Bryant that wasn't enough .He knew Lucky had a graveyard under his belt and he believed that at least four of the murders committed by Lucky were hits ordered by Lil' Billy. Taking down Lil' Billy, Lucky and anybody else affiliated with the Stay Solid Boys had become the defining theme in Detective Bryant's life.

Detective Bryant thought that with Lucky in jail it would be easier to get info about his past crimes, but that wasn't the case. When asked about Lucky, people were still being tight lipped.

Detective Bryant's most reliable source of information was a barber named L.A. L.A. was the barber of choice for most of the drug kingpins in Akron.

For over a decade L.A. had been giving Detective Bryant the inside scoop on Akron's underworld, but recently L.A. had disappeared. At first Detective Bryant feared the worst, but then he received a tip that L.A. was out of town. He had recently received another tip that L.A. was back in town but keeping a low profile. In response to that tip, Detective Bryant had initiated a stakeout of L.A.'s mama's house.

Three days after the stakeout began, L.A .showed up at his mama's house. Detective Bryant waited about ten minutes before approaching the door. Ironically, as soon as

Detective Bryant was about to knock on the door, it opened. L.A. stood there frozen like a deer caught in the headlights.

Detective Bryant smiled, "You ain't in a hurry are you?" he asked.

L.A. swallowed hard and replied, "I was gon' call you."

"I'm sure you were," Detective Bryant smirked, "but anyway we need to talk. Can I come in?"

"Yeah come on."

Detective Bryant followed L.A. to the living room and took a seat. "L.A. you been missing in action, what's your problem?" Detective Bryant asked.

"Ain't no problem, I'm just tryna change my life," L.A. replied.

"Change your life how?"

"I'm through with the dope game."

"Okay, so you've had spiritual awakening, but what does that have to do with you staying in contact with me?"

"If I ain't in the mix no more that means I don't have any info for you." L.A. wasn't really trying to stop hustling, he just wanted to stop being an informant for Detective Bryant. Lately Detective Bryant had been pressing L.A. to gather info on Lucky and L.A. was nervous. He didn't mind snitching on drug dealers, but snitching on killers was dangerous.

"L.A. I think you got a misunderstanding about our relationship," Detective Bryant began, "You work for me until I say you're done."

Detective Bryant let his words sink in and then continued, "Now before you think about going missing again check this out, not only will I stick you with a major drug offender case, but I'll make sure the Beacon Journal runs a story about how you've been an informant for the past decade."

"Come on man, I'll get killed," L.A. protested.

"Yeah I know, so if you wanna live stop playing games with me."

"You already got Lucky on a murder case, what else do you want?"

"I want info about his other murders and I want it fast."

Detective Bryant had L.A. boxed in and L.A. knew it. Since he had no way out, L.A.'s mental wheels started turning in hopes of coming up with a way of giving Detective Bryant what he wanted.

"Okay look, I think I got a avenue to find out some things about Lucky, but you need to back off a little bit. I can't operate under the pressure," L.A. said.

"Don't worry buddy, there'll be no pressure from me," Detective Bryant said with a smile.

Yeah whatever, L.A. thought. He had reached the point where he hated Detective Bryant's guts. Detective Bryant had tricked L.A. for years into thinking they had a real friendship. Now that L.A. knew the truth he felt emotionally scarred. L.A. was a vindictive creature and while Detective Bryant had the upper hand at the time, L.A. was determined to have the last laugh.

Lil' Billy, T-Man, and Rick had been moving stuff from Lil' Billy's mama's house in Akron to her new home in Pepper Pike since six in the morning. Now at six in the evening they were finally on the last load.

"Man I swear y'all had enough stuff in that house to

fill up two houses," T-Man said as he shut the back of the U-Haul truck.

Lil' Billy laughed, "You know Mama don't believe in throwing nothing away."

"Let's chill for a sec before we get on the road. My body starting to ache," T-Man said.

"Where yo pain pills?" Rick asked.

"I been selling them muthafuckas," T-Man replied. "I ain't tryna be strung out on pain killers."

"Yeah, I can feel you on that," Lil' Billy said. He had been prescribed pain pills too after he was shot and just like T-Man he had refused to take them.

The fellas sat on the porch for a while talking about the good old days, but talking about the past meant talking about Cash and that was too painful for them. Because of that, the conversation switched to the future.

"I been meaning to tell y'all," T-Man began, "I'm moving to Columbus in a couple of weeks."

"Who you know down there?" Lil' Billy asked.

"My daughter's mama Tammy, got family down there."

"I heard it's a lot of money in Columbus, so whenever you ready I'll shoot you a couple bricks."

T-Man shook his head, "Thanks , but no thanks my nigga, I got a job waiting on me, so I ain't gon fuck around in the game."

"You a smart man. I'm proud of you bruh," Rick said and gave T-Man some dap.

"What y'all niggas got planned besides taking over the rap industry?" T-Man asked.

"Right now, I'm focused on putting together this Stay Solid Black Cartel concert," Rick replied.

"Y'all gon throw it in Akron?"

"Naw we gon have it in Cleveland. This gon be Young Skrilla's first show in Ohio, so I'm thinking we might be able to fill up an arena."

"Well make sure y'all let me know when it's going down." T-Man paused then turned to Lil' Billy, "What's up nigga, why you so quiet?"

"Ain't shit my nigga, I'm just thinking. A nigga got a lot on his plate right now, ya feel me?" Lil' Billy replied.

"Yeah I feel you." T-Man nodded. They were all dealing with the pain of Cash's death, but while T-Man saw it as a sign to at least try to put the street life behind him, Lil' Billy was taking the opposite approach.

Lil' Billy had decided that the best way to honor Cash's memory was to do what Cash would want him to do = ball hard. In a few days Lil' Billy would be picking up fifty kilos of cocaine, fifty kilos that were originally meant to be placed in Cash's hands. Because of that, Lil' Billy felt obligated to not only stay in the game, but to win in the game.

T-Man on the other hand was through with the game, at least for now. When it came to hustling, Cash had always been his backbone and now that Cash was dead, T-Man didn't have it in him to keep hustling. On top of that, T-Man didn't play with guns, but he knew if he stayed in Akron he would have to carry a gun just to survive. T-Man had come to the conclusion that it was time for him to take a step back until the smoke cleared. The future was full of unknowns, but one thing for certain was that Lil' Billy was working hard to find out who killed Cash and once he did, T-Man would be back on the frontline.

Chapter 4

Back In Business

"Ooh Baby, you taste so good," Dasha purred as she kissed Molly passionately on the neck.

Since coming back from Atlanta, Dasha had been so busy she hadn't had a chance to be intimate with Molly and she was overflowing with desire.

While Molly moaned with pleasure Dasha ran her tongue down to Molly's nipples and began sucking on them. Dasha was totally in tune with Molly sexually, so she knew when to suck, when to lick, and when to bite. By the time Dasha's tongue reached Molly's pussy, the pussy was soaking wet with anticipation. Dasha spread Molly's pussy lips and began licking the walls which caused Molly's legs to shiver. Molly's reaction aroused Dasha even more and she began working her tongue even faster.

As Dasha moved in on Molly's clit, she lifted up and pinned Molly's legs all the way back.

"Oh yes!" Molly screamed out in ecstasy while Dasha sucked on her clit like a baby sucking on a pacifier. Molly could feel her orgasmic tide rising, so she grabbed

Dasha's head and prepared to ride the wave. Molly wanted to scream but when she opened her mouth nothing came out. The sheer joy of the orgasm had left her speechless.

Molly's body jerked uncontrollably for thirty seconds in response to the multiple orgasms she was having. She felt like she was floating and after the wave of orgasms subsided she laid there in a daze holding Dasha tight.

Meanwhile, even though Dasha's body was next to Molly's, her mind was somewhere else.

Dasha was happy to be back home, but she could tell that things were not the same. Beside her conversation with Jack, Dasha felt like everything else she was hearing was synthetic. Nobody was telling Dasha what she needed to hear, only what they wanted her to hear. Dasha was getting frustrated, but she knew she couldn't make too much noise. Lil' Billy had given Dasha strict instructions about how he wanted her and Molly to move around Akron. He told her not to ask questions about Cash's murder, just let all the info come to her naturally, so that's what Dasha had been doing.

Dasha had spent a lot of time analyzing the things Jack had told her, but was unable to reach any conclusions. She had known Fat Chad since they were kids and she had never known him to be a snake type nigga. Trying to buy the strip club was one thing, but killing Cash was something else completely. On top of that it was Fat Chad and his Gorillaz who were doing all the retaliating in regards to Cash. Somebody on the Hill may have been helping the Eastside, but Dasha didn't think that it was Fat Chad.

Dasha's period of analysis was interrupted by the sound of her cellphone. *I wonder what this bitch want,* Dasha thought when she saw it was Peaches' number. Dasha wasn't really in the mood to talk to Peaches, but she answered the phone anyway.

"Hello," she said.

"Hey girl, what's up?" Peaches asked.

"Nothing, half asleep," Dasha replied dryly. She could tell by the excitement in Peaches' voice that Peaches had breaking news to report.

"Guess who got killed," Peaches said, confirming Dasha's suspicions.

"Who?"

"Tiny."

"Tiny the stripper?"

"Yeah girl, ain't that crazy?"

"What happened?" Dasha asked, somewhat floored by what she was hearing.

"They say she was getting off work at the strip club and somebody shot her in the head while she was getting in her car," Peaches replied.

Damn these niggas killing bitches too! Dasha thought.

"I swear it's getting to the point where I'm scared to even leave the house," Peaches continued, "but anyway, what you doing this weekend?"

"Nothing really. Why?" Dasha asked.

"I was thinking maybe we could get a bottle and hangout for a little while."

"We can do that, just call me."

"Oh, by the way, if it ain't a problem I would prefer it if you came by yourself." Peaches was in no hurry to encounter Molly again.

"That's not a problem. I'll come by myself," Dasha smiled and looked at Molly.

"Who was that?" Molly asked after Dasha hung up

the phone.

"That was Peaches," Dasha replied.

"Ooh Peaches… just hearing her name makes my pussy tingle," Molly said seductively.

"Baby you done scared her, you was too aggressive that day at the car wash."

Molly laughed, "You think that was aggressive, wait until I really turn it up on that bitch!"

After Lil' Billy moved into an apartment at the Qua 55 he was ready to get down to business. Using the cellphone he was given specifically for Black Cartel business. Lil' Billy called Atlanta and gave the green light. 48 hours later Lil' Billy received a callback from Atlanta and was given address to a warehouse in Macedonia, a small industrial suburb located halfway between Akron and Cleveland.

One of Ace's coke customers owned a carpet cleaning business, so in an attempt to be low key, Lil' Billy and Ace used one of the company vans for the trip to Macedonia. The police in Macedonia were known for pulling Blacks over, so Lil' Billy knew he had to have his fronts up.

Lil' Billy was good with directions, so it didn't take him long to find the warehouse. It was a typical warehouse surrounded by shipping containers and cargo vans. The warehouse bustled with activity, with forklifts moving to and fro. Lil' Billy couldn't help but wonder how much of the activity going on was illegal.

Lil' Billy pulled the van up to the front gate and pressed the button on the intercom. A few seconds passed before there was a response.

"Yeah!" A voice yelled through the intercom.

"I'm here to pick up order 720," Lil' Billy said.

There was no response and for a second Lil' Billy hoped he hadn't given the wrong order number, but those worries were put to rest when the front gate slid open.

Lil' Billy drove through the gate. Up ahead he saw a heavy set older white guy waving for him to come that way. The man was wearing a hard hat, flannel shirt, and work boots. In other words, he looked nothing like a drug dealer.

"Order number," the man said to Lil' Billy in a no nonsense tone.

"720," Lil' Billy replied.

The man stepped away from the van and spoke into a two-way radio. About two minutes later another white man driving a forklift loaded with a large box approached.

Lil' Billy and Ace got out and opened the back of the van. The box was stamped with the words *Columbian Select* and Lil' Billy could smell the coffee grounds that were inside the box.

"Better than Taster's Choice," the man on the forklift said in an attempt at humor.

Lil' Billy ignored the remark and finished loading the box into the back of the van. Being that he was a Black man now in possession of fifty kilos of cocaine, Lil' Billy wasn't in the mood for small talk.

Lil' Billy and Ace were both on pins and needles and the tension only increased now that it was time for the most dangerous part of the whole process, transporting the cocaine from the warehouse to the stash house.

With fifty kilos of cocaine in the van, the twenty minute drive from the warehouse in Macedonia to the stash house in University Heights felt like twenty hours. Lil' Billy and Ace rode in complete silence. Lil' Billy focused on staying within the speed limit, while Ace kept his eyes on the rear view mirror. When they finally pulled into the driveway of the stash house they breathed a collective sigh of relief, each of them thinking the same thing… *we made it!*

———————————

About an hour after Lil' Billy made the pick-up, Sincere received word in Atlanta.

Considering the fact that Sincere was moving thousands of kilos on a regular basis, he usually wouldn't keep up with a fifty kilo pick-up. What made this pick-up so different were the high hopes Sincere had for Lil' Billy.

Sincere had a net worth of close to 400 million dollars and the foundation of his empire was drug trafficking. Besides his fortune, the other thing that separated Sincere from the other Black kingpins was his connect. Sincere had a direct line to Columbia, the largest cocaine producing country in the world, and the leader of Columbia's largest drug cartel, Angel Salazar.

After meeting each other at the 96 Atlanta Summer Olympics, Sincere and .Angel began a business relationship that proved to be a financial windfall for both of them. Now Sincere was ready to do something most hustlers never got a chance to do; walk away from the game on top.

Angel was unhappy with Sincere's plans to become a legitimate businessman. His attitude was, why fuck up a good thing? Angel's initial reaction when he first heard that Sincere wanted to get out of the game was to have him killed As far as Angel was concerned, Sincere knew too much plus without Sincere, Angel's American cocaine trafficking operation would come to a standstill. Who else could move thousands of kilos with the speed and efficiency that Sincere did?

After giving it much thought Angel gave Sincere an ultimatum; find someone to take his place and Angel would let him get out of the game with his life. There was only one hitch, if the person Sincere chose turned out to be a bad apple, Sincere would still lose his life.

Therefore with his life literally hanging in the balance, Sincere began the process of finding his replacement.

When Sincere met Lil' Billy, he knew instantly that he had found his man. In Sincere's opinion Lil' Billy had all the qualities necessary to be a boss, but he couldn't be 100% certain until he saw how Lil' Billy handled larger amounts of cocaine.

As Sincere reflected on his life in general, he was pleased with the position he was in. He was close to leaving the dope game with a fortune and he had finally met the woman who seemed liked the final piece of the puzzle. *Pretty soon you'll be my wife*, Sincere thought as he watched Cassandra swim laps in the pool.

Sincere was relaxing in a lounge chair under one of the London plane trees that surrounded the pool area at his mansion. Sincere had been taking phone calls and reading the newspaper while Cassandra took her morning swim.

Cassandra, whose real name was Sandy, liked to use her morning swim as a time to collect her thoughts, because to say she had a lot on her mind would be a major understatement. Sandy was living a double life.

Sincere may have thought meeting Sandy was just a chance encounter, but it wasn't, it was all by design.

What Sincere didn't know was that Sandy had a son by his brother Cedric, the same brother that Sincere killed many years ago and collected $100,000 for doing it. He took the $100, 000, bought ten kilos of coke from a Cali Crip and never looked back. So much time had passed that Sincere thought his treacherous act would remain buried in the past, but what's done in the dark eventually comes to the light.

The last time Sandy had returned to her hometown of Detroit, an old school hustler named Sugarman had told her the shocking truth about Cedric's death.

At the time Sandy was engaged to Lil' Billy, so she pushed the drama of what happened to Cedric to the back of her mind, but after her and Lil' Billy broke up, Sandy returned mentally to the world that made her – the world of her and Cedric.

For Sandy, being back in that world meant finding out what really happened to Cedric. She had to know if Sincere's empire was built on the blood of the man who had fathered her only child.

After Sandy and Lil' Billy broke off their engagement, Sincere became Sandy's focus, so after a quick trip to Detroit to see her son, she headed to Atlanta. Once there, Sandy put herself in position to meet Sincere.

Sincere may have been used to being with some of the most beautiful women in the world, but he still fell for Sandy hook, line, and sinker. Sandy was at the top of her game, using everything in her repertoire to blow Sincere's mind. Sincere hadn't said as much, but Sandy knew she was gaining his complete trust and that was her goal. There was only one problem; Lil' Billy.

Sandy was still in love with Lil' Billy. Their breakup had been so abrupt that Sandy hadn't been able to get any closure. The fact that Lil' Billy was now dealing with Sincere only complicated matters. Sandy had figured that since her and Lil' Billy would be in different cities, that closure would eventually come as a result of separation. Now Sandy realized that she might be dealing with Lil' Billy again a lot sooner than she expected which presented a major problem.

If Sincere found out about her past with Lil' Billy it would blow Sandy's cover and possibly cost her life. Sincere was obviously a dangerous man, he had killed his own brother.

Sandy was playing a high-stakes game of chess, so she had to think many moves ahead. Once Sincere turned over his Columbian plug to Lil' Billy, their dealings with each other would end. In the meanwhile Sandy needed to stay in the background and make sure that she didn't cross paths with Lil' Billy. Any unresolved issues Sandy had with Lil' Billy would have to be worked out at a later date. Right now the only issue that mattered to Sandy was the mystery of Cedric's death and that was an issue she was determined to resolve.

———————

For Peaches, Big Mike having a cell phone in the joint was the hassle she thought it would be. He was calling or texting her 24/7, only taking breaks when the phone needed charging.

Even though Peaches kept denying it, Big Mike knew she had to be fucking somebody and he was obsessed with finding out who it was. Not once did the thought of Fat Chad fucking Peaches ever cross Big Mike's mind. He didn't think Fat Chad was shrewd enough to pull a snake move like that and he thought Peaches was too top notch to fuck with a hood nigga like Fat Chad.

Big Mike was wrong on both counts.

Despite Big Mikes unlimited phone access, Peaches was constantly finding ways to spend time with Fat Chad. Peaches was playing it so close that one time Fat Chad ate her pussy while she had phone sex with Big Mike.

Fat Chad enjoyed the ego boost that came from fucking the boss' wife, while Peaches on the other hand enjoyed the sex and power. Fat Chad had the sexual stamina needed to beat the pussy up for hours, but more importantly for Peaches, he had power in the streets.

One day Big Mike went on a round trip to the prison hospital in Columbus. He had broken his ankle playing basketball and the doctors needed to check and make sure it was healing properly. Since Big Mike wouldn't have access to his phone all day, Peaches would have a chance to do something she had been wanting to do for a long time; have hours of uninterrupted sex with Fat Chad.

"Baby if I woulda knew you was gon be this turned up, I would have brought some Gatorade with me," an exhausted Fat Chad said.

Peaches smiled, "You ain't through is you?" she asked, wanting more of the pussy pounding.

"Naw, just give me a minute to reload. I gotta admit, I ain't never met a female whose pussy stay wet like yours."

"And I ain't never met a nigga that keep it wet like you," Peaches shot back, stroking Fat Chad's ego as usual.

"I see you got good game and good pussy!" Fat Chad laughed.

"That ain't no game, it's the truth," Peaches protested, "Let's be real, you know and I know that I can have any nigga in this city, but I'm fucking with you. "

"Okay, so what is it about me that made you wanna fuck with me?"

"Cause you're a real boss. Believe me, after years of being with a fake boss, I know a real one when I see one."

"So you saying that Big Mike is a fake?" Fat Chad questioned. Even though he knew he was crossing Big Mike by fucking Peaches, he still had the utmost respect for him.

Peaches sat up in the bed and looked Fat Chad in his eyes. "A real boss got power and Big Mike don't have any power," she began, "Without you, Big Mike would just be another nigga in the joint. You the one with all the power, don't you see that?"

"I hear what you're saying, but Big Mike had enough power to give me the connect and now I'm seeing real paper."

"He gave you the connect!" Peaches smirked. "I coulda gave you the connect. I know the syndicate niggas in New York personally. Them niggas been chasing this pussy ever since they met me. Whatever type of deal you got with the syndicate, I can make it sweeter, believe that."

What Peaches was saying sounded good, but Fat Chad was still skeptical. Fucking his bitch while he was in the joint was one thing, but to go behind Big Mike's back and deal with the syndicate directly would be an act of war. Besides all that, Fat Chad couldn't figure out what Peaches' motives were. Big Mike was taking care of Peaches, so why was she crossing him in every way possible?

"Peaches, keep it real with me, is you and Big Mike going through something I don't know about?"

Peaches took a deep breath before answering, "I know from the outside it look like Big Mike is taking care of me, but he only do that to make up for the hell he done put me through."

"What kinda hell?"

"That nigga fucked my mama and both of my sisters."

"Since y'all been together?"

"Yeah!" Peaches lied, "Then he almost got me killed sending me to that stash house. A real boss wouldn't use their main bitch as no mule," Peaches paused before going in for the kill, "I know you got a woman, but I'm choosing you. I'm the bitch that can help you get to the next level, Just think you already got the power and once I get you really connected with the syndicate you gon have the money."

Fat Chad reflected on what Peaches was saying. Big Mike had shown him a lot of love, but at the same time he was treating him like a lil' nigga, especially when it came to dealing with the syndicate. Big Mike had it arranged so that he was getting a bigger slice of the pie than Fat Chad was, even though Fat Chad was the one moving the bricks. Fat Chad was seeing a few dollars, but he had a hunger for more and what Peaches was offering him was an opportunity to satisfy that hunger. "Okay, so what we gon do about Big Mike?" he asked.

"Let me handle Big Mike," Peaches said, "I gotta keep playing the role with him, but you my daddy now. I just want you to promise me one thing."

"What's that?"

"That you ain't gon let them Stay Solid niggas get away with what they did to me"

"Baby don't worry I got you. When the time is right I'll finish the job."

"I love you Daddy." Peaches began kissing Fat

Chad's chest. The intoxicating effects of Peaches mouth and the words that came out of it was giving Fat Chad's third eye blurred vision. He couldn't see that right beneath the surface of his dreams of money and power lurked a nightmare and Peaches was the female Freddy Kruger.

L.A. had known Dasha since she was a little girl. Back in the day when he was still selling rocks, Dasha's mama Nicki was one of his main customers. L.A. felt sorry for Dasha because he could see that she was living in hell. Her clothes were hand-me downs and there was never any food in the house.

In a show of compassion, when L.A. would stop by to sell Nicki dope, he would bring some fast food with him to give to Dasha. On the occasions he didn't bring food, he would slide Dasha ten or twenty dollars.

By the time Dasha was a teenager, she had gotten thick and she had gotten fast and those tens and twenties had turned into fifties and hundreds. Dasha had a crush on L.A. and even though he tried to resist, the invitation to hit that fat ass was something he couldn't pass up.

L.A. didn't have a pimp bone in his body, so despite the fact that he had Dasha's mind, he was content with using her body. When L.A. was entertaining friends he would call Dasha over to really get the party started. Dasha would suck and fuck the whole house if L.A. told her to, she was young and didn't know any better.

As L.A. moved up the totem pole in the game, he started fucking with a higher caliber of women and Dasha didn't make the trip. Every blue moon L.A. would cross paths with Dasha, but for the most part they existed in two different worlds.

L.A. didn't know Dasha was affiliated with the Stay Solid Boys until she caught a dope case. Cash had sent Dasha to drop off 62 grams of coke to a guy named Amp King. Amp King turned out to be an informant and Dasha got jammed up. The situation exposed Amp King as a snitch and was a hot topic in L.A.'s barbershop for weeks.

L.A. figured if he could rekindle his relationship with Dasha, he might be able to pump her for information about Lucky.

Between Molly and the Beamer truck, Dasha's name had been in heavy rotation in the streets ever since she got back from Atlanta. According to street gossip, Dasha had really stepped up her game and the days of throwing her a few dollars for sexual favors were over with. These days, Dasha was strictly business.

Nevertheless, L.A. knew Dasha would be happy to hear from him and he was right. Despite all the sexual abuse Dasha had suffered at the hands of older men, she considered L.A. one of the good guys. He may have used her sexually, but he had showed Dasha love at a time in her life when nobody was showing her love.

After tracking Dasha's number down, L.A. gave her a call. "Hey lil' mama," he said when Dasha answered.

"Is this L.A.?" an excited Dasha asked.

"Yeah, how did you know so fast?"

"Cause ain't nobody ever called me lil' mama but you."

"Well you know I been hearing some good things about you."

Dasha laughed, "Muthafuckas been talking bad about me so long it's about time they said something good!"

"Baby the way you handling business, they ain't got no choice but to say something good. But anyway, I called you cause I was thinking that maybe we could go have a drink and catch up on old times."

"Yeah I'm down with that, but I ain't tryna fuck with no hood bars."

"Shit me neither! Not the way niggas been dying round this muthafucka. I got a "in the cut" spot I drink at in Merriman Valley. It's a mostly white crowd, so ain't no drama."

"That's cool, when you tryna hook up?"

"How bout later tonight, around nine?"

"Okay, just call me then and I'll meet you."

Dasha was somewhat surprised by hearing from L.A., but the more she thought about it, the more she realized that she should have expected it.

Ballers had been on Dasha's trail since she had got back from Atlanta and most of them had the same goal in mind; a ménage a trios with Dasha and Molly. They didn't realize that they weren't dealing with the old freaky, free fucking Dasha. The new Dasha had rules and one of them was that nobody could have her and Molly at the same time, except Lil' Billy. Nevertheless, Dasha was looking forward to hooking up with L.A.

The possibility that L.A. was on some deep cover police shit was a thought that never crossed Dasha's mind. Nobody in Akron had ever suspected that L.A. was an informant. He wore the camouflage of a street nigga and that is what made him so dangerous.

Chapter 5

Land Of The Heartless

After hitting Stan off with ten bricks, Lil' Billy pulled back and let Ace work the other forty. Lil' Billy was determined not to let his name start floating around in the Cleveland underworld mix. He wanted his whole persona to be that of an up and coming rapper.

Despite the fact that Akron was only thirty minutes away from Cleveland, Stay Solid Records was virtually unknown in Cleveland. The Rap scenes in Cleveland and Akron were totally different. In Akron, a rapper could move units through word of mouth, while in Cleveland it was hard to get exposure without radio play.

Since Young Skrilla and Raw Breed had a large following in Cleveland, Lil' Billy and Rick decided to use their alliance with Black Cartel Entertainment to open up the Cleveland market for Stay Solid Records .

While he was in Atlanta Lil' Billy had recorded a joint mix tape with Raw Breed, so Rick suggested that they release a single from the mixtape to Cleveland's hip-hop radio station and all the club DJ's. Rick also made contact with a rapper from Kinsman named Showtime. Showtime was connected with a rap label in Akron called Flamboyant Records, so he was already familiar with Stay Solid.

When Showtime got the call from Rick, he was more than happy to help Stay Solid Records. He connected them with record stores, club owners, and most important of all, a venue to hold the Black Cartel-Stay Solid concert. In exchange for all his help, Rick promised Showtime a spot as an opening act at the show.

Since returning from Atlanta, Lil' Billy had become a lot more involved in the business side of Stay Solid Records and while Rick was pleased with Lil' Billy's renewed enthusiasm he was worried about him.

There was emptiness about Lil' Billy that Rick couldn't explain. Rick could really notice the change when they were in the studio. Lil' Billy's lyrics had taken on a darker tone. It was as if Lil' Billy was on a different planet.

Rick also knew that Lil' Billy had went in deep with the Black Cartel on the dope side and that bothered him also. The whole purpose for going to Atlanta was to make a clean break from the dope game, not go in deeper. Lil' Billy claimed he had got the plug for Cash, but Cash was gone, so what did he need the plug for now?

As long as Lil' Billy was in the dope game, he was putting everything him and Rick had built at risk. Rick didn't want to pressure Lil' Billy, but they needed to be on the same page. If Lil' Billy planned on selling dope for infinity, Rick needed to know that, because if that was the case, Rick had concluded, they would have to end their business partnership.

Over the years Ace had formed some strong alliances with solid dudes from all over Cleveland and now those alliances were coming in handy.

Ace knew if word got out that he had bricks on deck it would bring heat cause his name was already known, so he used his niggas on Buckeye and Harvard to push the heavyweight. In his own hood he operated the way he always had; serving tracks and nine packs to the young hustlers on 134th and Kinsman.

Ace's Puerto Rican bitch Maria was still moving powder for him at the G.P. club on 93rd and Nelson. Ace might not have realized it yet, but Maria was slowly but surely becoming the closest thing he had to a main bitch. Every dollar she made from shaking her ass to shaking his powder, she put in Ace's hand.

The G.P. was packed as usual when Ace came through the door. He gave the bouncer Big Tone some dap then stepped in and took a look around. Strippers of all shapes and sizes were bouncing their ass for dollar bills, while the bass from the speakers pulsated through the club.

Maria was in a booth giving a lap dance when her and Ace made eye contact. Ace gave her a nod then stepped to the bar and ordered a shot of Grey Goose. Maria showed up about ten minutes later. "Hi Papi!" she greeted Ace as she sat on the stool next to him.

"What's good baby?" Ace replied.

"The money," Maria smiled and handed Ace a wad of cash.

"What time you getting off?" Ace asked.

"I think I'm gon leave early. That cop I told you about is here," Maria cut her eyes to the end of the bar where

Officer Strawberry was sitting.

Officer Strawberry was bar-none the dirtiest cop in Cleveland. Whether it was police brutality, planting drugs on innocent people, or extorting drug dealers, Officer Strawberry was involved in all of it.

Officer Strawberry was also known for using his position as a cop to pressure women for sex, especially strippers. He had his eye on Maria for a while, but she had spurned his advances. Most of the strippers at the G.P. considered fucking and sucking Officer Strawberry the cost of doing business there. One stripper had even told Maria, "Just give him what he wants and he'll leave you alone," but Maria wasn't having it.

Like every other hustler from Up The Way, Ace was familiar with Officer Strawberry, but luckily thus far Ace had been able to stay out of his way. *Maybe I need to set her up in another strip club*, Ace thought while listening to Maria tell him about Officer Strawberry's latest stunt.

Ace knew it would be hard to find another spot that did the numbers that the G.P. did, but at the same time he wasn't trying to be at odds with a dirty cop.

"Yeah baby, I don't want you tussling with that fool, so if you gotta leave early that's cool," Ace said.

"You coming over tonight?" Maria asked.

"Yeah I'll be through, just call me when you get home."

"Okay Papi." Maria got up and headed towards the dressing room while Ace finished his drink.

Meanwhile Officer Strawberry was still sitting at the end of the bar, nursing a drink, and watching Maria like a hawk.

Ever since Kat's murder, Stan had been wearing a bullet proof vest. Tension was thick throughout the city, but for Stan the tension level was the highest in his neck of the woods, the Eastside.

Because of Stan's close relationship with the Stay Solid Boys he was catching crooked looks from niggas mourning Kat's death. Stan had gotten word that there had been discussions amongst Kat's closest allies about blowing down on Stan in an aggressive manner.

Under normal circumstances Stan would be approaching niggas about what he was hearing, but right now he had more important issues on his plate.

When Lil' Billy gave Stan the ten bricks to move, he let Stan know that there was a lot more where that came from. With that in mind Stan had been busy building up his clientele so he could handle a bigger load. Stan understood that now that he had a major plug it was time to push it to the limit.

Stan's other big issue was Lucky's case. It was Stan's understanding that the only thing the police had on Lucky was one eyewitness and that eyewitness was old man Mr. Thomas who lived on McKinley. Trina and Monique were going to testify that Lucky never left their house on Talbot, so Lucky had a 50/50 chance at trial. If Mr. Thomas changed his story or better yet didn't show up for court then Lucky was a free man.

Stan, like everybody else that grew up around Baird Hill knew Mr. Thomas. His late wife Mrs. Thomas used to be the neighborhood candy lady. Mr. and Mrs. Thomas had a granddaughter named Nicole that Stan had a history with. As a teenager Stan had fucked Nicole a few times, but with age they had grown apart.

Nicole ended up having three kids by three different niggas and rumor had it that she was an alcoholic nutcase. She was also a compulsive gambler and her game of choice was Pity-Pat. Pity-Pat is a popular card game in Akron, so in hopes of running into Nicole Stan started going to Pity-Pat games.

It didn't take long for Stan to cross paths with Nicole and the first thing that caught his attention was how she looked. The bottle was obviously taking a toll on her.

Nicole was more than happy to rekindle the relationship with Stan, so damn near every night he was at her house. For Stan fucking with Nicole was a hard grind, she was an outright drunk. All she did was drink and yell at her kids, plus she kept a nasty house. On top of that her sex game was garbage. She couldn't suck dick without biting and she always wanted to get fucked in the ass, something Stan really wasn't into.

It was a strain, but Stan kept in mind that dealing with Nicole wasn't about pleasure, it was about the business of freeing Lucky, because Lucky's trial date was fast approaching.

The best time to get a coherent conversation out of Nicole was in the morning before she started drinking. So one morning after spending the night with her Stan asked Nicole about Mr. Thomas .

"How yo grandfather doing? He still living on McKinley?"

"Yeah, his mean ass still over there, why what's up?"

"I was just wondering cause I noticed you don't never talk about him."

"Ever since my Granny died, he been on bullshit, so I don't even go around him. He bout to lose the house cause he spend all his money in West Virginia at the dog races."

This might not get messy after all, Stan thought while listening to Nicole talk.

When Lucky sent word to handle Mr. Thomas, Stan knew what Lucky meant, but hoped it wouldn't come to that. Now with the info Nicole had just provided, Stan could see a way to handle the situation without any blood being shed. All he had to do was use Mr. Thomas' money problems as a way to solve Lucky's legal problems. Hopefully, Mr. Thomas would play ball, because if he didn't shit was going to get hectic.

————————————

Peaches was overcome with so much jealousy and envy while listening to Dasha talk that she was literally gritting her teeth. Peaches was a bad bitch, but she was local. While Dasha, on the other hand, had been sliding through Atlanta pushing a Bentley and rubbing elbows with athletes and rappers.

For the first time in their lives, Dasha was making Peaches feel small. Dasha had big city ambition, while Peaches was content with being a big fish in a small pond.

Peaches had invited Dasha over to her house in an attempt to get information from Dasha about Lil' Billy. Dasha was the only avenue Peaches had to keep up with Lil' Billy's movements.

It didn't take Peaches long to realize that Dasha had changed. In the past Peaches had always been able to dominate the conversation, but now Dasha was more self-assured and in control. Peaches was beginning to hate the new Dasha almost as much as she hated Lil' Billy.

"So what's going on with Lil' Billy?" Peaches asked hoping to change the direction of the conversation.

"He good, he just focused on his rap career and putting the streets behind him," Dasha knew Peaches would eventually ask about Lil' Billy, so she was prepared. Dasha didn't trust Peaches at all and she wasn't about to tell her anything that she could use against Lil' Billy.

"He done put Akron behind him too, huh?" Peaches asked.

"Girl, Lil' Billy moving on to bigger and better things, ain't nothing goin on in Akron but a bunch of drama."

"You right, I just hate the way the streets be talking about him."

"Talking 'bout him how?"

"You know, shit like he scared to show his face in Akron and how he ain't got no strength without Lucky."

"They got Lil' Billy fucked up!" Dasha snapped, "That nigga putting together a real shrewd play and when it's all said and done, the whole city gon bow down to Stay Solid."

Without realizing it, Dasha had just allowed Peaches to bait her. Peaches had lied about what she was hearing in the streets. Her whole purpose was to get under Dasha's skin in hopes that Dasha would get so emotional that she would say something that would expose Lil' Billy's plans.

Peaches was attempting to bait Lil' Billy through Dasha. Like any other nigga who was a factor in the streets, Lil' Billy had a big ego. Peaches was hoping that once Dasha told Lil' Billy what she said, he would come back to Akron just to prove a point. Once Lil' Billy was back in Akron, Peaches could turn up the pressure on Fat Chad to kill him.

While Dasha went on and on about how strong Stay Solid was, Peaches sat there quietly nodding her head in agreement, anticipating the day Dasha fell off her high horse. *Bitch you talking that boss shit now, but once Lil' Billy is dead you'll be back in the gutter where you came from.*

————————————

While Lil' Billy's single with Raw Breed was getting increased spins on the radio, it was the chopped and screwed version that was getting heavy play in the streets. The chopped and screwed movement that had originated in Houston had taken Cleveland by storm. It was 2004 and the whole city was listening to screw music and sipping on codeine laced syrup.

With a hot track out Lil' Billy and Rick decided it was time to get out and mingle, and Showtime's annual Up The Way cookout at Woodhill Park was the perfect place to do it.

The cookout was a go-to event for hustlers from all over Cleveland, so the cleanest rides and baddest bitches were on the scene. Not to be outdone Lil' Billy brought out his Denver Bronco Chevy, sitting on 24 inch chrome with Molly looking good in the passenger seat. Rick was behind the wheel of Lil' Billy's old school van which was wrapped in the graphics for Lil' Billy and Raw Breed's upcoming mix tape.

Ace was posted up at his brand new 2004 Chevy Suburban chopping game with all the factors from 134th and Kinsman. Ace always enjoyed the Up The Way cookout, but this year was even better, cause this year his name was on everyone's lips and he was enjoying the attention.

Having Lil' Billy on the scene brought even more attention. Ace had turned everybody in the hood on to Stay Solid's music, but because Lil' Billy had been keeping such a low profile, nobody had seen him in person.

While Rick and Molly mingled and passed out promotional CD's, Lil' Billy sat in the Suburban with Ace politicking.

"What's up family, you alright? You seem kinda tight," Ace said as he twisted up a blunt.

"Shit I'm cool, I'm just checking out all these new faces," Lil' Billy replied, "It lightweight seem like everybody looking at me ."

"They might be my nigga, you know everybody bumping that cut you got out with Raw Breed."

"You think anybody connecting me to what you doing?"

"Hell naw! The niggas I'm dropping bricks on think I got a Puerto Rican plug on the Westside. Then my hood niggas don't even know I got heavyweight like that cause I'm still running the same regulation I always been running . All these niggas know about you is that you my cousin and you doing yo thang in the rap game."

"Good, cause the last thing I need is the dope man tag on me."

Ace laughed, "Don't worry, don't nobody know you Tony Montana but me!"

While Lil' Billy and Ace sat in the truck relaxing and smoking some good weed, Ace pointed out all the niggas and bitches that were about something . "See that light skinned chick standing in front of that silver Benz?" Ace pointed in her direction.

"Yeah, what's up with her?" Lil' Billy asked.

"Her name Constance, she from Shaker Heights," Ace hit the blunt and continued, "Her people got long dough. Her daddy a doctor at Cleveland Clinic and her mama teach at Case Western Reserve. She been riding a Benz since she was sixteen."

"Somebody need to be charging that ho," Lil' Billy said from a pimp's perspective.

"Well the bitch been eyeing you since you got here, so maybe you the one to put it down where other niggas done failed."

"If the ho at a cookout like this she must be tryna choose."

"Yeah she tryna choose, but not in the way you talkin' about."

"What you mean?"

"Fam the bitch is a groupie. She fuck whoever got a name, but she don't get attached to nobody. A lot of niggas done tried to make her they main bitch, but she change niggas like she change clothes."

Lil' Billy knew exactly how to play a bitch like Constance. She was used to niggas jumping at the chance to fuck her cause of her looks, but pretty women were old news to Lil' Billy and besides that he didn't have time to waste on groupies. Not even a pretty one driving a Benz.

"Who is these niggas?" Lil' Billy asked referring to a caravan of cars and trucks that was rolling through.

"That's them St. Clair niggas," Ace replied, "They always come through deep."

Deep was an understatement. There were at least twenty cars and trucks lined up back to back and they were all sitting on twenty inch rims or better. There were old school drop-tops, big boy trucks, and foreign luxury cars, but the car that really caught Lil' Billy's attention was the car leading the pack. It was a brand new Maserati riding on chrome .

The Maserati stopped right where Lil' Billy was standing. The driver's side window came down and Lil' Billy saw a familiar face.

"Hey nigga, what you doing in the Land? I thought you was an Akron nigga now," the driver of the Maserati said with a big smile on his face.

"Nigga you ain't heard? I'm cross-country with the game these days," Lil' Billy said.

The man driving the Maserati was Walt, Lil' Billy's best friend from junior high.

Walt got out of the car and gave Lil' Billy a big hug, "How long you gon be up here? You know we got a lot of catching up to do," Walt said.

"Shit, I'm back my nigga," Lil' Billy replied, "I got a spot down at the Qua 55."

"Qua 55! Nigga you musta made it in the NBA."

"Naw, I'm just fuckin with the rap game. I gotta single out with Raw Breed right now."

"I heard that cut, but I thought it was some other Lil' Billy. I forgot you was the best rapper at F.D.R ."

"And the best hooper," Lil' Billy added.

"I don't know about all that," Walt smiled. Lil' Billy and Walt had been basketball rivals since they were kids.

Lil' Billy and Walt spent the next thirty minutes chopping game and catching up. Walt knew some young niggas over on St. Clair that were trying to make moves in the rap game, so he thought it might be a good idea to introduce them to Lil' Billy and Rick.

"Make sure you call me in a couple days," Walt said

as he got back in his Maserati.

"That's a bet my nigga," Lil' Billy replied then walked over to his Chevy where Molly was standing," Baby what 's up, you enjoying yourself?" he asked.

"Yeah I'm cool," Molly replied. "It's a different flavor than Atlanta, but I like it." Besides a trip to Chicago years back, Molly had never been to the Midwest.

Lil' Billy was liking the atmosphere in Cleveland too. He finally felt like he had some room to breathe. In Akron a rich nigga was never too far away from a broke nigga with jealous thoughts. In Cleveland a nigga with money could separate himself easier. Lil' Billy knew eventually he would have to deal with his unresolved issues in Akron, but meanwhile he wanted to enjoy the fruits of his labor. *It might be time to treat myself to a trip to the car lot*, he thought.

While Lil' Billy thought about new cars, Constance stood by her brand new Benz looking at Lil' Billy like she wanted to eat him alive.

Chapter 6

A Tangled Web

Because of a disturbance at his barbershop, L.A. had to postpone his original date with Dasha, but he wasted no time in scheduling a make-up date.

With Detective Bryant breathing down his neck, renewing his relationship with Dasha had taken on an added importance for L.A., so instead of dealing with Dasha like she was a freak he decided to wine and dine her.

L.A. picked up Dasha in his brand new Corvette and took her to the Red Lobster in Montrose for dinner. Afterwards they headed to a bar in the Merriman Valley that catered to an upper echelon white crowd and had a few drinks.

All evening L.A. kept telling Dasha how proud he was of her. Even though he was pouring it on thick for strategic purposes, in all sincerity, he was impressed by the progress that Dasha had made. Most girls who grew up in households as dysfunctional as Dasha's, ended up broke and on drugs.

By the time Dasha had finished her drink she was

tipsy and ready to fuck and she made sure L.A. was aware of this. She didn't have to tell him twice, L.A. downed his drink and said "Let's go."

L.A. had a couple of houses at his disposal, but he decided to take Dasha to the one in Kenmore. It was a long drive from Merriman Valley to Kenmore and Dasha gave L.A. some of the best head he had ever had in his life on the way there.

This dog done learned some new tricks, L.A. thought as Dasha's head bobbed up and down. When Dasha felt L.A.'s balls tighten up she sucked even faster. L.A . took one hand off the steering wheel and grabbed Dasha's head as he came in her mouth. Dasha swallowed every drop just to remind L.A. how freaky she could get.

Once they reached the house, L.A. led Dasha straight to the bedroom, "Take off your clothes," he instructed her. While Dasha undressed, L.A. stood there admiring her thickness. Once Dasha was completely naked, L.A. handed her a bottle of baby oil.

While Dasha oiled her body up, L.A. laid back on the bed and stroked his dick. *I wish I had a pill*, he thought as Dasha got on top of him and began to ride.

For the next few hours, Dasha rocked L.A.'s world for old times sake. It had been a while since they had hooked up, but Dasha still knew what L.A. liked in bed. On top of that, she had picked up quite a few new skills over the years.

L.A. was enjoying himself, but he hadn't lost focus on his real mission, so after Dasha drained him he engaged her in some pillow talk. For the first few minutes Dasha talked about Atlanta and her future plans, but when the subject of Amp King came up L.A. saw an opening, "What happened with that case anyway?" he asked.

"Pellini got me probation," Dasha replied, "You know Stay Solid keep him on the payroll."

"That nigga Amp must wasn't hip to what happened to the last nigga that tried to snitch on Stay Solid."

"I don't know what he hip to. Fuck that snitch nigga."

"What's up with Lucky, is he gon shake that case or what?"

"I'm sure he is but he don't discuss his business with me."

Without realizing it L.A. had fucked up when he alluded to the snitch nigga Joe's murder, then immediately shifted to Lucky, whom most of the streets assumed was responsible for Joe's murder. Alarms went off in Dasha's mind.

Despite the fact that a blind man could see that Dasha had stepped up her game, L.A. still didn't respect her mind. He still thought he could manipulate her like he used to when she was a teenager, but he was wrong.

"I'm gon give you a couple hundred to put on his books and tell that nigga if he need anything else just send word," L.A .said.

"Okay," Dasha nodded.

Lil' Billy had always told Dasha to follow her gut instinct and right now her gut was telling her that something about L.A.'s conversation wasn't right. Dasha made a mental note to watch what she said around L.A.

Meanwhile, L.A. was also making mental notes. Dasha was being tight-lipped when it came to Lucky, but it was still early in the process. L.A. knew he had to be patient and earn Dasha's trust and eventually she would start talking. L.A. felt like running off at the mouth was just in a bitch's nature. They couldn't help but do it.

———————————

When Peaches told Big Mike she was going to New York to do some shopping, his only request was that she take some pictures while she was there to send to him. Big Mike would have never fathomed that the real reason Peaches was going to New York was to negotiate a side deal for Fat Chad with the syndicate, but that was exactly what she was doing.

As soon as Peaches left Akron she called Premo, the leader of the syndicate on his private line. Premo had slid Peaches the number behind Big Mike's back the first time he met her, but Peaches had never used it.

Peaches told Premo that she was on her way to New York to discuss some important business with him. Premo in turn told Peaches when she arrived in New York to go to the Waldorf-Astoria hotel on Park Avenue in Midtown Manhattan and there will be a suite reserved for her. Premo had no idea what type of business Peaches wanted to discuss, but he couldn't wait to find out.

After listening to Peaches explain the dynamics of the side-deal that she was trying to orchestrate for Fat Chad, Premo came to two conclusions; Peaches was more than just a pretty face and she was one of the most ruthless women he had ever met.

Nevertheless, Premo agreed to do the deal because at the end of the day it made good business sense. Fat Chad was obviously a young nigga in a position of power and powerful men generate more money.

When Peaches got back to Akron and gave Fat Chad the good news the reality of his life really hit him; he was the most powerful young nigga in the city. He had an army that would kill on his command, he could fuck any bitch he wanted, and now thanks to Peaches, he had a real plug.

Fat Chad had spent a lot of time and energy making sure that it never got out that he was behind Cash's murder, but now he didn't give a fuck. As far as he was concerned, Stay Solid was history. Without Lucky they weren't equipped to go to war and Lil' Billy seemed more like a man on the run than the strong nigga people thought he was.

Fat Chad had promised Peaches he would finish off the Stay Solid Boys and when the opportunity presented itself he intended to keep that promise, but until then his focus was on money. He was even putting his unresolved issue with Lil' Man on the back burner.

Lil' Man was a loyal to the highest bidder type of nigga and right now Fat Chad was the highest bidder. Fat Chad knew he would eventually have to kill Lil' Man. but right now Lil' Man served an important purpose. With Lil' Man controlling the block business, Fat Chad had more time to concentrate on kingpin operations.

It's time for me to cop a big boy truck, Fat Chad thought as he reflected on his newfound baller status. Fat Chad wasn't a flashy guy, but dealing with Peaches was having an effect on him. She was constantly telling him what real bosses do, so subconsciously he was, in essence, competing with Big Mike. He may not have realized it, but surpassing Big Mike had become the driving force in Fat Chad 's life. It was just one of the many side effects of good pussy.

This gon be my last dance, Maria thought as she gave a lap dance to a middle aged black man known as

Preacherman. On Sunday Preacherman was a pastor at one of Cleveland's largest Black churches.

For Maria, dancing was secondary to selling powder, so once she ran out of coke she usually called it a night. She had sold her last gram an hour ago and would have left if not for Preacherman showing up. He was one of her main tricks.

While the R. Kelly strip club favorite "Sex Me" played in the background, Maria grinded up against Preacherman's groin, rotating her hips in a slow circular motion. When Preacherman closed his eyes Maria knew it wouldn't be long, so she leaned forward and whispered in his ear, "Ooh Papi… you so big," which took him to his peak.

When the song ended the fantasy ended and Maria got off Preacherman's lap and headed to the dressing room.

While Maria cleared out her locker, a stripper named Jackie approached her.

"Can you sell me another gram?" Jackie asked.

"That last one I sold you was it," Maria replied.

"Can you call Ace for me?"

"Girl you know Ace ain't making no moves this late."

Jackie was flying high. Her eyes looked like they were about to pop out of her head and her nose was running like a faucet. Maria noticed her condition and said, "Don't you think you need to slow down a little bit on that powder?"

"I'm cool, I only fuck with it when I'm dancing." Jackie replied.

And you dance all the time, Maria thought but kept it to herself. It was late and she didn't feel like doing a long drawn out drug intervention. Jackie was a grown woman. If she wanted to fuck her life up, that was on her.

While walking to her car, Maria gave Ace a call to

let him know she was on her way home. He informed her that he was already at her crib, which put a smile on her face. After being around tricks all night she couldn't wait to be in the arms of a solid nigga.

Maria stayed on the Westside, on 83rd and Madison, which was a nice distance from the G.P. To get home she always took 93rd to Harvard, which took her to Broadway, which took her to the 490 freeway.

When Maria got to the corner of 93rd and Harvard she noticed the flashing lights of an unmarked police car in her rearview. *What the fuck!* she thought as she pulled over. *It's a good thing I sold all that powder.*

Maria's relief was replaced by anxiety when she saw that it was Officer Strawberry who had pulled her over.

"Is there a problem officer?" A nervous Maria asked after rolling down the window.

"You driving pretty fast Senorita," Officer Strawberry replied, "What's the big rush?"

"I'm sorry, I didn't know I was going that fast. I'm just tryna make it home from work."

"How many dicks you suck tonight?"

"Excuse me?"

"Bitch you heard me! Matter of fact, get out the car!"

Now Maria was scared to death. There's no greater fear than the fear of the unknown and Maria had no idea what Officer Strawberry had up his sleeve.

Maria got out of the car and Officer Strawberry proceeded to pat her down as if they were husband and wife. It took everything within Maria to maintain her composure. She kept her hands on the hood of the car while Officer Strawberry molested her under the guise of a police search.

Don't move bitch!" Officer Strawberry snarled as he took out a flashlight and began searching the car. "You got anything in here I should know about?"

"No," answered Maria.

"See ya just told a lie," Officer Strawberry held up a half a blunt he found in the ashtray.

Maria didn't say anything, she just stared straight ahead. At this point the whole episode had her at a loss for words. Officer Strawberry continued his search and a few seconds later yelled, "Jackpot!"

"That ain't mine!" Maria yelped when she saw the small baggie of white powder in Officer Strawberry's hand.

"It is now!" Officer Strawberry fired back, "Let me see what else you got." Officer Strawberry dumped the contents of Maria's purse on the hood of the car.

"Well goddam ! You musta sucked a whole lotta dicks tonight," Officer Strawberry said referring to the wad of cash that fell out of Maria's purse. He smiled and put the money in his pocket.

"You can't take my money!" Maria shrieked, by now she was in tears.

"Bitch I'll take more than that if you don't start playing ball!"

Officer Strawberry let his thinly veiled threat hang in the air for a few seconds before speaking. "You have a nice night and drive safely," he stated calmly before getting in his car and leaving.

Maria stood there stunned. *What the fuck just happened?* she wondered. She got in her car and sat there for fifteen minutes collecting her thoughts before she called Ace. "Papi, we got a problem," she said as soon as Ace answered the phone.

———————

All these channels and ain't shit to watch, Lil' Billy thought as he flicked through the channels on the 65 inch plasma screen T.V. He was at his apartment at the Qua 55 relaxing and trying to recuperate from the night before.

Lil' Billy went to the Mirage with Walt and had the time of his life. They popped so many bottles Lil' Billy was pissing Moet. Bad bitches were everywhere and they all stopped at Walt's table to pay homage and meet Lil' Billy.

Amidst all the partying Lil' Billy and Walt did talk business. Walt had St. Clair in a chokehold from 105th to 141st Street. He was even supplying formaldehyde, more commonly known as "water," to the niggas on Hough. Walt had a nice operation in place and he made it clear to Lil' Billy that he could move fifty kilos easily.

Lil' Billy had come to the conclusion that it was time to go to Atlanta and talk to Sincere. He had moved a hundred bricks over the past month and with Walt on deck he could move even more.

Lil' Billy reflected how back when he was young, Cash would always talk about making a million dollars. Back then a million dollars seemed like a fantasy, but now it was a reality. The more Lil' Billy thought about it, the way things were going, two million could soon become the reality. This was all because Lil' Billy had what all hustler's dreamed of having. He had a plug and as long as he had one, Lil' Billy planned to continue selling dope.

Molly interrupted Lil' Billy's thoughts with a kiss on the cheek, "Good morning Baby how you feeling?" she asked.

"Like shit," Lil' Billy answered.

"I bet you do! I ain't never seen you as drunk as you were last night."

"And I'm paying for it now, my head is pounding."

"Baby give me a second to get dressed and I'll run to the drug store and pick up some aspirin for you."

"Okay."

Molly headed back towards the bedroom then stopped, "Oh by the way, you know ole girl still here," she said.

"Ol' girl who?" Lil' Billy looked confused.

"The one you brought home last night."

I must have been sloppy drunk, Lil' Billy thought as he tried to remember what girl he brought home.

As if on cue, the girl in question, who happened to be Constance, walked out of the bedroom. "I left my number on the nightstand, call me later," she said.

Lil' Billy nodded while Molly smiled and said, "I'll call you sooner."

After Constance left, Lil' Billy looked at Molly and said," You know I don't even remember talking to her last night, let alone bringing her home."

"Well you better believe the party went on without you," Molly laughed."

Oh yeah, just so you know, we gon slide down to ATL next week," Lil' Billy said changing the subject.

"Good cause I need to do some recruiting," Molly said.

"You tryna bring some of that ATL ass up this way huh?"

"Baby between here and Akron we can make a killing in the pussy game. Matter of fact we can run them hoes through the whole Midwest."

"Fuck it then, let's turn the Stay Solid van into a ho hauler!" Lil' Billy laughed, but in reality, he was dead serious. Lil' Billy's hustle was relentless. He was always thinking of ways to make money. He knew no matter how good things looked on the surface there was always a bullet to the dome or a federal indictment lurking in the background, so while he had momentum in the game, he had to ride it to its highest level.

Lil' Billy was headed to the top and when he got there, he wasn't going to stop. He would just find another mountain to climb.

Chapter 7

The Hunger for More

No matter how many times she had been there, Sandy never got tired of going to the Georgia Aquarium. Even since her father bought her some goldfish when she was a little girl, Sandy had been infatuated with sea creatures.

Sandy and Sincere had just done some shopping at The Underground and came to the Georgia Aquarium afterwards to walk and talk.

Sandy was a keen observer and since they had been together she had studied Sincere closely. In Sincere, Sandy saw a very intelligent man, but she also saw a very cold-hearted man and this coldness came out when Sincere talked about his father.

What Sincere felt for his father was pure hatred. He felt like his father was responsible for his mother's drug overdose.

On the other hand, when the subject of his brother Cedric came up Sincere's whole mood changed. He talked about Cedric as if they had been inseparable, when in reality, Cedric had never even known Sincere. The more Sincere lied about his relationship with Cedric, the more it confirmed in Sandy's mind that everything Sugarman had told her was the truth; Sincere was the one who killed Cedric.

Revenge is a dish best served cold, but Sandy was still setting the table, so in the meanwhile she played the role of a woman in love. "Baby I want one of these for my birthday," she said as she and Sincere stood in front of a shark tank holding hands.

Sincere smiled, "Cassandra, where we gon keep a shark at?"

"I don't know, but I'm sure you can think of something."

"I guess I'm the man with all the answers, huh?"

"You sure are," Sandy kissed Sincere.

"Well Baby, I don't know if I got all the answers, but I do have a question."

Sincere reached into his pocket and pulled out the biggest diamond ring Sandy had ever seen in her life, as he got down on one knee. "Cassandra I knew you was the one the day I met you and I'm ready to make it official. Will you marry me?"

Sandy stood there feigning surprise, when in reality she had been expecting a marriage proposal from Sincere for some time.

"Baby, I'm sorry," Sandy said as her eyes welled up with tears, "I love you, but I can't marry you."

Sincere stood up, "Why Baby? What's wrong?"

"Because you still in the game and I can't commit to you until you commit to living a righteous life."

"Baby I told you that I am in the process of putting that life behind me."

"And when the process is over, and that life is completely behind you, then I'll marry you."

Sincere didn't respond, he just stood there staring into the shark tank. He was disappointed that Sandy turned down his proposal, but he understood her reasons and it made him want even her more. Now he was more determined than ever to get out of the game and that meant turning over the plug to Lil' Billy sooner rather than later.

––––––––––––––

The most important time of the week for Lucky was the hour he spent on the visit with Dasha. Outside of Dasha, Lucky didn't communicate with anyone on the streets. The police were trying to pin multiple homicides on him, so the less people he dealt with, the better.

Lucky always brought a pad and pencil to the visits. The visits were held behind glass with phones to talk on. Lucky wrote down questions on the pad and held them up to the glass for Dasha to read. Dasha would always respond with yes or no answers.

Lucky's visits with Dasha were taking on even more importance because his trial started in about a month and he needed to know what to expect.

"What's up nigga?" Dasha said when she picked up the phone.

"I'm cool, what's up with you, you staying solid?" Lucky replied.

"You know it, by the way somebody gave me some money to put on your books."

"Who?"

Dasha used her fingers to form the letters L and A. In response, Lucky wrote on the pad *the barber?*

Dasha nodded yes and Lucky shook his head in disapproval and wrote, *I don't trust him.*

Dasha asked why and Lucky wrote down his reasons which were, in essence, nothing more than gut feelings.

Dasha breathed a sigh of relief because despite the gut feelings she had herself, she didn't want to believe that L.A .was working with the police. She liked him too much.

Next, Lucky moved on to the subject of Stan. Dasha smiled and gave Lucky the thumbs up.

"So everything cool?" Lucky asked.

Dasha nodded yes with a big smile on her face.

I wonder what Stan got up his sleeve, Lucky thought. Stan's word was his bond and if he said things were cool, Lucky figured he had nothing to worry about. Nevertheless, as long as the State's only eyewitness was still alive, Lucky wouldn't, and couldn't feel completely comfortable.

Lucky and Dasha spent the remainder of the visit engaged in small talk. At the end Lucky did what he always did. He held up the pad with a list of whatever assignments he wanted Dasha to carry out before their next visit.

This week the main issue was Trina and Monique. Lucky's lawyer, Pellini, had informed him that because Trina and Monique were his alibi witnesses, the State would do everything they could to attack their credibility. Trina and Monique didn't have a criminal record, so according to Pellini, the police were probably watching them for any signs of illegal activity. If the police could pin a case on Trina and Monique before Lucky's trial, they would become worthless as witnesses.

Lucky knew Trina and Monique were probably still hustling, so he told Dasha to let Stan know they needed to shutdown shop until after the trial.

After the visit Dasha walked to her car with tears in

her eyes. She was always emotional after seeing Lucky. Even though Stan had said Lucky was going to beat the case, public opinion was saying otherwise and Dasha was worried.

Whenever Dasha would share her worries with Lil' Billy, he would always reassure her by saying "*Our team gon win as long as we stay solid.*" Dasha was praying that Lil' Billy was right because after losing Cash she couldn't handle losing Lucky too.

———————

Thoughts of losing weighed heavily on Detective Bryant's mind also. His murder case against Lucky was weak and he knew it. Outside of the lone witness, Mr. Thomas, Detective Bryant hadn't been able to gather any additional evidence against Lucky. He tried to put pressure on a Arab store owner named Ahmed, who he thought knew more about Bulldog's murder than he was admitting, but that plan didn't work out. Detective Bryant's repeated attempts to pressure Ahmed led to a heated phone call from a city councilman telling him to back off.

When Detective Bryant heard that Lucky had two alibi witnesses, he knew his case was in trouble. The lead prosecutor, afraid of suffering a defeat at trial, had threatened to drop the case if Detective Bryant didn't bring him more evidence.

Trina and Monique had clean records, but according to one of Detective Bryant's street level informants, they sold coke on the side. Detective Bryant knew if he could stick Trina and Monique with a dope case before the trial started it would destroy their credibility, so he gave his old partner in narcotics Detective Hilton a call to see what they could come up with.

Trina and Monique only dealt with a small circle and when none of Detective Bryant's or Detective Hilton's informants could penetrate that circle, they did what they always did in a crucial situation; they broke the law.

To obtain a warrant to raid Trina and Monique's house on Talbot St., Detective Hilton claimed that one of his confidential informants had bought drugs from them. This was a complete fabrication, but Detective Hilton knew it would work because Trina and Monique *were* selling drugs, so they would think they really had sold to an undercover and try to cop a plea. If for some reason they decided to go to trial Detective Hilton would tell prosecutor that the confidential informant was missing in action and to drop the case. By then Lucky's murder case would be over with and it would no longer be necessary to pursue a case against Trina and Monique anyway.

Detective Bryant was sitting in an unmarked car down the street from Trina and Monique's house waiting for SNUD to execute the warrant. He had been watching their house all night and judging from the traffic he was certain that there were drugs in the house.

Detective Bryant checked the time then turned up his police radio. It was 8:58 A.M. and the raid was scheduled for 9:00 A.M. Two minutes later, right on schedule, an all-white van turned off 5th Avenue onto Talbot Street. The van screeched to a halt in front of Trina and Monique's house. The SNUD team jumped out and kicked down the front door.

Once Detective Bryant received word over the radio that the scene was secure, he drove down the street, got out the car, and entered the house.

Trina and Monique were sitting on the couch in

handcuffs with nothing on but their bra and panties. "Y 'all can at least let us put some clothes on!" Trina snapped.

Detective Bryant ignored Trina's remark and walked into the kitchen where Detective Hilton was waiting.

"Hey Hilt, what ya got?" Detective Bryant asked.

"A quarter ounce of crack, twenty ecstasy pills and about an ounce of marijuana," Detective Hilton replied.

"In other words, probation," Detective Bryant had hoped that there would be enough drugs in the house to charge Trina and Monique with a Major Drug Offender specification which carried ten years mandatory. He thought if they were facing serious time they might be willing to recant Lucky's alibi. Nevertheless, the fact that they had a case pending, albeit a minor one, would still hurt their credibility.

While the police were in Trina and Monique 's house, Stan was down the street watching the show from a safe distance. He had missed Dasha's call the night before, so when he woke up and saw her number in his phone he called her immediately. Dasha gave Stan the message from Lucky, so as soon as he got off the phone with Dasha he tried to get in touch with Trina and Monique. When they didn't answer the phone Stan decided to go by their house, but when he got to the corner of Talbot and Baird, he knew he was too late. Police were everywhere.

As soon as Stan saw the police bringing Trina and Monique out in handcuffs he called his lawyer Angelo Pellini on their behalf. Pellini said he would know in a couple of hours what the police found in the house and he would call Stan back.

With Trina and Monique caught up, Stan knew Lucky's freedom was completely in his hands. *I gotta make sure my plan for Mr. Thomas is all the way solid*, he thought. With that in mind Stan headed to Nicole's house.

———————————

There was no doubt that being at odds with Officer Strawberry was a major problem, but Ace was a true hustler and true hustlers know how to make adjustments.

Officer Strawberry took $4,000 from Maria the first night he pulled her over. To ensure that Maria never got caught slipping with that much money again, Ace changed the way they conducted business.

Now instead of Maria leaving the club with money she would pass it off to another stripper who would deliver it to Ace, who would be waiting outside the club.

Officer Strawberry continued to pull Maria over when she was leaving the G.P., but now he was coming up empty handed because Maria never had more than a hundred dollars on her.

Officer Strawberry knew he was being out smarted and that made him more determined to break Maria. For her to work in the G.P. and not give him any pussy was an affront to his authority and he could not accept that.

Ace knew that Officer Strawberry was a sick individual, so besides the money pickups, he stayed away from the G.P. He was even considering taking Maria out of the G.P. because the money she was making there wasn't worth the headache of dealing with Officer Strawberry.

In reality Ace didn't even need the G.P. anymore. He had made $250,000 in the past 30 days moving bricks and Lil' Billy had just left for Atlanta to go holler at his plug about increasing the load.

Ace was approaching a level of the game where the

main concern was the Feds, not the local cops. Officer Strawberry preyed on street-level hustlers and Ace was way past block bleeding.

Ace concluded that it was time for him to change up his operation in a way that reflected the type of money he was playing with. That meant taking Maria out of the G.P. and no more selling work on 134th & Kinsman. He had too much to lose to get caught up in Officer Strawberry's world.

At first Maria was resistant to the idea of not working at the G.P. anymore because she worried about losing Ace. Their relationship had began as a business venture and Maria thought that if she wasn't able to hustle for Ace he would eventually phase her out of his mix.

Ace had no plans of getting rid of Maria. Besides the fact that he had developed feelings for her, he realized her true value. Being around Lil' Billy had opened up Ace's eyes to a different level of the game. He saw how thorough Dasha and Molly were and how much of an asset they were to Lil' Billy's operation. He realized that Maria had the potential to be just as thorough.

"Here baby count this for me," Ace told Maria as he got in his Suburban and handed her a duffle bag. He had just made a money pickup at a bar on 116th & Buckeye.

Since she had stopped working at the G.P. Maria had been spending most of her free time riding shotgun with Ace while he took care of business. It only took one money pickup for Maria to realize why Ace said they didn't need the G.P. anymore.

"Twenty-Two Five," Maria said when she finished counting the money.

Ace stopped by his mama's house to drop off the money. "I'm hungry, where you tryna eat?" he asked when he got back in the truck.

"Let's stop at the Shack and get some wings," Maria replied.

"That's cool, but anyway, I know you tired of riding around with me all day every day, so watcha wanna do?"

"Papi you my man, I'm gon do whatever you want me to do."

This a bottom bitch for real, Ace thought before saying, "I want you to do what you best at and that's catching tricks."

"So you want me to go back to the G.P.?"

"Hell naw! Not as long as Strawberry's bitch ass hanging around there. What I want you to do is put together a team."

Ace noticed the confused look on Maria's face, so he explained, "There ain't no doubt you was the main attraction at the G.P. and you capable of being the main attraction on any stage in any city."

"Okay, but if I'm the main attraction. What I need a team for?"

"Mo money baby…Not only can you charge the tricks, but you can charge the other dancers. You the main attraction and they gon pay you to let them be yo opening act. I'm talking bout putting it down at events like the NBA All-Star game and the Super Bowl where the big money tricks be."

As Maria sat there soaking up the game she could finally see the vision. There was too much money in the world to keep being a local ho and with a nigga like Ace behind her she was inspired to fulfill her potential.

When Ace pulled up at the Shack on 143rd & Kinsman, the first thing that caught his attention was the fact that nobody was hanging out in front of the Shack. There were usually at least one or two young hustlers posted up, but today it was a ghost town.

While Ace and Maria walked in the Shack to order their food, the reason the block was a ghost town was sitting across the street in the Family Dollar parking lot in an unmarked car. Officer Strawberry had come to 143rd & Kinsman to shakedown the small time drug dealers for money, but one of them noticed him and discretely spread the word to the other hustlers, who in turn got off the block.

When Officer Strawberry saw Ace and Maria go in the Shack he immediately sprung into action. He wasn't about to pass up an opportunity to show them who's boss.

Ace and Maria were in the Shack about ten minutes. When they came out they stopped in their tracks.

"This your truck?" Officer Strawberry asked while looking in the passenger window of the Suburban.

"Yeah, what's the problem?" Ace replied.

"Boy I ask the muthafuckin questions!" Officer Strawberry barked, "Now open up these doors!"

Ace gritted his teeth and did as he was told. He wasn't riding dirty, so he figured Officer Strawberry wouldn't be able to squeeze him the way he did niggas, when he caught them dirty.

"Keep y'all hands on the hood," Officer Strawberry ordered as he began searching the truck.

It began as a routine search until Office Strawberry realized that the truck was clean. He wanted to make Ace beg for mercy in front of Maria, but since his search came up empty and he didn't have any drugs on him to plant in the truck, he didn't have any leverage.

Officer Strawberry decided to try a different tactic in

hopes of provoking Ace.

Ace's Suburban had T.V. screens in the headrests, the dash, and the doors. Officer Strawberry yanked the T.V. screen out of the front passenger door and threw it on top of the truck.

"Come on man! Why you tearing up my shit?" now Ace was boiling.

Officer Strawberry ignored Ace and continued yanking the screens out of the doors. When he was finished, he began a aggressive pat down of Maria which included squeezing her ass and titties.

"Senorita, you need to invest in some pussy powder cause I can smell the dick on you," Officer Strawberry smirked.

"And I can smell the pussy on you," Ace muttered.

"What the fuck you say?" Officer Strawberry grabbed Ace's neck in an attempt to smash his face into the hood, but Ace reacted and hit Officer Strawberry with a vicious right cross. The punch knocked Officer Strawberry on his ass, but he quickly got back on his feet and drew his gun.

"Nigga, you a dead man!" Officer Strawberry barked as he put the gun to Ace's head.

"Please don't shoot!" Maria screamed and tried to grab Officer Strawberry who then pointed the gun at her and spat, "Bitch back up!"

Meanwhile Ace stood frozen, expecting to die at the hands of a crooked cop, but instead Officer Strawberry proceeded to place Ace in handcuffs.

"Nigga, me and you bout to take a little ride," Officer Strawberry said as he led Ace to the unmarked car.

"Baby, go to my mama's house," was the last thing

Cellini

Maria heard Ace say before Officer Strawberry stuffed him in the backseat.

Chapter 8

Hotlanta

Upon landing at Atlanta 's Hartsfield International Airport , Lil' Billy , Rick and Molly all headed in different directions.

Rick's girlfriend Melissa was there to pick him up. Molly's sister Mia was there for her and Raw Breed was waiting on Lil' Billy.

Lil' Billy hopped in Raw Breed's black Hummer and they headed to the luxurious Bedford Pine Townhouse Lil' Billy stayed whenever he was in Atlanta.

After taking a quick shower and changing clothes, Lil' Billy stepped into the living room where Raw Breed was waiting with a fresh blunt.

"I don't know if you know it or not," Raw Breed began, "but you the talk of the town my nigga."

"Oh yeah?"

"Hell yeah, when you came up with Molly you came up with one of the ATL's finest and the real players is tipping they hat to that."

"Ah Man, you know Dasha is the one who knocked her for real."

"See that's pimp shit right there!" Raw Breed

laughed, "Where Dasha's fine ass at anyway, I was looking forward to seeing her."

"She in the AK handling some important business for the team, but speaking of the AK, after we do the show in Cleveland we gon do a stripper fest in Akron the next day. I know Skrilla gon probably need to get back down here right after the show, but I'm hoping you can hang around and host the stripper fest."

"Bruh you got that coming and while ya bullshittin, Skrilla might stick around too. The Black Cartel and Stay Solid is family my nigga."

"No doubt," Lil' Billy replied.

In a lot of ways Lil' Billy considered the stripper fest in Akron more important than the concert in Cleveland. With Lucky's murder trial coming up, Lil' Billy believed that it was important that he make a statement in Akron and that statement was: Stay Solid may have taken some blows, but they were still stronger than ever.

———————

The Bank of America Plaza was the tallest building in the State of Georgia and Sincere's office was located there on one of the top floors of the building, which was appropriate considering that Sincere was a towering figure himself.

Whenever Sincere encountered a dilemma, the view from his office window always helped him put things into perspective. The bird's eye view of Atlanta was a reminder to him of how far he had risen above the slums of Detroit.

Sincere was sitting in his office staring out the window when he received word that Lil' Billy was in Atlanta. Sincere knew that meant that Lil' Billy wanted to talk business and for Sincere the timing couldn't have been better.

The clean break Sincere had been trying to make from the game, had been up until recently, fueled by his desire to remain free, but now it was fueled by something even stronger; love.

Sincere had never loved a woman as much as he loved Sandy. She stimulated his intellectual and sensual sides at the same time. It was as if she had touched his soul.

When Sandy issued her ultimatum to Sincere that there would be no marriage until he was completely out of the dope game, fulfilling Sandy's wish became the center of Sincere's life.

Sincere was an avid reader of astrology books and he felt like all the signs were pointing to him giving the Columbian connect to Lil' Billy sooner rather than later. At the same time, he didn't want to rush things to the point where he was being reckless because besides the millions of dollars that were at stake, his life was hanging in the balance.

Nevertheless, Sincere had taken note of how quick Lil' Billy was moving bricks, so he figured that Lil' Billy had come to Atlanta to talk about increasing his load.

That was a good thing, but Sincere knew for Lil' Billy to be an acceptable replacement in Angel's eyes Lil' Billy would have to expand his operations beyond the state of Ohio.

Sincere's thoughts were interrupted by a knock on the door. "Come in," he said.

Sincere's Hispanic secretary Rosa walked in and handed Sincere a folder, "Here's the report you requested on commercial real estate in North Carolina," she said.

"Thank you Rosa," Sincere replied as he glanced at

the report.

"Is there anything else you need?" Rosa asked.

"No that'll be all," Sincere checked his watch, "You know what, it's two o'clock, why don't you take the rest of the day off."

"You sure you don't need me to stick around?"

"I'm sure. Go ahead and start your weekend early."

"Thanks boss," Rosa smiled and walked out of the office.

Meanwhile, Sincere sat the folder on his desk and went back to his previous activity; analyzing Lil' Billy.

For Rick, being back in Atlanta meant being able to spend quality time with his girlfriend Melissa. Rick had met Melissa on his previous visit to Atlanta and they immediately hit it off.

Melissa had a college degree, owned a clothing boutique, and worked in the A&R department at a major record label. She was a true Southern Belle with brains and beauty to match.

Rick had always dreamed of meeting a woman like Melissa and now that he had, he planned on holding on to her.

"You know Baby, I think I'm ready to make some changes," Rick said as him and Melissa were strolling through Piedmont Park holding hands and enjoying the nice sunny day.

"What kind of changes?" Melissa asked with anticipation.

"Well first of all, I think it's time that I make Atlanta my permanent home."

Melissa squeezed Rick's hand. "Oh Baby, that would make me so happy. After what happened to your friend Cash, you being in Ohio really worries me."

"It worries my parents too and they been on me a lot lately about relocating."

"Well what is there to think about? You can move into my place right now or if you think that's moving too fast, I'll help you find your own place."

"Baby living arrangements ain't the big issue. The main thing I need to figure out is what exactly is the future for Stay Solid Records."

Melissa looked confused, "I don't understand, I thought the plan for Stay Solid was to build on your underground buzz and eventually sign a big distribution deal with a major label."

"That was *my* plan, but I think Lil' Billy got his own plans."

"Why do you say that?"

"Because the main reason we came to Atlanta in the first place was to put the streets behind us and focus on our music, but instead Lil' Billy done got even deeper into the streets."

Melissa knew exactly what Rick was talking about. Even though she had never been a part of street circulation, she was familiar with the unsavory elements of Black Cartel Entertainment. Since day one, rumors had been floating around the music industry that Black Cartel Entertainment was nothing more than a front for a real Black Cartel. Because of that, Melissa had been working behind the scenes trying to secure for Stay Solid what she considered a more legitimate entrance into the music industry.

Melissa worked in the A&R department at Big Time

Records. The founder of Big Time Records was a man named D.C. Walker. D.C. was a legend in the music industry. He had discovered some of the biggest stars in the history of R&B.

Melissa had slid D.C. a Stay Solid C-D to listen to and while he liked the music, he was particularly interested in Rick's beats. D.C. knew that singers and rappers come and go, but good producers were hard to find.

Melissa had held back from telling Rick about D.C.'s interest in him because she didn't want it to seem like she was planting seeds of separation between him and Lil' Billy, but after listening to Rick talk she realized those seeds were already there, so she might as well talk to him about D.C.

"Baby since we on the subject of your future, I got something I been meaning to tell you," Melissa began.

"I hope this ain't bad news," Rick sighed.

"No this is good news... At least I think it is."

"Okay, what's up?"

"I gave my boss one of y'alls C-Ds and he loved it."

"For real!" Rick was grinning from ear to ear.

"Yeah. He wanted to hear more."

"I can't wait to tell Lil' Billy about this!"

"Baby, hold up," Melissa interrupted, "There's something else you need to know."

"What's that?"

"D.C. is only interested in you. He said Lil' Billy is too street for his tastes, but your production skills are extraordinary."

Rick sat down on a park bench and thought about what Melissa was saying. Working with D.C. Walker was a once in a lifetime opportunity, but at the same time, he couldn't turn his back on everything he had built with Lil' Billy.

"Melissa I'm flattered that D.C. likes my stuff, but me and Lil' Billy are a team. I wouldn't be comfortable making a move without him," Rick said.

"Baby, I understand," Melissa said. "I just wanted you to know that you have options."

Rick was taking those options seriously. Life is about choices and if Lil' Billy chose to stay in the dope game, then Rick would be forced to make a choice of his own.

Between the show with Black Cartel and Lucky's murder trial, Stay Solid had a lot on its plate and Rick didn't want to throw in the added drama of a possible split between him and Lil' Billy.

Nevertheless, Rick knew that he and Lil' Billy were approaching a fork in the road and the time was fast approaching when a decision would have to be made about which direction they were going to take.

_____

When Sincere and Sandy arrived at Justin's Restaurant for dinner, as usual there was a nice crowd on hand. Justin's was the go to spot for Atlanta's Black Elite and without a reservation it was next to impossible to get a table.

"You expecting someone else?" Sandy asked, noticing a third chair at the table.

"Yeah, a friend of mine is going to join us for dinner," Sincere replied while looking over the menu.

About two minutes later Sincere saw the hostess leading his dinner guest to the table. Sincere checked his watch, "Right on time as usual!" he smiled as he stood up to shake Lil' Billy's hand.

The smile on Lil' Billy's face disappeared as soon as he saw Sandy sitting at the table. *What the fuck!* he thought. Lil' Billy felt like he had just been blind- sided in a car accident. Seeing Sandy so unexpectedly had him in a state of shock.

"Everything alright?" Sincere asked, noticing the change in Lil' Billy's demeanor.

"Yeah everything's great," Lil' Billy replied trying to regain his composure.

Sincere turned to Sandy who was dealing with her own inner turmoil, but doing a better job of concealing it. "Baby this is Lil' Billy, the guy I'm always talking about," Sincere began, "Lil' Billy this is my soon to be fiancé Cassandra."

Sandy nodded politely and shook Lil' Billy's hand. Just touching Lil' Billy set off sparks inside Sandy, but she remained ice cold on the surface.

"Cassandra you say?" Lil' Billy asked, voice full of contempt.

"Yeah, *Cassandra*," Sandy shot back with emphasis on the name.

For the next few minutes Lil' Billy and Sincere engaged in small talk while Sandy sat there in silence, smiling and nodding at the appropriate times. The initial panic Sandy had felt when she first saw Lil' Billy had subsided somewhat now that she realized Lil' Billy wasn't going to expose her to Sincere, at least not yet.

Sincere looked at his phone, "Excuse me for a second, I need to take this call," he said.

"No problem," Lil' Billy replied.

When Sincere stepped away from the table Lil' Billy

and Sandy sat there for a few seconds in an uncomfortable silence until Lil' Billy broke the ice, "You sho get around," he smirked.

"Look whatever issues you got with me let's just keep 'em between us," Sandy said.

"I don't have any issues with you Sandy, oops, I mean Cassandra. Do you even know who the fuck you are, cause I sho don't."

"Nigga I was the woman who loved you and treated you like a king and you talked away from it all. That's who I am." Sandy was getting emotional.

"And now you love and treat Sincere like a king and oh let's not forget how you was on tape sucking Big Mike's dick like he was a king," Lil' Billy shot back.

Sandy shook her head and laughed, " Nigga you funny as hell, you portray this role like you such a straight up and down street nigga, but you really just a young ass square!"

"Baby the only thing square in my life is the knots of money in my shoebox."

"Humph!" Sandy grunted, "Yo money still fitting in shoeboxes?"

Before Lil' Billy could respond Sandy added, "Just remember, you work for *my* man, so don't bite the hand that feed you."

The conversation was cut short by Sincere's return.

"Sorry about that. That was some after hour's business that needed to be addressed," Sincere said.

"Being successful is a 24 hour job," Lil' Billy replied.

"See that's wisdom right there." Sincere turned to Sandy, "Baby I told you this guy was sharp."

Sandy smiled and gritted her teeth at the same time. Running into Lil' Billy was a game changer. The scars from their break-up hadn't healed yet.

Sincere usually told Sandy his plans, so she figured that when he did meet up with Lil' Billy she would know ahead of time and be able to make the proper preparations, but instead she had been ambushed.

Making matters worse was how nasty Lil' Billy was towards her. To Sandy it seemed as if his attitude hadn't changed one bit since the day he received the sex tape.

Sandy understood that Lil' Billy was hurt, but what she still couldn't understand was how he could let one incident from her past wipe away all the good she had brought into his life.

Sitting so close to Lil' Billy while her mind wrestled with unanswered questions was making Sandy uncomfortable, so immediately after dinner she told Sincere she wasn't feeling good and needed to go home. Sincere sent for a car to take Sandy home and after she departed he stepped to the bar to talk business with Lil' Billy. "I see the transition to Cleveland is paying off for you," Sincere began.

"Yeah, that's what I wanted to talk you about," Lil' Billy said. "I'm ready to at least double my load."

"You saying at least leads me to believe that you feel like you can handle even more than that."

"I can, but I don't wanna move too fast."

"You shouldn't move too fast or too slow. You should move at the speed that the circumstances dictate."

"I don't understand what you mean."

"What I mean is that if you've built a machine that can handle more, then you should give it more while you have the opportunity," Sincere paused then continued, "If you ask me, I think you can handle a thousand."

"Whoa! I don't know about all that. I'm only dealing with a small part of Akron and a small part of Cleveland," Lil' Billy countered.

"Okay so imagine if you was dealing with a bigger part of those cities and other cities. Being in the Rap game puts you in the position to travel and meet people. It was the Rap game that put you in the position to meet me." Sincere was trying to plant the seeds of expansion in Lil' Billy's mind before he even began the discussion of him possibly dealing with Angel.

Lil' Billy was in total agreement with what Sincere was saying, but while half of his mind was analyzing his conversation with Sincere, the other half of his mind was still dealing with the shock of seeing Sandy. He thought that part of his life was over, but now he realized that it wasn't.

"So what you telling me is that I should step my game up?" asked Lil' Billy, trying to stay focused on the matter at hand.

"That's exactly what I'm telling you, Sincere replied. "What I'm offering you is a chance to supply the entire Midwest."

"Shit, it's gon take a lot of cocaine to do that."

"And you have access to a lot of cocaine, so supply will never be an issue."

This man has all the answers, Lil' Billy thought. It didn't make sense for him to keep coming up with excuses when Sincere obviously had everything laid out for him. The bottom line was; he could either shit or get off the pot.

"Let's increase the load to 200 and from there we'll just let nature take its course," Lil' Billy concluded.

"Agreed," Sincere said and raised his glass to toast.

After downing their shots of Louis the Thirteenth, Sincere motioned to the bartender that they needed a refill. Meanwhile Lil' Billy remembered another issue he needed to talk to Sincere about. "I got something else I need to holler at you about," he said.

"What is it?" Sincere asked.

"Can you connect me with a good price on water?"

Sincere smiled, "I can connect you with anything, including water if when you say water you mean formaldehyde."

"Yeah that's what I'm talking 'bout."

"No problem, I'll have my affiliates in Chicago take care of whatever water needs you may have."

Damn! This nigga is like the street messiah, Lil' Billy thought. *I wonder what it feel like to have that much power.*

Chapter 9

The Show

Dasha stuck her face into the pillow and screamed. L.A. was pounding her pussy doggy style and the combination of pleasure and pain was overwhelming Dasha. She had cum so many times she had lost count and L.A., who was high on Ecstasy, was showing no signs of letting up.

"Throw it back!" L.A. commanded as he smacked Dasha's ass. It seemed like the harder he drilled Dasha's pussy the wetter it got. They had been going at it for three straight hours and were dripping in sweat, but L.A. was still searching for that elusive nut.

Dasha grabbed the headboard and used it as leverage as she threw her ass back to meet L.A.'s violent thrust head on. Dasha was used to Ecstasy dick but L.A. was performing on a totally different level. She could usually suck at least one nut out of him, but not tonight.

Dasha was a cum freak. Whether it was in her mouth, pussy or her ass, she enjoyed the feeling of a man cumming inside of her. Dasha was known for her ability to make any man or women cum no matter what type of drug they were on. She considered anything less to be an insult to her sexual ability, so she was determined to bring L.A. to full satisfaction.

"Hold up," Dasha said, putting L.A.'s pussy pounding frenzy on pause.

Dasha moved to the edge of the bed while L.A. stood in front of her. She placed one hand on L.A.'s hip while her other hand clutched his balls and took all of his manhood in her mouth. The taste of her pussy on L.A.'s dick made Dasha hornier and she sucked his dick with so much enthusiasm and spit that it was running down her chin.

Even though L.A. was enjoying the treatment he was receiving from Dasha's mouth, he knew it was her thickness that was going to take him where he needed to go. "Turn around," he instructed her as he pulled his dick out of her mouth. Instead of getting in a doggy style position, Dasha stood straight up then bent down and grabbed her ankles. L.A. spread Dasha's ass cheeks and slid his dick inside her sloppy wet pussy.

"Hit that pussy Daddy! Hit it hard" Dasha yelled.

L.A. followed Dasha's instructions and started pounding the pussy like he was trying to knock the bottom out. Realizing the effect her dirty talking was having on L.A., Dasha continued edging him on. "Ooh Daddy, this yo pussy," she moaned. That was all L.A. needed to hear. Finally after hours of trying, he shot his seed inside Dasha who fell out on the bed, exhausted with a sore pussy.

"Damn nigga, I ain't gon be able to walk tomorrow," Dasha sighed.

L.A. smiled and headed to the bathroom to take a quick shower.

L.A. had been spending a lot of time with Dasha, but he hadn't got any closer to getting information about Lucky.

Whenever L.A. would bring up Lucky, Dasha would freeze up. With Detective Bryant breathing down his neck, L.A. was becoming frustrated. He had been doing all he could to gain Dasha's trust, but their relationship, for the most part, was the same as it had always been; a sexual partnership.

Dasha wasn't the type of woman that ran her mouth and after Lucky told her he didn't trust L.A. she was even more tight lipped around L.A. Nevertheless, she enjoyed having sex with L.A., so whenever he wanted to spend time she tried to make herself available.

Dasha was laying in the bed relaxing when she heard the vibration of L.A.'s cell phone on the nightstand. Dasha looked at the bathroom door while she debated within herself whether or not to be nosy. *A quick peek won't hurt*, she thought as she proceeded to pick up the phone.

Dasha looked at the phone screen and saw the initials "J.B." and a number that caught her attention. *Where do I know that number from?* Dasha racked her brain trying to figure out why the number seemed so familiar. *Detective Johnny Bryant!* The name exploded in her head.

When Dasha caught her dope case Detective Bryant interrogated her about a few murders he thought the Stay Solid Boys were responsible for. Dasha didn't cooperate, but Detective Bryant still gave her one of his business cards just in case she had a change of heart.

Dasha quickly grabbed her purse and began rummaging through it, in hopes that she still had the business card. She did, and after comparing the number on the card to the number in L.A.'s phone everything became crystal clear to her.

Lucky was right, Dasha thought as she sat there clutching Detective Bryant's card with a blank look on her face. She wondered if she should confront L.A., but decided not to. She wanted to see what Lil' Billy thought about the situation first.

Dasha heard the shower cut off, so she quickly put the business card back in her purse. When L.A. came out of the bathroom, Dasha greeted him with the fakest smile she could come up with.

When Lil' Billy and Rick got back to Cleveland they got right down to business. For Rick that meant making sure everything was on point for the concert and the after party. The Black Cartel had shown Stay Solid a lot of love in Atlanta, so Rick planned on doing all he could to return the favor.

Meanwhile, Lil' Billy was making sure his team was ready to take things to the next level. Sincere had offered him the keys to the kingdom and Lil' Billy planned on accepting them. Since everything would be moving through Walt, Stan and Ace, Lil' Billy had one on one meetings with each of them at his apartment to make sure they were all on the same page.

Walt and Stan were on board, but Ace was having serious problems that were making it hard for him to make moves.

"Shit Bruh, just pay that muthafucka off," Lil' Billy suggested after Ace told him about the issues he was having with Officer Strawberry.

"Dude don't want no money, he want my bitch," Ace replied.

"Okay, so what's the problem?"

"Maria ain't tryna fuck with dude on no level."

Lil' Billy shook his head, "That ain't her call though. You the coach, she just a player. Fam look, you got too much going on to be beefing with a cop. Maria need to do whatever she gotta do to get dude off yo trail."

Molly walked in the living room from the kitchen," I ain't tryna be all in yo business, but I think I got a solution to yo problem," she said.

"Oh yeah?" Ace's face lit up.

"Yeah," Molly continued, "Tell Maria to give me a call."

"Shit, I'm bout to call her right now then." Ace pulled out his phone.

While Molly went to the bedroom to talk to Maria, Lil' Billy and Ace continued talking business.

"The ticket on the bricks done dropped to twelve-five a piece," Lil' Billy said. Ace gave Lil' Billy a look of surprise. "And the price gon get lower than that," Lil' Billy continued, "The higher the load, the lower the price. We got 200 bricks to pick-up right now and a year from now I wanna be picking up a thousand bricks."

"Fam hold up," Ace interrupted, "That's a lot of coke, how we gon move all that shit?"

"It ain't gon be hard. We already got the best product and now we gon have the best prices."

Ace didn't question Lil' Billy any further. It was obvious that Lil' Billy had momentum, so Ace figured he might as well just go with the flow and get rich in the process.

"What you got planned for the concert?" Ace asked, changing the subject.

"You know Rick really handling all that," Lil' Billy replied. "I know the after party at the Mirage, then the next day we gon do the Stripper Fest in Akron."

"A Stripper Fest?"

"Yeah Molly got some thick hoes from Atlanta flying up to show the Ohio hoes how to put it down ."

"Shit, I might have to slide through the G.P. and see if them hoes up to the challenge."

"The more the merrier my nigga!" Lil' Billy laughed.

After a few more minutes of small talk Lil' Billy checked his watch.

"Fam I gotta get up outta here. I'm running late," he said.

"Where you headed?" Ace asked.

"I gotta go out to Randall and holla at the Chinaman."

"What he hooking up for you?"

"Something real shiny for the concert."

Chinaman was the go-to jeweler for all the hustlers in Cleveland. Besides watches and chains, he also specialized in money laundering. If you wanted to spend over ten thousand on some ice and not have to worry about the IRS, the Chinaman was the man to go see. On top of that, his diamonds were never cloudy, they were always top of the line.

Lil' Billy wasn't really into jewelry, but the concert was a special occasion, so he gave the Chinaman forty thousand to design a special chain for him.

Sincere had advised Lil' Billy not to be too flashy, but always show up when it's time to show out. Lil' Billy felt like he was a king ascending to the throne and he planned on making the Black Cartel-Stay Solid concert his coronation.

———

"You know Stay Solid having something at Jack's strip club," Peaches yelled from the kitchen where she was fixing Fat Chad something to eat.

I knew this was coming, Fat Chad thought. "Yeah, I saw one of the flyers," he replied.

Fat Chad knew that Peaches was only bringing up the Stripper Fest so he would know that she hadn't forgot that he promised to finish the job on the Stay Solid Boys. Fat Chad had hoped that the Stay Solid Boys would stay away from Akron long enough, that by the time they did return, Peaches would be over the issue she had with them. Instead she was just as relentless as she had always been.

"So what you gon do?" Peaches asked as she sat Fat Chad's meal down on the coffee table in front of him. She had cooked him a T-Bone steak with a baked potato on the side.

"About what?" Fat Chad asked, stalling for time.
"About them Stay Solid niggas!"

"Okay, hold the fuck up!" Fat Chad snapped, "Gangsta shit is my business, not yours, so let me handle shit the way I handle it. That Stripper Fest gon have APD security, only a fool would try something there."

"Daddy I'm sorry," Peaches sighed, "I didn't even think about all that."

"Baby the shit gon get handled, but in the right way. I ain't gon send my Gorillaz on no suicide mission, ya feel me?"

Peaches nodded.

The furthest thing from Fat Chad's mind was making a move on the Stay Solid Boys at the Stripper Fest. Orchestrating Cash's murder had left Fat Chad mentally fatigued. After having Cash murdered, he had also had Kat and the stripper Tiny killed just to cover his tracks. All the bloodshed had drained him.

Now that Fat Chad was rising in the game his focus was on money, not murder. He had just copped a new Cadillac Escalade and bought his mama a house. The last thing he wanted to do was play the murder game again.

Nevertheless, Fat Chad was always true to his word, so he intended to keep his promise to Peaches. After the play she turned with the syndicate for him, Fat Chad felt like he was indebted to Peaches. In addition, he was in love with Peaches. He wasn't as wide open as Big Mike was, but it was love nonetheless, and love has a tendency to be blind.

Fat Chad decided to have his hitters on deck at the Stripper Fest just in case. He wasn't going to force anything, but if he saw a chance to hit one of the Stay Solid Boys then he would give the green light. With that in mind, Fat Chad picked up his phone and gave his people in Youngstown a call.

————————

When Young Skrilla, Raw Breed and their entourage arrived at Cleveland Hopkins International Airport, a black stretch Hummer limo was there to pick them up. From there they were taken to the Tower City Hotel in downtown Cleveland, where Rick had reserved the entire top floor for not only them, but also the five strippers Molly had flown up from Atlanta for the Stripper Fest.

Lil' Billy and his entourage, which consisted of Ace, Walt, T-Man, Dasha and Molly, were already at the hotel when Rick arrived with Young Skrilla and the Black Cartel in tow.

After everybody was introduced to each other, Rick ran down the itinerary for the day, "In about two hours we gotta stop by the radio station for an interview," he began, "then we gon make an appearance at City Blue clothing store out at Randall Park Mall. We got sound check at six, then after that we can relax until show time."

"They sell gators at City Blue?" Young Skrilla asked.

"I don't think so, why?" Rick said.

"I heard the Midwest is the best place to buy gators."

"If you tryna get some gators you gotta check out Mr. Albert's," Walt cut in.

"You think we gon have time to slide through there?" Young Skrilla looked at Rick.

"If you want some gators, we gon make time my nigga," Rick replied.

"Right now it's time to hit this G-13," Lil' Billy smiled and handed Young Skrilla a blunt stuffed with the high-potency weed."

After the smoke session, the Black Cartel headed to the radio station for the interview, then out to City Blue, where the crowd was so large that extra police were called in. Young Skrilla cut his appearance at City Blue short, so he could do some gator shopping at Mr. Albert's. After spending $20,000 on gator shoes, boots and belts, Young Skrilla headed to the arena for the sound check where all the performers for the show were already waiting.

"Showtime you up first tonight," Rick began, "you got thirty minutes to get the crowd cranked up. Me and Lil' Billy going on next, then Raw Breed gon come on and do three tracks with Lil' Billy. Breed you gon finish the set by yoself, then Skrilla it's on you to bring the house down."

"I think I can handle that," Young Skrilla smiled.

After running through the sound check Rick, Young Skrilla, and the rest of the Black Cartel headed back to the hotel, while Lil' Billy went to his apartment to prepare for what he knew was going to be the biggest night of his life.

———————

Meanwhile, back in Akron it was a big night for Fat Chad too. He felt like he was stepping onto the big stage. Hustler's from as far away as Pittsburgh and Detroit were going to be at the Black Cartel-Stay Solid concert and Fat Chad wanted to make sure he was recognized.

Fat Chad was parked on Peckham in his sparkling new Cadillac Escalade with Lil' Man in the passenger seat rolling blunts. Behind them in a stretch Escalade limo, were ten young Gorillaz dressed from head to toe in Bathing Ape.

Fat Chad had selected these Gorillaz to accompany him to the concert based on their loyalty and earning potential. He wanted to show them some of the rewards that came with being on his team.

On top of that, no matter how much money he made, Fat Chad was determined not to lose touch with the streets. In his analysis that was the mistake Lil' Billy and the Stay Solid Boys had made and it cost Cash his life.

Fat Chad's goal was to die from old age, so to achieve that goal every move he made was pre-calculated. Playing chess in the joint with Big Mike had taught Fat Chad the value of thinking a few moves ahead.

The all expenses paid trip to the concert was Fat Chad's way of countering any possible seeds of betrayal before they had a chance to take root in his closest Gorillaz. Fat Chad knew from experience how dangerous a soldier could be once they started dreaming of becoming a general, so he planned on making sure his soldiers were content with their position.

Fat Chad was also hoping that after the concert he'd get a chance to talk to Lil' Billy. He wanted to get a read on Lil' Billy's future plans, in particular whether or not the Stripper Fest was just a onetime thing or if it meant the Stay Solid Boys were back in Akron permanently.

Even though his killers would be there on standby, Fat Chad didn't like the logistics of making a move on the Stay Solid Boys at the Stripper Fest. His gut instinct told him it wasn't right.

At the same time Fat Chad knew the quicker he took care of this unfinished business the quicker he could focus completely on what really mattered to him; shining like a star in the sky.

———————

"Damn Daddy, you shining like a muthafuckin superstar!" Dasha said, grinning ear to ear.

Lil' Billy didn't respond, he just stood there staring at the man in the mirror, also impressed by what he was seeing. Lil' Billy was in the dressing room preparing to go on stage in front of a packed arena, and his outfit alone was going to be the star of the show, He had on black Mauri gator boots, black jeans with gator pockets, and a black gator jacket. His jewelry consisted of a platinum Rolex with the iced out bezel, diamond pinky rings on both hands, and a platinum chain that said "CASH" in canary yellow diamonds. Lil' Billy was a man at the top of his game and his appearance reflected that.

Rick stuck his head in the dressing room and said,

"It's show time my nigga."

"Alright y'all, let's roll," Lil' Billy said to the Atlanta strippers that would be coming out on stage with him. He looked at Molly and Dasha and added, "I'll holla at y'all when I get through turning this muthafucka out!"

With his adrenalin pumping to the max, Lil' Billy proceeded to hit the stage and work the crowd into a frenzy. The bone jarring bass, Lil' Billy's aggressive lyrics and the visual effect of the strippers shaking their ass non-stop had the entire arena charged up.

By the time Raw Breed joined Lil' Billy on stage most of the crowd realized that they were witnessing a concert that would be talked about for years to come.

Last but not least Young Skrilla took the stage and did what he was asked to do; he brought the house down. He performed all the dope boy anthems he was famous for and for the grand finale he brought Raw Breed and Lil' Billy back out to perform a new track the three of them had recorded the last time Lil' Billy was in Atlanta called "It's Nothing."

After the show it was time for the after-party at the Mirage, which was sold out. Despite all the stars that were already in the building Lil' Billy's arrival still caused a stir. He was the epitome of a twenty-first century pimp as he walked through the club with Molly and Dasha on each arm.

When Lil' Billy reached the V.I.P area Young Skrilla, Raw Breed, Rick, T-Man, Ace, Walt, Stan and Showtime were already there popping bottles and celebrating the success of the concert. As soon as Young Skrilla saw Lil' Billy he stood up. "Here go the star of the show right here!" he exclaimed.

Lil' Billy laughed," I appreciate the compliment, but

you the reason the whole city came out."

"That might be true my nigga, but after tonight you the reason they gon keep coming out."

"Spoken like a true player!" Lil' Billy smiled and gave Young Skrilla a hug.

While Lil' Billy basked in the adulation he was receiving, Fat Chad was in awe of the whole scene. For the first time in his life he was in a room full of real bosses and he could feel the energy.

Seeing Lil' Billy shine made Fat Chad realize how conflicted his feelings about Lil' Billy were. On one hand it made Fat Chad feel good to see a nigga from the Hill putting it down like Lil' Billy was, but at the same time he felt a twinge of envy because Lil' Billy had out of town success while Fat Chad was still, in essence, a local nigga. Nevertheless, Fat Chad put his emotions on the backburner and headed towards Lil' Billy's table in hopes of striking up a conversation.

"Hey bruh, I just wanted to let you know, that was the livest show I ever seen," Fat Chad said when he reached Lil' Billy's table.

Lil' Billy nodded his head in approval as Fat Chad continued, "Yeah you really put it down for the Hill."

"Naw, I put it down for Stay Solid," Lil' Billy shot back, but not wanting to seem like he was on bullshit, he added, "But shit that is the Hill, so I guess you right."

There was an awkward silence before Fat Chad said, "Imma get back over here to my young Gorillaz, but maybe we can chop it up at yo Stripper Fest tomorrow."

"Fa sho," Lil' Billy replied, giving Fat Chad the brush off somewhat.

Lil' Billy spent another hour at the Mirage before

him and the entire Black Cartel and Stay Solid entourages headed to the Tower City Hotel for the real after-party.

The affair at the hotel was strictly for the upper-echelon crowd, but the lobby was still packed with fans trying to gain access to the top floor by any means necessary. The top floor was only accessible by key, so unless a person had been personally escorted by someone with a key, or in possession of one of the special invitations that had been passed out at the Mirage, they were left on the outside looking in.

What was going on the top floor could only be described as a baller's paradise. In addition to the ten Atlanta strippers, there were another ten strippers from the G.P. on the scene ready to provide whatever sexual services were needed. There was also a high-stakes dice game going on with a minimum bet of $5,000.Some of the richest street niggas in the State of Ohio were at the table winning and losing brick fare with a roll of the dice.

Lil' Billy had also kept in mind what Sincere had told him, so in the midst of all the celebration he was also politicking with some of the out of town bosses who were in attendance. Most of them were Rap label heads who still had one foot in the dope game. In other words they were just the type of guys Lil' Billy needed to expand his cocaine operation.

After exchanging phone numbers with some hustlers from Columbus, Lil' Billy stepped out into the crowded hallway where he ran into Rick who greeted him with a big smile on his face.

"Follow me," Lil' Billy said as he led Rick to his suite. With so much going on they hadn't had a chance to talk one on one, and Lil' Billy was looking forward to hearing Rick put their night to remember in its proper perspective. "Well my nigga, what you think?" Lil' Billy asked Rick once they were in the suite alone.

"I think we put it down," Rick replied.

"Naw, you put it down. You made all this shit happen."

"*We* made this happen. Stay Solid is a team. Always has been and always will be."

"Yeah you right. I just wish the whole team was here to witness this."

Lil' Billy looked at the canary yellow diamonds on his chain that spelled out Cash's name.

"His body ain't here, but you better believe his spirit is all around us," Rick said.

Rick had wanted to talk to Lil' Billy about his continued involvement in the dope game, but decided not to. He figured they could have that conversation in a few days, once things had returned back to normal .Tonight was all about celebration.

"Hand me a bottle of that Moet," Rick said as he stood up to leave.

"Ah shit, Mr. Clean and sober drinking tonight!" Lil' Billy laughed.

When Rick opened the door to leave Molly and Dasha were standing there about to knock."Perfect timing!" Rick smiled. "See you in a few hours my nigga."

"Stay Solid!" Lil' Billy said and held up a bottle of Moet.

Rick held up his bottle in return then turned and headed down the hallway towards his suite.

As Rick made his way down the hall he saw T-Man and Stan coming towards him escorted by four Atlanta strippers.

"Hey my nigga, I left something in yo room, but I'll pick it up in the morning," 'I'-Man said.

"Alright, I'll see you then," Rick said and continued down the hall.

As soon as Rick stuck the key in the door to his suite his phone rang. It was Big Moe calling.

Big Moe worked security for Showtime and tonight he had been posted in the hotel lobby in front of the elevator. His job was escorting those lucky few who had invitations to the top floor.

"Yo Big Moe, what it do?" Rick answered the phone.

"It's still pandemonium down here, but I'm calling cause some of yo people from Akron down here," Big Moe said.

"Shit if they was my people they would already be up here."

"Yeah I was thinking the same thing, but they pressed me to call, they say they name is Fat Chad."

Before Rick could reply his suite door opened and standing there butt ass naked was one of the thickest women Rick had ever seen in his life. *I left something in yo room*, Rick thought about what T-Man had said and smiled. "Yo if they ain't got no invitation fuck 'em," Rick said before he hung the phone up and stepped into his suite.

Meanwhile Big Moe gave Fat Chad the bad news," It's a no go Bruh," he said.

Fat Chad stood there for a split second not only stunned, but feeling disrespected. *Do them niggas know who the fuck I am*! he thought angrily.

Fat Chad had been lightweight offended by Lil'

Billy's demeanor when he tried to holler at him at the Mirage, but he overlooked it. Now he felt like the Stay Solid Boys had played him like a off-brand and that was something he couldn't overlook. *Y'all niggas better enjoy ya self tonight cause tomorrow y'all gon get a reality check.*

Chapter 10

WELCOME HOME

As bad as he wanted to disappear, L.A. mustered up enough courage to show up at Detective Bryant's house for his weekly haircut, slash debriefing.

L.A.'s scheme to get info about Lucky through dealing with Dasha hadn't panned out. All the sex in the world hadn't been able to loosen Dasha's lips and now L.A .didn't even know how to get in touch with her. Dasha had changed her number and for reasons L.A. was in the dark about, hadn't given him the new one.

Lucky's murder trial would be starting in two days and that was the deadline Detective Bryant had given L.A. to get info about the other murders Lucky had already committed. L.A.'s mission had turned out to be unsuccessful and now it was time to give Detective Bryant the bad news.

"Here check it out," L.A. said as he handed Detective Bryant a the mirror to inspect his haircut.

"We're good," Detective Bryant said and handed the mirror back to L.A.

"Well about that one demo I was telling you

about...It didn't work out," L.A. said nervously.

"Don't worry about it," Detective Bryant replied. "Everything is A-okay."

"Huh?" L.A. was lost.

"Don't worry about Lucky, I got that situation under control."

L.A. was relieved, but curious, "Under control how?" he asked.

"Sorry L.A., I can't go into all that. That's official police business and you're not an official cop...yet," Detective Bryant smiled.

Man, fuck you! L.A. thought. Despite the fact that the information he had provided Detective Bryant over the years had led to the arrest of over a hundred people, L.A. still didn't consider himself to be part of law enforcement. He was suffering from snitch denial.

Meanwhile, Detective Bryant felt like a game of golf. Even though he hadn't been able to gather more evidence about the other murders he believed Lucky had committed, the case he did have on him was strong enough for a conviction.

Lucky's two alibi witnesses were now convicted felons. The prosecutor offered Trina and Monique a take it or leave it probation deal and they took it. The prosecutor had rushed through the plea deal to make sure Trina and Monique had the convictions on their record before Lucky's trial started.

Now the jury's choice would come down to believing an elderly eyewitness with a clean record or two convicted drug dealers. In Detective Bryant's opinion, Lucky was up shit creek without a paddle.

Even though Lil' Billy knew the stripper fest would have a capacity crowd he wanted to create even more buzz, so instead of laying back and recuperating from the night before, Lil' Billy, Young Skrilla and Raw Breed were riding around Akron in Lil' Billy's new black on black BMW 750, smoking blunts and being seen.

To a certain extent, Lil' Billy considered Akron enemy turf, so following behind his BMW in a Ford Expedition were four of Walt's best shooters from St. Clair. Lil' Billy was making sure he was prepared if his unknown enemy tried to make a move.

After giving Young Skrilla and Raw Breed a tour of the city and stopping to sign a few autographs, Lil' Billy took them back out to their room at the Holiday Inn in Montrose, so they could rest up before the Stripper Fest.

Meanwhile, Lil' Billy headed to the strip club to make sure everything was on point for the evening's festivities and to meet with Jack.

While his personal security detail waited outside, Lil' Billy stepped in the strip club, "Guess who's back!" Lil' Billy greeted Jack who was sitting at the bar talking to Lexus.

"Well I'll be damned! I finally got to see what a million dollars look like!" Jack replied as he got up to hug Lil' Billy. All the planning for the Stripper Fest had been handled by Rick and Molly, so Jack hadn't seen or talked to Lil' Billy since Cash's funeral.

Lil' Billy took a seat at the bar, "Jack I want you to know I appreciate you letting us throw this event at yo club," he said.

"Come on now, you know I woulda' been upset if

you hadn't had it here," Jack replied. "I was ready to have one last big shindig anyway."

"What you mean, one last shindig, you goin somewhere?"

"Lexus baby, could you excuse us for a sec?"

"No problem boss," Lexus replied and walked to the end of the bar. Once she was out of ear shot Jack continued, "Lil' Billy I'm tired," he began, "I been in this business since hoes was selling pussy up and down Howard Street and I thought I had seen it all, but this new generation is like something I ain't never seen."

"What type of issues you having? You already know I'm down to help you anyway I can," Lil' Billy said.

"This issue is them muthafuckin Gorillaz. I mean shit, they done took over my damn club. They disrespect my dancers, they sell dope in here like they own the place…Don't get me wrong, I knew you and yo niggas was hustling in here, but y'all did it with polish, These lil' muthafuckas got crack heads coming in here to buy dope!"

"Did you ever talk to Fat Chad about this shit?"

"Yeah and you know what he did? He laughed in my face. He said if I can't control what goes on in my club I need to sell it to him."

As Lil' Billy sat there listening to Jack, he could feel his temperature rising. Ever since Sandy had introduced Jack to Lil' Billy, Jack had been a street mentor to Lil' Billy giving him insight on the finer points of the game. Because of that, Lil' Billy had the utmost love and respect for Jack.

Despite all the other issues Lil' Billy had going on in his life, he felt obligated to help Jack with his problem .To turn a blind eye to Jack's dilemma would go against everything Lil' Billy stood for.

"You know me and Fat Chad suppose to holla tonight anyway, so when we do I'll see if we can get a understanding about the issues you having," Lil' Billy said.

"Good luck," Jack said. "That nigga Fat Chad got so big he think he invincible."

"Well hopefully our egos' don't clash, cause shit, I got a nice size one my damn self."

"Yeah I was thinking the same thang."

Jack's remark made Lil' Billy laugh, but for Jack the situation was no laughing matter. Lil' Billy may have thought clashing with Fat Chad wasn't a big deal, but in 2004 clashing with Fat Chad and his Gorillaz was a death sentence. Jack knew better than to underestimate Lil' Billy cause through the years Lil' Billy had proven himself to be game tight, he just hoped that Lil' Billy didn't underestimate Fat Chad, cause that would be a fatal mistake.

Sunday's at the G.P. were always slow, but this Sunday was especially slow. Most of the hustlers who would usually come through the G.P. were tapped out from the Black Cartel-Stay Solid concert from the night before.

Normally Officer Strawberry wouldn't come to the G.P. on Sunday either, but he was horny, so he figured he would stop by and get a quick blowjob from Jackie. Even though he knew Jackie would probably be there shaking her ass to support her powder habit, he still called ahead of time to let her know he was on the way.

Well ain't this a pleasant surprise, Officer Strawberry thought when he walked in the G.P. and saw Maria on stage dancing. He hadn't seen her in a while and it was his understanding that she had quit dancing.

Since Jackie was nowhere in sight, Officer Strawberry figured he might as well have a drink and enjoy Maria's ass clapping show before he took Jackie to the parking lot. As Officer Strawberry sipped on his drink and watched Maria dance, he couldn't help but notice that it seemed like she was performing for him.

The whole time Maria was doing the splits and bouncing her juicy ass, she was licking her lips and looking Officer Strawberry dead in the eyes.

Officer Strawberry was confused by Maria's sudden interest in him. *The bitch must be high on something,* he thought. Nevertheless he planned on taking full advantage of the situation.

When Maria got off stage she walked straight over to Officer Strawberry, "Do you think we can go somewhere and talk?" she asked getting straight to the point.

"Yeah sure, we can talk in my car," Officer Strawberry replied.

"Give me a second to get dressed and I'll meet you in the parking lot," Maria said and headed to the dressing room while Officer Strawberry went outside to his car.

Officer Strawberry couldn't believe his luck. Even though Maria hadn 't come right out and said it, she was obviously ready to play ball cause every stripper at the G.P. knew what it meant to get in Officer Strawberry's car.

"Well Senorita what ya wanna talk about?" Officer Strawberry asked as soon as Maria got in the car.

"I wanna know how I can work at the G.P. without you taking my money," Maria replied.

"Come on now, let's not play dumb. I think you know what it takes to operate in Officer Strawberry's district."

"Okay, but how often?"

"Just every once and awhile. I know you got a man that loves you," Officer Strawberry lied. In reality, now that he believed he had broken her down, he planned on fucking Maria every chance he got.

"So Papi you promise if I suck yo dick here and there you'll stop taking my money?"

"I promise."

"Lean yo seat back."

Officer Strawberry followed Maria's instructions while she unzipped his pants. "Ooh Papi it's so big," she purred. Maria was lying through her teeth because Officer Strawberry's dick was no longer than four inches at best. Because of his lack of length Maria had no problem taking his entire dick in her mouth.

"That's right bitch suck it all!" Officer Strawberry snarled. He enjoyed degrading women, so while Maria was busy gobbling him up, he hurled a steady stream of insults at her.

Hurry up and cum you sick muthafucka! Maria thought. This was hands down the worst sexual experience of her life, but Officer Strawberry wouldn't know the difference. What he thought was an enthusiastic blowjob was in reality, Maria trying to hurry up and end what was for her a gut wrenching ordeal.

As soon as Maria felt Officer Strawberry cumming, she attempted to take his dick out of her mouth, to no avail.

"Swallow it bitch!" Officer Strawberry barked as he held Maria's head down with two hands and filled her mouth up with cum. Once he was completely spent he pulled her head up, "Open yo mouth!" he spat.

Maria did as she was told and opened her mouth.

"Bitch I told you to swallow it!" Officer Strawberry said as he backhanded her so hard across her face that she saw stars.

After Officer Strawberry inspected Maria's mouth again he unceremoniously kicked her out of his car and just like that her nightmare was over.

As Maria made her way back into the G.P. she stuck her hand in her jacket pocket and cut off the miniature tape recorder.

Akron's entire underworld came out for the Stay Solid Stripper Fest. Ballers and wanna-be ballers, from every side of town considered it a can't miss event. Most of them were there for the egotistical purpose of letting everybody know they were getting money, but at the same time a lot of them had come out to show Lil' Billy support. The Stay Solid Boys had taken some hits, but were still standing and that was something everybody respected.

The Akron Police were providing security for the event and that put everyone in attendance at ease. When street niggas got together in large numbers, the result was usually violence, but with the police on the scene, even the craziest niggas were in chill mode.

Outside, tickets that had cost fifty dollars were being scalped for two to three hundred dollars and every fifteen minutes the price was rising.

Once word got out about what was going on inside, people were willing to pay whatever it cost to witness the festivities.

To say it was going down in the strip club would be an understatement. What was going on that night was nothing less than ghetto erotica, decadence and opulence at the same time. The strippers had nothing to strip out of because they were already completely naked. While some of them were spinning around on the pole doing typical stripper feats, others were on stage eating each others' pussys to the shock and enjoyment of the capacity crowd.

A cameraman was on the scene filming everything for a DVD Stay Solid planned to release in the future, while a photographer from a urban men's magazine was there taking pictures for an upcoming issue.

At the center of the entire extravaganza was Young Skrilla and Lil' Billy, who were relaxing in V.I.P. area with their respective entourages.

Lil' Billy was wearing a gator outfit, the exact same style as the one he wore on stage at the concert. The only difference was the color. The one he wore at the concert was black and the one he wore at the Stripper Fest was blue.

A lot of the tension Lil' Billy had originally felt about being back in Akron disappeared. He was having a good time and everyone seemed to be happy that he was back in town.

When Fat Chad sent Lil' Billy a bottle of Dom Perignon, Lil' Billy figured that it would be a good time to talk to Fat Chad one on one about the issues Jack was having with the Gorillaz.

Lil' Billy grabbed the bottle of champagne and headed over to the area of the club where Fat Chad and his Gorillaz were posted up.

Lil' Billy noticed Lil' Man by Fat Chad's side and greeted him first, "What's up lil' nigga?" Show me some love!"

Lil' Man stood up and gave Lil' Billy some dap and

a hug. "What's good big homie?" Lil' Man said.

"Boy, ya look like ya out here shining! Cash always said you was a lil' hustler."

Lil' Man didn't respond, he just stood there silent and uncomfortable. Seeing Cash's name hanging around Lil' Billy's neck had unsettled Lil' Man. Add that to the fact that he was high on powder, ecstasy, and weed, and the feelings of guilt and paranoia were intensified.

Fat Chad noticed how rattled Lil' Man looked, so he quickly stepped in to change the subject, "Bruh, this a helluva event you put together," he said to Lil' Billy.

"Thanks, I just wanted to show the city that I ain't gon never forget where I came from," Lil' Billy replied, "but yo, lets pop this bottle, I need to holla at you on the one on one anyway."

Fat Chad told his Gorillaz to give him some space then him and Lil' Billy slid in a booth and sat across from each other. After they popped the bottle and made a toast to the Hill, Fat Chad was ready to hear what Lil' Billy had to say, "What's up Bruh? You said you needed to holla at me," Fat Chad said.

"You know this strip club is like a million dollar spot right?"

"Hell yeah, I wish I had a spot like this."

Yeah I bet you do, Lil' Billy thought before saying, "Well anyway Jack is getting old and he ready to walk away from all this, but he leaving the club in good hands."

"Who taking over?"

"I'm taking over, but Molly gon run the day to day operations."

"Okay so where do I fit in in all this?" Fat Chad asked, not liking the direction the conversation had taken.

"It's like this," Lil' Billy began, "Molly got big plans for the club. She plan on making what you see tonight a normal thang. Out of town strippers and some of the biggest rappers in the game gon be coming through here on the regular. Now with this new level of entertainment there has to be a new level of customer. This club is gon be the place where the Players' play, so we can't have niggas in here that wanna disrespect dancers or to be serving fiends in here, ya feel me?"

"Yeah I understand all that, but I still don't understand what this has to do with me ."

"I need you to control yo lil' niggas when they up in here. All the disrespecting dancers and using this spot as a dope house is over with. If the police raid this spot, that's gon cost me money and I ain't tryna take no losses."

This nigga tryna check me like I'm a little nigga! Fat Chad thought. *Well nigga you about to get put in yo place tonight, right in front of all these out of town niggas you brought with you.*

"Bruh, don't worry bout nothing, if any of my Gorillaz get out of line in here I'll handle it personally . You got my word on that," Fat Chad said in the most sincere voice he could come up with.

"That's what's up," Lil' Billy smiled. "Yo check this out, after this is over with, we gon have a private party at the Holiday Inn in Montrose and I want you to be there."

"Then I'll be there my nigga!" Fat Chad gave Lil' Billy some dap.

With his business with Fat Chad taken care of Lil' Billy headed back to the V.I.P. section. "What's up with that nigga?" T-Man asked Lil' Billy referring to Fat Chad.

"He cool my nigga… Everything is all good," Lil'

Billy replied, then turned to Sean Linen and said, "What's up nigga you ready?"

"Hell yeah! I'm just waiting on Molly to pass me the mic," Sean Linen replied.

Sean Linen was a young rapper from St. Clair that Walt had under his wing. Walt had the money, but he didn't have the expertise necessary to really make moves in the rap game, so he had brought Sean Linen to Lil' Billy and Rick.

All it took was hearing one verse and Lil' Billy and Rick knew Sean Linen would make a great addition to Stay Solid Records.

Sean Linen was still rough around the edges, so Lil' Billy decided to let him perform a song at the Stripper Fest, so he could get some experience in working a crowd.

"How y'all doing? Is y'all enjoying the Stripper Fest?" Molly asked the crowd in her thick southern accent as she took the stage. The crowd roared their approval and Molly continued, "Well since y'all like it so much, we gon keep doing it big every week with Stay Solid Sundays and just like tonight some of my thick home girls from the ATL gon be in the building and some of the best rappers in the game... With that said, I'd like to introduce the newest addition to the Stay Solid family coming from Cleveland, Ohio ... Sean Linen!"

While Sean Linen proceeded to rock the crowd, Lil' Billy sat back somewhat amazed at how good everything was going. The concert and the Stripper Fest had been a roaring success.

There had been a capacity crowd at both, without any of the drama that was usually associated with hip-hop related events. Besides a few skirmishes between some females, everyone had been on their best behavior.

After Sean Linen performed his song, Lil' Billy was ready to head to the hotel. He figured it would be best if they left in groups instead of all at once, so while Young Skrilla, Raw Breed and their entourages left first, Lil' Billy decided to leave last with Molly and the strippers.

Lil' Billy had told his personal security detail to take the rest of the night off, but they had refused. They were under strict orders from Walt not to let Lil' Billy out of their sight, so while everybody else was partying, they had remained sober, keeping their eyes on Lil' Billy at all times.

Lil' Billy, Molly, and Sean Linen were sitting at the bar having a celebratory drink with Jack, while they waited on the strippers to get dressed.

"What's up O.G., you sure you don't wanna come out to hotel with us?" Lil' Billy asked Jack in a playful tone.

"I think I done seen enough activity for one night. I'm in the mood for a private party," .Jack smiled and looked at Lexus.

"I can dig that!" Lil' Billy laughed. "By the way, I talked to ole boy about the problems you been having and he assured me that he was gon straighten it out."

"Good," Jack nodded his approval.

When the strippers came out of the dressing room that meant it was time to go. Everyone gave Jack a hug and headed out to the parking lot.

Molly, Sean Linen, and two of the strippers got in Molly's truck, while the rest of the strippers were riding in two rented Escalades. They pulled out of the parking lot with Lil' Billy in his BMW in the lead and his security team bring up the rear.

Meanwhile, sitting in the back of the parking lot in his Cadillac Escalade by himself was Fat Chad. As soon as he saw Lil' Billy pull out of the parking lot, he made a phone call.

———————

When they got the call from Fat Chad, Buddha, and Meech, were sitting in a stolen Crown Victoria in Wooster-Hawkins Plaza. Buddha and Meech were professional hit men from Youngstown and lately, Fat Chad had been their main customer.

"The target in a black BMW and they coming our way," Buddha said after hanging up the phone.

Meech didn't say anything, he just nodded and grabbed the Tec-9 from under the seat. He covered his face with a red bandanna and Buddha did likewise. The red bandannas were Fat Chad's idea. He wanted the Eastside to be blamed for the hit.

Buddha pulled the car up to the corner of Hawkins and Wooster and waited for the BMW to come into sight. The strip club was across the street from Rolling Acres Mall and since Buddha and Meech had rode past it earlier that night they knew it wouldn't take long for the BMW to make it from the strip club to the intersection where they were waiting.

"Here it come," Meech said when he saw the BMW approaching from the distance.

Now it was all about timing. Buddha had the green light, so he had to wait until the BMW pulled up to the red light before he pulled out into the intersection.

A split second after the BMW stopped at the red light the Crown Victoria pulled in front of it and Meech started pumping slugs from the Tec-9 into the BMW's windshield.

In the midst of the gunfire and broken glass Meech

could see the figure in the front seat of the BMW laying stiff which meant his mission was complete.

"Go!" he yelled and Buddha hit the gas.

Lil' Billy's security team jumped out of the Ford Expedition and returned fire to no avail as the Crown Victoria sped off into the night.

Chapter 11

TRIALS AND TRIBULATIONS

Sugarman had learned a long time ago how to live life without regret, but as he sat in his office listening to Sandy talk, regret was exactly what he was feeling.

About a year ago Sugarman had told Sandy what he believed to be the real story behind her baby's father Cedric's murder. He told her because he and Sandy had always been close, plus he felt like she had a right to know.

Now he realized that he had made a mistake. "Sandy, are you sure you really wanna pursue this? I mean shit, you're dealing with a very dangerous individual," Sugarman said referring to Sincere.

"Look Sugarman, I'm past the point of no return," Sandy replied. Sandy had returned to Detroit to spend time with her son and make arrangements just in case something went wrong in Atlanta.

After much observation and careful planning, Sandy came up with what she thought was the perfect way to avenge Cedric's death. She knew if Sincere uncovered her plot he would probably kill her, so she wanted to make sure in the event of her demise that her son would be well taken care of.

"Okay, just out of curiosity, what exactly are you going to do?" Sugarman asked.

"Now you know I can't tell you that," Sandy smiled, "The bottom line is that this is Sincere's fate and I'm just the vessel of karma."

With that statement, Sugarman realized that it would be fruitless to continue trying to intervene in Sandy's plans. He had no grounds to stop her from pursuing what he had to admit was a righteous cause.

Sincere taking the contract on his own brother was without question the most treacherous act Sugarman had ever seen in his entire life in the streets. It was the type of act that the devil didn't even like.

In Sugarman's opinion, Sincere deserved to die for what he had done, he just hoped that Sandy didn't lose her life trying to bring about vengeance.

Sugarman opened the safe behind his desk and put the $50,000 Sandy gave him to hold for her son in it.

"Well hopefully I'll see you in six months," he said. Sandy had told him she would be back to Detroit in six months and if she wasn't back, she was more than likely dead.

"Sugarman you ain't gotta hope, I'll be back, believe that," Sandy insisted.

"What makes you so sure?"

"Cause I'm true to the game, so the game will always be true to me."

———————

After watching what was meant to be his murder take place, Lil' Billy was literally in a state of shock. He knew he had come within sixty seconds of death.

When Lil' Billy and his entourage pulled out of the strip club parking lot, they drove down Romig Road until they came to a red light across from Primo's Deli.

While waiting for the light to change Molly pulled up next to Lil' Billy in her BMW truck with Sean Linen in the passenger seat. Molly rolled her window down, so Sean Linen could remind Lil' Billy what he promised him earlier that night; that he could drive Lil' Billy's BMW.

Lil' Billy, always being a man of his word, got out of his car and hopped into the truck with Molly, while Sean Linen got behind the wheel of the BMW.

Sixty seconds later Sean Linen was dead behind the wheel of that BMW.

The local news media was all over the story of Sean Linen's murder, placing extra emphasis on the fact that he was a rapper affiliated with Stay Solid Records and had just performed at a Stay Solid event when he was killed. Also at the behest of Detective Bryant, the Beacon Journal ran a related story about Lucky's upcoming murder trial and referred to Lucky as an artist on Stay Solid Records, despite the fact that Lucky had never even breathed on a microphone before.

Immediately after the shooting, Rick took Young Skrilla and the rest of the Black Cartel to the airport, so they could get back to Atlanta before the Akron detectives could question them.

Walt's shooters also made a beeline out of town which was understandable considering that they had fired weapons at the scene of the murder.

Lil' Billy, Molly and the strippers were taken downtown for questioning. When they arrived, Angelo Pellini was already there waiting. After everyone was tested for gun powder residue, they were put in separate rooms to be interrogated.

This was Detective Bryant's first time meeting Lil' Billy face to face, but instead of interrogating him himself, he watched everything on camera from another room.

Throughout the interrogation, Lil' Billy maintained the same stoic expression on his face. To Detective Bryant this meant that Lil' Billy was cold hearted and more than capable of signing off on murders. Nothing the detectives asked Lil' Billy seemed to rattle him.

Beneath his cool demeanor Lil' Billy was dealing with a mind full of chaotic thoughts. Somebody wanted him dead, but who and why was still a mystery to him.

After the police were finished with him, Lil' Billy went to his mama's house in Pepper Pike and let her know he was alright, then went to his apartment to try to relax and figure things out.

Lil' Billy took a quick nap then called Ace and Walt and told them to come by so they could talk.

"Make sure you let Sean's family know I'll pay for the funeral," Lil' Billy said to Walt.

"Don't worry about that Bruh, I was gon take care of it," Walt replied.

"Naw, I wouldn't feel right if I didn't do it… that nigga lost his life because of me."

"I feel you Bruh," Walt paused before asking, "What happened though?"

"Somebody was tryna hit me," Lil' Billy replied. "A Crown Vic pulled up and unloaded on my Beemer."

"Like I told you before, I got young niggas that will go and air shit out, all you gotta do is say the word," Ace said.

"Yeah, that's cool but, I don't even know who to go at…at first I thought I was at war with the Eastside, but now I'm not so sure," Lil' Billy continued, "Whoever behind this shit got money. Them niggas that tried to hit me was professionals. Them wasn't no young niggas tryna collect five thousand."

"Well unless you gon turn yo back on Akron completely, you need to find out who behind this shit and hit 'em hard," Walt said.

"That's what I plan on doing, but first I gotta make sure my nigga Lucky straight. His trial starts tomorrow." Lil' Billy wasn't just issuing idle threats, he meant what he said. He refused to continue being on the receiving end of gangsta shit. With or without Lucky, Lil' Billy knew he had to show the streets that Stay Solid was still built for war.

If not, his only option would be to do what Walt said and turn his back on Akron completely and Lil' Billy had too much pride to do that.

Damn this pussy wet! Fat Chad thought while Peaches bounced up and down on his dick like a pogo stick.

Fat Chad and Peaches were under the impression that Lil' Billy was dead, so Peaches figured she would reward Fat Chad with some good sex for completing her mission.

Peaches had never felt more powerful in her life and that power had the effect of an aphrodisiac on her. Peaches squeezed her titties and bit her bottom lip as she had orgasm after orgasm. *Maybe I should keep him around a little longer*, Peaches thought while enjoying the ride on Fat

Chad's dick. She had originally planned on phasing Fat Chad out after he killed Lil' Billy, but now she was thinking it might be in her best interest to hold on to him. Fat Chad was the most powerful young nigga in the city and on top of that he knew how to beat the pussy up the way Peaches liked it.

Fat Chad wasn't as polished as Peaches would have liked him to be, but she figured he could keep her occupied until Big Mike came home or she came across another boss she wanted to conquer.

Fat Chad grabbed Peaches' hips giving her advanced notice that he was approaching his peak. Peaches leaned forward and whispered in Fat Chad's ear, "Come inside me Daddy," and right on cue Fat Chad released his seed inside Peaches.

Fat Chad and Peaches spent the next few minutes lying in each other's arms enjoying the after sex euphoria.

Fat Chad's phone rang and he reached over and grabbed it off the night stand. It was Lil' Man calling.

Even though he wasn't saying much, Peaches could tell by his body language that Fat Chad was being told something on the phone that he didn't like. When Peaches heard Fat Chad ask, "Who was in his car?" she knew that the phone conversation was about Lil' Billy and that made her even more alert.

After hanging up the phone, Fat Chad sat there stunned. He couldn't believe what he had just heard. *I saw that nigga get in that car*, Fat Chad thought. *How the fuck is he not dead?*

According to Lil' Man, it was the rapper that performed at the Stripper Fest, who was killed in Lil' Billy's BMW and not Lil' Billy.

Peaches couldn't wait any longer, she had to know what was up. "What's wrong?" she asked.

"Dude still alive," Fat Chad replied.

"Lil' Billy?"

"Yeah."

"How?" Peaches was shocked.

"Shit, I guess he wasn't in the car."

"I thought you said you saw him get in the car."

"Look, don't start asking me a bunch of muthafuckin questions! The bottom line is the nigga ain't dead." Fat Chad was salty about the whole situation, but first and foremost for financial reasons.

Buddha and Meech charged $20,000 for hits, which was high, but reasonable considering the fact that they were professionals. Fat Chad paid them to kill the driver of the BMW that's what they did. The fact that it ended up not being Lil' Billy didn't matter. They didn't give refunds, so for Fat Chad that was $20,000 wasted.

Fat Chad could see that Lil' Billy was moving up the totem pole and the window of opportunity to kill him was closing, if not closed already. The more Fat Chad analyzed things he realized he had fucked up. He should been more patient and gave Lil' Billy time to feel comfortable again in Akron, but instead, he let his ego drive him into making a move too quickly.

Fat Chad wasn't completely game shy, so he recognized that he had only went at Lil' Billy to pacify Peaches and to retaliate for the embarrassment he felt when he couldn't get into the hotel after party after the concert in Cleveland.

Big Mike had warned Fat Chad never to make moves based on emotion, but that was exactly what he had done.

Fat Chad came to the conclusion that to continue pursuing Lil' Billy would be counter-productive to his goal of getting rich. He had just met a nigga from Canton at the Stripper Fest who wanted to buy ten bricks and that could be the beginning of him expanding into new markets.

Fat Chad decided that killing Lil' Billy was an issue that was going on the back burner, temporarily and maybe even permanently and Peaches was just going to have to accept that. *If she want him dead that bad, then she can kill him herself,* he thought.

———————

When Lucky stepped off the elevator at the Summit County Courthouse, Lil' Billy was the first person he saw. Lil' Billy smiled and gave Lucky a look that said *I'm still standing my nigga!* Lucky smiled back, then the deputies escorted him into the chambers of Judge Unger's courtroom.

Lucky had heard the rumors that Lil' Billy was dead, but the night before Pellini had come on an attorney visit and informed him that Lil' Billy was alive and well. Not it was time to focus on the matter at hand; saving his own life.

The first order of business would be picking a jury. The prosecutor Kevin Mason had just offered Lucky a ten year plea deal which he had refused, so the bailiff cleared the courtroom and brought in the prospective jurors.

As usual, with Summit County jury pools there weren't a lot of black people to choose from, so Lucky ended up with ten whites and two blacks.

After the jury was picked, there was a short recess before opening arguments began. During this time, the public was let back in the courtroom. Lucky's mama sat with

Lil' Billy, T-Man, Rick, Dasha, and Molly in the front row, while the rest of the courtroom was filled with the usual assortment of characters that always show up at ghetto funerals and murder trials.

Because the case against Lucky was so weak, the prosecutor's strategy was to engage in courtroom theatrics, beginning with the opening arguments. While Pellini on the other hand planned on keeping the focus on the state's lack of evidence.

After opening arguments were done it was time for the state to present its case. The first witnesses were the owner of the house that Bulldog was killed behind, the 911 operator, the first cops on the scene, and finally the coroner. Pellini gave them a basic cross examination. He saw no need to go on the offensive yet, it was still early. He was saving his best punches for the later rounds.

At 4:30 the judge called the evening recess. The trial would resume at 8:00 o'clock in the morning at which the state would call their only eyewitness, Lucious Thomas.

———————

The next morning Lucky felt something that he wasn't used to feeling. He was nervous.

What took place in Judge Unger's courtroom today would determine the rest of his life. He would either return to the free world or join the long list of street commandos who spend the rest of their lives rotting away in a prison cell.

Stan had sent word to Lucky that Mr. Thomas was taken care of, but Pellini had just informed Lucky that Mr. Thomas was outside the courtroom ready to testify. Lucky was confused, but one thing he knew for sure was that Stan had never let him down before.

"All rise!" the bailiff called out as Judge Unger entered the courtroom. After the judge took her seat on the bench, the rest of the rest of the courtroom sat down and the proceedings began.

The prosecutor stood up, "For the next witness the state calls Lucious Thomas to the stand."

The door to the courtroom opened and Mr. Thomas walked in. His walk more a akin to a shuffle and with the blue jean overalls he was wearing he looked like a sharecropper from the deep South. After swearing to tell the whole truth and nothing but the truth, Mr. Thomas took a seat on the witness stand and the questioning began.

After asking Mr. Thomas basic questions about his background and how long he had lived on McKinley, the prosecutor got to the heart of the matter.

"Now Mr. Thomas, on the day in question tell me what you saw when you looked out your bathroom window."

"I saw a guy shooting into the ground."

"Shooting into the ground?"

"Well that's what I thought at first."

"When did your thinking change Mr. Thomas?"

"When the detective came and talked to me," Mr. Thomas pointed at Detective Bryant who was seated at the prosecutor's table.

The prosecutor continued, "Now after talking to Detective Bryant you learned that the guy you thought was shooting into the ground was in fact shooting into a man's body, is that correct?"

"Yes sir."

The prosecutor walked over and stood next to the jury box, "Mr. Thomas is the man you saw shooting into what you thought was the ground in the courtroom right now?"

"No sir."

The courtroom let out a collective gasp.

"Excuse me, would you repeat that answer?" the prosecutor asked.

"I said *no sir*," Mr. Thomas leaned toward the microphone.

"So Mr. Thomas, what you're telling this courtroom is that the man you saw shooting into what you thought was the ground is *not* in the courtroom?"

"Objection!" Pellini yelled, "The state is badgering the witness. Mr. Thomas has already answered the question."

"Objection sustained," Judge Unger said, "Mr. Mason you need to ask a different question."

"Your Honor, the state requests a sidebar," the prosecutor was visibly shaken by the shocking turn of events.

"Sidebar granted, attorneys may approach the bench," Judge Unger replied.

"This should be good," Pellini whispered to Lucky before he headed to the bench.

Nobody could hear what was being discussed during the sidebar, but the body language displayed by Pellini and the prosecutor conveyed that there was a heated debate taking place.

Meanwhile, Lucky scanned the courtroom for familiar faces and seated behind his mama was Stan and Nicole. Stan gave Lucky a reassuring smile and Lucky nodded in return. There was no doubt in Lucky's mind that Mr. Thomas' performance on the witness stand was a Stan production.

After the sidebar, the prosecutor had no further

questions for Mr. Thomas. Instead he called Detective Bryant to the stand to give testimony about how Mr. Thomas had picked Lucky out of a photo line-up. It was a last ditch attempt to save what was in essence a sinking ship.

When it was the defense's turn to present their case, Pellini only called one witness, Mr. Thomas. Mr. Thomas explained how he had picked Lucky out of a photo line-up, but once he saw Lucky in the courtroom, he knew he had picked the wrong guy.

Before closing arguments Pellini filed a motion for acquittal which the judge denied, so the state proceeded with what had be one of the most bizarre closing arguments in history. The prosecutor asked the jury to disregard the testimony of Mr. Thomas who was technically the state's witness. For Detective Bryant and the rest of the prosecution it was painful to watch, but for Pellini it was a joyous scene.

Pellini knew the State's case was dead, so during his closing argument he delivered the nail in the coffin. Pellini was a master of courtroom melodrama and the jury sat there captivated as he labeled the state's case Lucky an example of judicial corruption.

The jury deliberated for no more than thirty minutes before coming back with the verdict everyone was expecting; not guilty.

Chapter 12

Back In The Saddle

This must be my lucky day, Buttaman thought as he headed towards the front door of the G.P. Buttaman was a known Up the Way crackhead and Ace had just promised him fifty dollars to give a manila folder to Officer Strawberry who was inside the G.P. Under most circumstances Buttaman would have looked inside the envelope, but Ace had given him strict instructions not to look inside and not to tell Officer Strawberry where he got it from.

When Buttaman stepped inside the G.P., Big Tone the bouncer stopped him dead in his tracks, "Hold it! Buttaman you know goddamn well you ain't allowed in here!"

"I swear I'll be in and out. I got a package for Officer Strawberry," Buttaman pleaded.

Big Tone looked at the manila envelope Buttaman was holding. "Alright Buttaman, hurry up. You got sixty seconds," he said.

Buttaman quickly made his way to the bar where Officer Strawberry was sitting.

"This is for you," Buttaman said and quickly made

his way out the door.

Meanwhile, Officer Strawberry opened the envelope and pulled out a mini-tape recorder and a typed letter. He immediately read the letter.

One more false move and a copy of this tape is going to the chief of police and the mayor's office.

Officer Strawberry felt like the room was spinning, but he regained his composure enough to go out to his car, so he could listen to the tape.

Officer Strawberry pushed play on the tape recorder and immediately heard his and Maria's voice. *This dirty bitch taped me!* he thought. There was nothing he could do. He had been outsmarted. If the tape got in the hands of his superiors, not only would his career as a police officer be over, but he would probably end up in prison.

Officer Strawberry needed to regroup. He had to find a way to neutralize the advantage that Ace and Maria had over him, but how?

Now, more than ever Officer Strawberry understood the old saying; it ain't no fun when the rabbit got the gun.

––––––––––––––

The not guilty verdict in Lucky's murder trial sent shock waves throughout Akron's underworld. With those two words, the entire equation of the streets had been changed. Factors all over the city were doing self-analysis to make sure they hadn't done anything while Lucky was in the county that would put them at odds with him or any of the Stay Sold Boys.

Lucky spent his first night of freedom at his mama's house, then Dasha and Molly took him to Lil' Billy's spot in Cleveland. Lucky didn't want to be visible in Akron until he had a clear understanding of what was going on.

When Lucky got to Lil' Billy's place, Lil' Billy, Rick, and T-Man were there waiting on him. Lucky was so happy to be in the company of the men he considered his brothers that his eyes teared up.

After all the hugs were out of the way, the fellas sat down so they could discuss everything that was going on. Without being told, Dasha and Molly went in the other room to give them some privacy.

"Well my nigga, how ya feel?" Lil' Billy asked.

"Real good Bruh," Lucky replied, "I feel like I'm in a dream."

"Well it ain't no dream my nigga, you out here as free as a bird," T-Man said.

"Where that nigga Stan at? I can't wait to hear how he put that play down with that old man," Lucky said.

"He up here fucking with one of his Cleveland hoes. He said he gon shoot through later on," Rick said before adding, "By the way, I brought my clippers, so come on, let me tighten you up."

While Rick cut Lucky's hair, the fellas had the conversation Lucky had been waiting months to have; who killed Cash?

"On the surface, it look like the Eastside did it, but my gut tells me somebody from the hood was involved," Lil' Billy began, "of course my first suspect was Fat Chad, but then I got word that he had the Eastside nigga Kat killed in retaliation for Cash getting killed."

"Them niggas that shot me at the Delia Market had on red," T-Man cut in.

"And the niggas that tried to hit me after the Stripper Fest had on red bandanas," Lil' Billy added.

"See that's the reason I know the Eastside ain't behind all this," Lucky said, "That's the oldest trick in the book, wearing another team's colors, so they'll get blamed. Another thing is if this was a Eastside operation they coulda hit me on Talbot. What sense would it make for them to go at us in our hood when they could catch one of us in their hood?"

"Okay, if it ain't the Eastside that brings up back to the hood which brings us back to Fat Chad," Lil' Billy said.

"Maybe, maybe not," Lucky said, "We can't just lock in on one person. We gotta be patient cause now that I'm out, niggas gon start talking."

"Just don't do nothing crazy, cause you know the police gon be on yo ass," Rick said.

"Shit, I'm already hip. I plan on staying in the shadows," Lucky replied.

"Well not too far in the shadows, cause I need you to ride shotgun with Molly," Lil' Billy said.

"What's the mission?"

"Making the strip club Stay Solid again."

"Okay, I'm down with that, but speaking of Molly, how you come up with that bad muthafucka anyway?"

Lil' Billy proceeded to get Lucky caught up on everything that took place in Atlanta, including his relationship with Sincere. Nothing Lil' Billy told Lucky surprised him cause Lil' Billy had always been the type of nigga that made shit happen. It wasn't until Lil' Billy told Lucky about his encounter with Sandy that Lucky raised an eyebrow, "Man, how she get connected with dude?" he asked.

"Bruh, I don't know and don't give a fuck," Lil' Billy replied.

"Do Sincere know you used to fuck with her?"

"Naw, he don't even know her real name. He think her name Cassandra...But shit, that might be her real name. Ain't no telling with her. The only thing I know for sure is that he done opened up a cocaine pipeline for me and pretty soon I'm gon be flooding the whole Midwest."

Lil' Billy spent the next hour or so explaining Stay Solid's new status in the game. Lucky and T-Man were impressed, but Rick just sat there silently, disappointed in what he was hearing. More and more he was realizing that him and Lil' Billy were on different paths in life.

Later that evening, Stan came through and the first question on everyone's lips was how did he get Mr. Thomas to change his story?

"Well, you know I used to fuck with his granddaughter Nicole back in the day," Stan began, "so I rekindled a relationship with the bitch and through her I found out that Mr. Thomas was having money problems and was on the verge of losing his house. After that, shit was easy. I shot him the $8000 to get his house out of foreclosure, plus gave him another $5,000 after he got off the witness stand."

I got a few dollars put up, so I'll shoot you the thirteen racks back this week," Lucky said.

"Bruh, come on with that bullshit," Stan was offended, "You don't owe me shit. I did that in the name of the game."

"You right, my nigga, I'm trippin," Lucky gave Stan a hug.

"By the way, you know Trina and Monique looking for you," Stan smiled.

"Oh, I was in the county working out, I'm ready for

them hoes!" Lucky laughed.

"Hold up, cause before you get to them, I got some Cleveland action for ya," Lil' Billy cut in, "then Molly got some Atlanta hoes for you to play with."

"Well fuck it! Pass me the muthafuckin Hennessey and let's get this party started!" Lucky stood up and everybody laughed.

Lucky had a good time that evening, on through the night into the next morning. In the midst of good liquor, good weed, and good pussy, Lucky remained conscious of how close he came to losing his life.

Lucky had always had the streets attention, but now he had the attention of the Akron police and he would be a fool to take that lightly.

While Lucky was in the county jail, he had read a book called The Art of War by Sun Tzu. In the book it talked about using deception to defeat your enemy and that's what Lucky planned on doing.

Everyone was expecting Lucky to get back in the trenches and avenge Cash's murder, but Lucky was smarter than that. On the surface, he planned on presenting the image of a changed man, but beneath the surface, he could be making moves to find out who Stay Solid's enemies were. Once he had that information, then Akron would see a spike in homicides.

———————

As a result of Lucky's acquittal, Detective Bryant's dream of becoming chief of police one day suffered a serious setback. He had gambled and lost and now the entire Summit County Prosecutor's Office had him on their shit list.

As soon as the not guilty verdict was read, Detective

Bryant started formulating a plan to rise from the ashes. He knew it would take something big to recover from the fiasco of Lucky's murder case and that's what he had in mind.

It was common knowledge in the city of Akron that Angelo Pellini was a crooked lawyer with mafia ties, but for some reason local or federal law enforcement had never gone after him. Rumor had it that Pellini had the goods on some of the most powerful political figures in Akron and because of that he was virtually untouchable, at least on the local level.

Detective Bryant felt like his back was against the wall, so he decided to call in a few favors. His first move was to make contact with his old friend from the FBI, Special Agent Tom Ryan. Agent Ryan specialized in government corruption and was more than willing to help Detective Bryant go after Angelo Pellini.

Next, Detective Bryant gave his contact at the Beacon Journal, a reporter named Phil Trotter, a call. He informed Trotter that he had a big story cooking and that he would make sure Trotter was the one to break it. In exchange, Detective Bryant had Trotter tell him everything he knew about Angelo Pellini.

Finally, at the weekly haircut slash debriefing, Detective Bryant filled L.A. in on his new assignment.

For L.A., going after Pellini was child's play compared to the drama of trying to gather info about Lucky, so he was more than happy to participate in what he considered a low risk endeavor.

Before L.A. became an informant for Detective Bryant Pellini was his lawyer, so he knew Pellini well. Pellini enjoyed Black women and powder cocaine and in the past, L.A. had supplied him with both.

"What exactly is it you want me to do?" L.A. asked Detective Bryant. They were in the basement of Detective Bryant's home.

"All you gotta do is place this under the seat in Pellini's car," Detective Bryant held up a small listening devise.

"Is there a certain conversation you need me to have with him?"

"Nah, just keep it normal. Y'all ain't had dealings in a while, so if you jump right into illegal shit he might get suspicious… here take this and give it to Pellini, as a retainer," Detective Bryan handed L.A. an envelope containing $5,000. This was a federal investigation which meant there was more money at Detective Bryant's disposal.

Now that he had given L.A. his assignment, all Detective Bryant had to do was sit back and listen to whatever discussions that the bug picked up. If things worked out the way Detective Bryant envisioned, once he put the squeeze on Pellini, Pellini would want to make some type of deal to avoid jail time and that's when things would really get interesting.

———————

Fat Chad was far from soft, but when he heard that Lucky had beaten his murder case, he was overwhelmed by anxiety. Just like everybody else in the city, Fat Chad knew that Lucky would be the one to get to the bottom of Cash's murder. A killer's greatest fear is death and for Fat Chad, Lucky represented for sure death.

Under normal circumstances, Fat Chad would just send his killers at Lucky, but Lucky was a totally different animal and it would be next to impossible to catch him slipping. With all the drama that the Stay Solid Boys had been going through, Lucky would definitely be on high alert, waiting on somebody to take a shot at him.

I gotta think of something, Fat Chad thought as he steered his Escalade around West Akron while smoking a blunt to the face. Fat Chad knew he had to make some type of move because three people knew he was behind Cash's murder and as far as he was concerned that was three too many.

Fat Chad had never known Big Mike to run his mouth, but even if he did he was in the joint, so Fat Chad had no way of shutting him up anyway.

Next was Peaches and since Fat Chad was in love with her, he couldn't help but analyze her in the most positive light. Nevertheless, he tried to give things an unbiased look and he concluded that Peaches knew a lot of secrets and she had yet to open her mouth, so that meant she could be trusted.

Finally, Fat Chad came to Lil' Man. From day one, Fat Chad had believed that he would one day have to kill Lil' Man, but he had thus far delayed that day of reckoning.

Lil' Man had not once showed Fat Chad any signs of betrayal, but Fat Chad couldn't get out of his head the fact that Lil' Man had betrayed Cash. At the same time, Fat Chad realized how valuable Lil' Man was to him.

Not only was Lil' Man controlling the cocaine traffic around Madison and Wildwood, but he was also the muscle. Lil' Man was the prototype crack baby; human life held no value to him. His propensity for wanton violence had made him feared by men twice his age. His liberal use of cocaine powder and ecstasy made Lil' Man even more unpredictable. Fat Chad may have founded the Gorillaz, but it was Lil' Man who kept them all in line. Despite all this, Fat Chad decided that allowing Lil' Man to live was a gamble he could not take.

Nevertheless, Fat Chad knew that before he could kill Lil' Man he would need to find his replacement and who better to help him with that mission than Lil' Man. With that in mind, Fat Chad headed to the hood to find Lil' Man.

Fat Chad found Lil' Man in his usual spot; on the corner of Peckham and Wildwood surrounded by Gorillaz. Upon seeing Fat Chad they approached his truck in order to pay homage.

"What it G like big homie? Lil' Man said.

"It's all good, hop in let's bend a few corners," Fat Chad replied.

"I'll catch up with y'all later," Lil' Man said to the other Gorillaz as he got in Fat Chad's truck.

What's the word in the hood?" Fat Chad asked.

"Shit everybody talking bout Lucky shakin' that murder case," Lil' Man replied.

"You seen him yet?"

"Who Lucky?"

"Yeah."

"Nah, ain't nobody seen him yet, but he out fa sho," Lil' Man felt some anxiety also about Lucky being out, but he believed as long as he kept his mouth shut he was cool. Furthermore, Lil' Man had decided that if shit did hit the fan, he would just shift the blame to Fat Chad cause in reality, Fat Chad was the one responsible for the whole thing.

"Well if you see him before I do, tell him I got something for him... but anyway I wanted to holla at you about our business," Fat Chad said.

"What's wrong? Is there a problem?" Lil' Man

asked.

"Nah, ain't no problem. I just think it's time for you to come off the block."

"I don't understand what you mean."

"I'm moving up the ladder, so that mean you gotta move up. It's time for you to start selling whole bricks."

Lil' Man sat there barely able to contain his excitement. For a young street hustler buying one kilo of cocaine is a major accomplishment, so being in a position to sell kilos is like dying and going to heaven.

"Big homie, I'm ready for the next level, but who gon hold down the block?" Lil' Man asked.

"That's a decision you gotta make," Fat Chad replied. "You out here in the jungle every day, so you know who the real Gorillaz is."

Lil' Man knew immediately who could take his place; his right hand man Pookie. Pookie was a certified hustler and he didn't have any qualms about taking a life. On a few of the murders that had been attributed to Lil' Man it was Pookie who had actually pulled the trigger.

Fat Chad was familiar with Pookie and on the surface he seemed like a good choice to replace Lil' Man. Fat Chad made a mental note to spend more time with Pookie, so he could see where his head was at.

Time was of the essence and even though Fat Chad didn't want to rush things, the bottom line was this = the sooner he got a read on Pookie, the sooner he could introduce Lil' Man to the next dimension.

CHAPTER 13

GAME CHANGERS

"After I add Sean Linen's vocals, we good to go," Rick said to Lil' Billy who had just walked out of the sound booth.

Lil' Billy had decided that the best way to honor Sean Linen's memory was to release a C-D in his name and give all the proceeds to his family.

After Rick cut off all of the studio equipment he figured it would be a good time to have the conversation with Lil' Billy that he had wanted to have for a long time. "Bruh, before you bounce I need to holla at you," he began.

"What's the deal? Talk to me," Lil' Billy replied.

"Well you know I ain't never got involved in yo personal life, and I never will, but I'm beginning to think that yo personal life might affect our business."

"I don't understand what you mean," Lil' Bully looked surprised.

"What I'm saying is, when we first went to Atlanta, the whole purpose was to get out of the dope game and focus on our music, but instead you done got even deeper in the shit."

"Okay, you said *I* done got deeper in the dope game,

so how is that affecting you?"

"Man, are you serious? If the police come after you, they gon come after Stay Solid Records and I'm a part of that."

Lil' Billy shook his head, "Nigga, fuck the police! You act like I'm standing on Madison serving fiends. The police can't see me. I'm too far behind the scenes."

Rick laughed, "Come on Bruh, don't fool yourself, you a Black man in America. You ain't never out of the sight of the police."

"Yeah, maybe so, but I ain't concerned with none of that. My only concern is being a rich Black man in America."

Rick paused then said, "Okay let me get this straight. You just gon sell dope forever?"

"Nah, I ain't gon sell it forever," Lil' Billy answered, "but I'm gon sell it until I'm ready to stop. I got too much momentum right now to just walk away and besides all that I'm doing what Cash didn't get a chance to do."

This nigga is too far gone, Rick thought. He couldn't believe that Lil' Billy was using Cash's death as an excuse to continue hustling. As far as Rick was concerned, it had nothing to do with Cash. It was all about Lil' Billy's greed. Rick had assumed that seeing Sean Linen die in a barrage of bullets that were really meant for him would have brought about a moment of clarity in Lil' Billy, but instead Lil' Billy was as focused as ever on being a drug kingpin.

Rick concluded that it was time to lay the foundation for what he now realized was the inevitable; the end of him and Lil' Billy's business partnership.

"Well I guess we can't see eye to eye on everything,"

Rick said, "but anyway, I'm bout to move to Atlanta permanently."

"You and Melissa getting serious, huh?" Lil' Billy smiled.

"Yeah, but that ain't the only reason I'm moving. I think to take Stay Solid Records to the next level, we need to have a bigger presence in Atlanta, plus I got some side projects I wanna pursue."

"What kinda side projects?"

"I wanna do some R&B production work."

Lil' Billy nodded his approval, but what he didn't know was that Rick was pursuing a lot more than side projects. He was pursuing a future that didn't include Lil' Billy.

Once the word got out that Jack's Strip Club was Lucky's headquarters again, the entire atmosphere in the club changed. No longer did Jack have to worry about the Gorillaz or anyone else disrespecting him or his dancers. Everyone was on their best behavior because nobody wanted to be on the receiving end of one of Lucky's violent episodes.

Lucky spent most of his time sitting at the end of bar listening to the parade of people who wanted his ear. After a few days, Lucky had heard every rumor and theory there was about what happened to Cash.

No matter what Lucky heard, he remained emotionless. He had conditioned himself not to react to anything he was told. Even though his engine was running hot for revenge, he knew he had to remain cold and calculating.

Besides Lucky's presence, Molly was the other reason the atmosphere in the club was different. She had turned the club into an Akron version of Sin City.

With the influx of Atlanta strippers, the local strippers were forced to step their game up. Some of them were up to the challenge, but quite a few were forced to relocate to smaller, hole-in-the-wall strip clubs.

With Molly in charge, the price of pussy at the strip club went up to $500 and the tricks were more than happy to pay the fee. Jack's strip club was gaining a reputation as a place where a trick could find whatever flavor he savored from snow bunnies to dark chocolate. Maria and her squad from the G.P. were even coming through once a week to provide a Spanish flavor.

In addition to top notch pussy, the strip club was also the place to find top notch Ecstasy. Using the strippers as mules, Molly's Atlanta connect kept her supplied with the best Ecstasy in the country.

The more time Lucky spent with Molly, the more he was impressed with her. He noticed how the Atlanta strippers showed her the utmost respect and obeyed her every command. He also liked the fact that even though Molly was a bad bitch, she was still down to earth.

Likewise, Molly also enjoyed Lucky's company. It was obvious that Lucky was feared by the entire city, but he didn't thrive on that and to Molly, that's what made him so thorough. When Molly had free time she would usually join Lucky at the bar where they would conversate about a variety of subjects.

Lucky had a cool exterior, but whenever the subject of Cash came up, Molly could see the change in his demeanor and to a certain extent it scared her.

As far as Molly was concerned, if the parties involved in Cash's murder had any sense, they should be as far away from Akron as they could get, because being at odds with Lucky was like being at odds with the devil himself.

For Peaches' mama Gloria, it was the straw that broke the camel's back.

Gloria had always had a love hate relationship with her youngest daughter, but for the past year the balance was more tilted towards hate.

Peaches treated her older sisters Crystal and Sonya like shit too, but they were too caught up in their own lives to really care. Gloria, on the other hand, was devastated by Peaches treatment of her.

Gloria was two decades past her prime, but in Peaches she saw what could have been if she hadn't experimented with drugs in her younger years.

Gloria was proud of Peaches, but at the same time she envied her success. Adding insult to injury was the fact that Peaches was living the life of luxury courtesy of Big Mike, the same man who had used and abused Gloria like she was a five dollar crack head.

Lately Gloria had been going through financial hardships and was on the verge of having her electricity cut off if she didn't come up with four hundred dollars. At the behest of Crystal and Sonya, Gloria decided to ask Peaches for the money.

Peaches' response was like a smack in the face.

Despite the fact that Gloria had never asked Peaches for anything, when she asked Peaches to loan her the money Peaches' response was, "You better suck somebody's dick."

What made Peaches' statement even more painful for Gloria was the truth behind it. Without Peaches' help the only option for Gloria *was* to suck a dick, an old school trick named King George's dick to be exact.

While Gloria's mouth was on King George's dick, her mind was on destroying Peaches.

Unbeknownst to Peaches, Gloria knew about her relationship with Fat Chad. A few months back, Peaches had a steamy conversation with Fat Chad at Gloria's house that Gloria had overheard from the next room. On top of that, Fat Chad had met Peaches a few times outside Gloria's house.

The first move in Gloria's takedown of Peaches was to write a letter to Big Mike asking him to send her visiting form A.S.A.P. because she needed to talk to him face to face. The fact that she told him not to mention it to Peaches was what piqued Big Mike's curiosity, so he immediately took the steps necessary to put Gloria on his visiting list.

When Big Mike walked into the visiting room, he was taken aback by how good Gloria looked for her age. Not only could her and Peaches pass for twins, but Gloria also had more ass than a donkey.

After the initial hugs and greetings were out of the way, Big Mike got to the business of why Gloria needed to see him so bad, "What's going on Glo, you having some type of problem you need me to help you with?" he asked.

"Not exactly, I'm here to let you know about a problem you got," replied Gloria.

"What problem is that?" Big Mike twisted uncomfortably in his seat.

"Peaches is playing you like a fool."

"Playing me how?"

"She fucking a young nigga named Fat Chad."

When Gloria saw the look on Big Mike's face she knew she had struck pay dirt. Big Mike had the look of a man who had just been sucker punched. Big Mike had imagined that Gloria wanted to see him because she needed a loan. He was totally unprepared for what she had brought to the table. Nevertheless, he wanted hear what evidence she had to back up what she was saying.

"How do you know she fucking him?"

"Because I've heard the way she talks to him on the phone and on top of that I done caught 'em fucking around at my house before."

"Fucking around how?"

"Well one night I woke up around midnight and there was a truck like the one you had in my driveway. I went downstairs to peek out the window and I saw Peaches in the front seat with her head in the nigga's lap." Gloria was lying about seeing Peaches and Fat Chad in the driveway, but she wasn't about to let a little thing like the truth get in the way of what she was trying to do.

Meanwhile, Big Mike sat there silently with blood in his eye, but all his murderous intentions were directed towards Fat Chad. Despite the fact that the sex was consensual, Big Mike considered Peaches the victim and Fat Chad the perpetrator and Big Mike was determined to make Fat Chad pay a heavy price.

"What made you decide to tell me all this?" Big Mike asked in an attempt to learn Gloria's motives.

Gloria was ready for that question, "You know me and you got history," she began, "back in the day I was willing to do whatever it took to be on yo team. When you got with my daughter it hurt, but I accepted it as a part of the game. What I can't accept is you being misused and taken for granted…Big Mike I still care about you and I'm down to do whatever you need me to do."

This bitch is delusional! Big Mike thought while listening to Gloria. When Big Mike first jumped off the porch, Gloria already had the reputation of being nothing more than eye candy that knew how to get in the bed and do what was dandy. At the time Big Mike was young and heartless and Gloria was old and desperate. The result was him using and abusing her sexually until the novelty wore off.

Now from what Big Mike could a certain, Gloria was now older and even more desperate. For her to think he would even consider being in a relationship with her was beyond his realm of comprehension. He didn't care what information she gave him about Peaches.

Nevertheless, Big Mike was never the one to pass up an opportunity to exploit somebody, so he figured he would use Gloria for what she was worth. "Check this out Glo," he began, "the fact that you still willing to keep it real with me after all these years speaks volumes about the type of woman you are… I definitely need a woman like you in my corner, but if you gon be on my team I need you to promise me something."

"What's that?" Gloria asked.

"That you'll keep our business between us."

"Baby, that ain't no problem. I promise you I'll keep our relationship between us."

Bitch I said business, not relationship! Big Mike thought as he gave Gloria a warm smile, "Okay good," he continued, "now look. I gon have my people bring you a few dollars to put in yo pocket, then I'll call later on so we can discuss a few things I need you to do."

Gloria nodded happily. She was bubbling with excitement. She believed she was well on her way to destroying Peaches' relationship with Big Mike, but in reality, she wasn't even close. The thought of leaving Peaches never crossed Big Mike's mind. Love is blind and the only betrayal he could see was Fat Chad's.

———————

Lil' Billy had reached a level that can only be described as supreme focus. Anything that wasn't conducive to him expanding his empire he blocked out. Besides Rick and his family, Lil' Billy didn't even interact with people who weren't participating in his cocaine operation. Even T-Man had come off the bench and got back in the game. He was moving bricks around the Cleveland Avenue area of North Columbus.

With Officer Strawberry off his trail, Ace was able to move like he wanted to Up the Way and as a result he had pretty much sewed up the Up the Way cocaine business and with Maria's help he was getting his foot in the door on the Westside of Cleveland.

Meanwhile, on the other side of town, Walt not only had St. Clair in a chokehold, but he had begun supplying hustlers from Wade Park, Superior, and East Cleveland with bricks. On top of that, the water Lil' Billy was getting from Chicago for $4000 a gallon, Walt was letting go for $20,000 a gallon to niggas on Hough and Down the Way.

The beautiful thing about Lil' Billy's Cleveland operation was that nobody knew that he was the plug behind Ace and Walt. The streets are always watching and gossiping so Ace and Walt were constantly throwing curve balls to keep the underworld off base as to who their plug was. The story on the streets of Cleveland was that Lil' Billy had made a few dollars hustling in Akron and now he was getting rich in the rap game.

Even niggas in Akron thought that Lil' Billy was out of the dope game. Lil' Billy wasn't letting Lucky touch anything and nobody knew he was supplying Stan.

Without making any direct sales, Stan was flooding the North, East, and South sides of Akron with cocaine. Stan only dealt with his childhood friends from Baird Hill and they took care of all coke distribution for him. Stan kept his fronts up by working the cash register for Ahmed at his Baird Hill corner store.

All in all, Lil' Billy's operation was running like a well-oiled machine. Along with his Ohio business, by using his rap career as a front he had also touched base with kilo shoppers in Indianapolis and Louisville.

Everything was panning out the way Sincere told him it would. Lil' Billy could see the beginnings of a Midwest drug empire. Even though he could hear Rick's warnings in the back of his mind, what Lil' Billy had was too much to walk away from.

The dope game had given Lil' Billy the type of power that black men dream of having; the power to change the lives of those you love in a positive way.

With that power Lil' Billy had moved his mama out of a west Akron ghetto into a beautiful home in Pepper Pike. That power had also allowed Lil' Billy to take his little brothers and sisters out of rundown city schools and put them in top of the line private schools.

Lil' Billy believed if he continued to make smart moves he would succeed where so many others had failed; he could leave the game when he was ready and on his own terms.

That was the future Lil' Billy envisioned, but in the meanwhile he was dealing with the present and dealing with the present meant dealing with more cocaine.

Lil' Billy decided it was time to talk to Sincere about taking things to the next level. Ironically as soon as the thought crossed his mind he received word from Atlanta that Sincere wanted to see him immediately.

Chapter 14

Ghetto Chess

For a city slicker like L.A., placing the bug in Pellini's car was a low-risk maneuver. L.A.'s cover story was that he thought he was being followed by the feds and if he was arrested he wanted Pellini already on retainer.

Pellini's antennas went up instinctively based on the fact that he hadn't heard from L.A. in over a decade, but before his suspicions could take root L.A. pulled out a hundred dollar bill filled with cocaine and Pellini's mind was consumed by thoughts of getting high.

L.A. and Pellini spent the next hour or so sitting in Pellini's Mercedes Benz 600 snorting coke and reminiscing about the good times they had in the past.

Detective Bryant waited a few days before he started reviewing what the bug was picking up, but once he did, he was blown away.

Pellini was as corrupt as they come. Not only was he using drugs, but he was orchestrating drug deals and helping drug dealers launder money too. Pellini had made himself a major component of Akron's underworld. He was the keeper of secrets. He knew who was who and what was what, but his power extended way beyond the streets. Pellini also had public officials caught up in his web of corruption. From procuring prostitutes for judges to paying off crooked cops, Pellini was doing it all.

The treasure trove of information Detective Bryant was getting off of the bug had presented him with somewhat of a dilemma.

Detective Bryant only wanted to take down Pellini and the street criminals he did business with. To go after judges and cops would result in a lot of bad blood between him and the folks downtown and that was something he didn't need if he ever wanted to become police chief.

Once Agent Ryan heard what the bug was picking up, Detective Bryant wouldn't be able to stop him from going after the crooked cops. He was a fed and could care less about offending anyone downtown.

Detective Bryant decided that the best plan of action would be to convince Agent Ryan to delay moving on the judges or cops until after they took down a few drug dealers. That way Detective Bryant could get the glory that would come from busting street kingpins then ride off into the sunset, while Agent Ryan could squeeze Pellini about the judges and cops and bust them later when Detective Bryant was out of the equation.

With that in mind, Detective Bryant called Agent Ryan and set up the time to meet for their next strategy session.

Big Mike's every waking moment was consumed by thoughts of Fat Chad fucking Peaches. He wasn't surprised that Peaches was fucking somebody, but the fact that it was Fat Chad was too much for Big Mike to handle.

Amazingly, in the midst of his emotional turmoil Big Mike was shrewd enough not to confront Peaches about the situation. He knew that the only way to keep Fat Chad in the dark was to keep Peaches in the dark.

Since Big Mike was unaware of the side deal Fat Chad had with the syndicate he believed he had the power to cut off Fat Chad's source of income. He even began entertaining thoughts of using the syndicate to cut off Fat Chad's life, but chose not to.

Big Mike called Premo and told him to freeze Fat Chad out on the bricks. When Premo asked Big Mike why, he told him that Fat Chad owed him money and was dragging his feet about paying him. Premo found this hard to believe because from what he could see Fat Chad always did good business. Nevertheless, if Big Mike wanted to end his business arrangement with Fat Chad, that was his prerogative. As far as Premo was concerned his side deal with Fat Chad was still in effect.

A week later, Premo received another phone call from Big Mike and this time Big Mike upped the ante; he wanted the syndicate to kill Fat Chad.

Premo was caught off guard by Big Mike's request and he responded as such. "Bruh you know that's quite a quantum leap from cutting off the man's product," he said.

"Yeah I know, but his behavior has led me to this position," Big Mike said.

"And what behavior is that?"

"I showed him syndicate love and he betrayed me."

"Betrayed you how?"

"He's sleeping with my woman."

No shit! Premo thought before asking, "And you want the syndicate to kill him because of that?"

"Hell yeah!" Big Mike shot back. "I put that nigga in the mix and he double-crossed me."

What Big Mike was saying confirmed what Premo had suspected ever since Peaches had negotiated the side deal for Fat Chad; Big Mike was a man in serious decline.

Premo believed that a man is only an asset while he is on the incline. Once he begins to decline, he becomes a liability and has to be removed from the equation. By exposing his emotional instability to Premo, Big Mike had in essence cut his own throat. Premo no longer planned on having any dealings with Big Mike that would put him or the syndicate at risk.

"Big Mike first things first, you need to calm down," Premo said. "What you have is a personal problem, not a syndicate problem, so I can't allow the syndicate to be used to solve it. Furthermore, I think you need to look at the whole picture."

"Shit, I am looking at the whole picture," Big Mike countered.

"Well if you looking at the whole picture you'll see that despite whatever is going on between youngsta' and yo woman, he has shown you real loyalty."

Big Mike knew Premo was referring to the fact that Fat Chad had killed the snitch that had set Big Mike up on his case. While Big Mike definitely considered that a show of loyalty, in his mind it didn't compare to what he considered the disloyalty of Fat Chad fucking Peaches. With or without the syndicate's help, Big Mike was dead set on getting Fat Chad killed.

Big Mike knew because of Fat Chad's reputation,

finding someone willing to kill him for money would be hard. Nevertheless, it wouldn't be impossible because in Akron when the price is right, even killers get killed.

While Big Mike focused on Fat Chad's demise, Fat Chad was busy planting the seeds he hoped would lead to Lil' Man's demise.

The old Fat Chad would have just killed Lil' Man himself, but the new Fat Chad was playing with too much money to get his hands dirty. Fat Chad still wore the persona of an untamed Gorilla, but in reality violence was something he wanted to put behind him.

Fat Chad had recently begun spending a lot of time with Pookie and he was convinced that Pookie would make a good replacement for Lil' Man.

Pookie was young and had the hunger for more, but even more important to Fat Chad was the fact that Pookie was from Uptown.

Fat Chad was from Uptown and when he started the Gorillaz it only consisted of niggas from Uptown. It eventually ended up including niggas from all over the Hill, but beneath the surface the Uptown Downtown divisions remained. Since Lil' Man was from Downtown, Fat Chad decided to use those divisions to take him out.

"Would you like anything else?" the waitress asked Fat Chad who was having dinner at a soul food restaurant on Copley Road.

"Nah, just yo phone number," Fat Chad replied and winked at the waitress causing her to blush before he turned to Pookie. "You cool lil' homie?" he asked.

Pookie nodded yes, too busy devouring the fried

chicken on his plate to respond verbally. The waitress smiled and walked away while Fat Chad sat there admiring the sway of her hips.

"You know lil' homie, I think our movement is getting watered down," Fat Chad said.

"Why you say that?" Pookie asked somewhat surprised by Fat Chad's remark.

"It's a lot of shit I'm seeing that you ain't hip to… The Gorillaz was really at its strongest when it was just a Uptown thang."

"Shit big homie we strong now… we got Gorillaz cross Copley on Mercer, down on Nome. We even got niggas in the Valley reppin the G."

"Yeah, we got numbers, but having loyalty is more important than having numbers. You know the only Gorillaz I trust"

"Who?"

"The ones from Uptown."

"You trust Lil' Man, don't you?"

Fat Chad chuckled and looked Pookie in his eyes, "Let me tell you a lil' bit about Lil' Man," he began, "he starting to let them drugs and all that street fame fuck with his head. Now you know we don't fuck with them Eastside niggas after what they did to Cash, so why the fuck am I hearing about this nigga snorting clam on the late night with them niggas?"

Pookie tried to respond, but Fat Chad cut him off, "Now hold up it gets deeper than that…I just got word that some of the big money niggas on the Eastside done pooled their money together to pay for hits on all of the major Westside factors and that Lil' Man let them know for $50,000 he would take care of me." Fat Chad was telling the truth about

Lil' Man's drug activity, but the story about Lil' Man possibly carrying out a hit on him was completely fabricated.

Pookie sat there stunned by what he was hearing. He knew about Lil' Man's late night drug excursions to the Eastside, but he also knew Lil' Man had family on the Eastside, so he didn't think anything of it. On top of that, Lil' Man had told him that going to the Eastside was his way of keeping up with the enemy.

On the other hand, Pookie knew how grimy Lil' Man was especially when it came to money and bitches.

One of Fat Chad's main rules was that no Gorilla could take a hit without running it past Fat Chad first, but Lil' Man was constantly violating that rule. On several occasions he had accepted $5000 for a hit, paid a younger Gorilla $2500 to pull the trigger, and kept the other $2500 for himself; all the while keeping Fat Chad in the dark about the hit.

Lil' Man also had another secret Pookie was aware of; he was fucking with Fat Chad's baby mama Felicia.

Pookie had told Lil' Man he was a fool to cross Fat Chad like that, but Lil' Man wasn't hearing any of it. Felecia was only 25, but she was a vet compared to the high school girls Lil' Man was used to fucking with. Felicia had pussy whipped Lil' Man and every chance he got he was creeping to her house on the Northside to fuck her.

Pookie had done a lot of dirt with Lil' Man, but after what Fat Chad said it was obvious that Lil' Man couldn't be trusted.

"So what you gon do?" Pookie asked

"I'm bringing our movement back Uptown," Fat Chad replied then added, "but besides all that I need to know where you stand in all of this."

"I stand with you big bruh!" Pookie fired back without

hesitation.

"Well, I need you to show me you stand with me," countered Fat Chad.

Pookie didn't respond. There was no need to. He knew exactly what Fat Chad wanted and he planned on giving it to him.

———————

Peaches rarely shopped at local malls. For one, she was obsessed with being the first or only one in Akron with certain clothes, plus she hated running into people. Peaches was probably the most talked about, but never seen woman in Akron, so when she was out and about she had to deal with a paparazzi-like level of attention.

Nevertheless, Peaches was bored and didn't feel like driving to Beachwood, so she went to Chapel Hill Mall. Most people from the Westside shopped at Summit Mall, so Peaches figured by going to Chapel Hill she wouldn't have to worry about seeing anybody that would want to stop and conversate with her.

Peaches had planned on only buying a pair of sneakers, but as usual once she got inside the mall her shopping addiction took over. By the time Peaches stopped in the food court to get something to eat, she was carrying bags from six different stores. Peaches ordered a slice of pizza then sat down at a table to relax before she drove home.

The food court had a children's area that included a merry-go-round. While watching the children running around enjoying themselves, Peaches thought about her desire to one day have children. The only man Peaches had ever even considered being pregnant by was Lil' Billy and that was another reason she hated him.

When Lil' Billy left Peaches it was as if he destroyed the dollhouse she had been playing with since she was a little girl. She had envisioned raising a family with him for years. Now she had to deal with the nightmare of him eventually raising a family with another woman.

Peaches was jarred out of her daydream by the arrival of a totally unexpected guest at her table.

"Hey girl! How you doing?" Molly said cheerfully.

"I'm fine," Peaches replied dryly.

"I don't know if you know this or not, but down in Georgia we *love* eating Peaches."

"Yeah, well maybe you should go back down there."

"Baby I would be a fool to do that, when I don' came across the juiciest peach of all," Molly's voice reeked of sexual undertones.

"Okay, check this out," Peaches began, "I don't know what lie Dasha done told you, but I don't get down the way she get down. I'm strictly dickly. Now if you'll excuse me I was just about to leave." Peaches grabbed her bags and stood up to leave.

"Sit down!" Molly snapped.

"Excuse me?"

"Bitch, I said sit down!" Molly's command scared the shit out of Peaches and she robotically sat back down. In an instant, Molly had taken control and now Peaches sat there like a student being reprimanded by a teacher.

"This lil' cat and mouse game you wanna play is cute," Molly said, "but understand that the bitch I want is the bitch I get and right now you that bitch."

"I told you, I don't fuck around," Peaches was trying to remain strong, but something about Molly was making her weak. *This bitch from down south, so she probably know Voodoo*, Peaches thought while Molly continued talking.

"That's what yo mouth say, but yo soul is telling me something else."

"No, that's where you wrong cause my mouth and my soul is saying the same thing."

"Ooh that's right girl put up a fight," Molly smiled, "but let's be honest, niggas don't know what to do with you do they?"

"What you mean by that?"

"I mean niggas look at you and they see a bad bitch with a fat ass and all they wanna do is beat the pussy up. I'll be the first to admit that ain't nothing like a big fat dick pounding the pussy, but sometimes the pussy needs that gentle touch, that touch that only a woman can provide…Peaches that's the touch I'mma give you."

"What makes you think that if I do need that touch, that I want it from you?"

"Cause I'm the baddest bitch you ever seen in yo life," Molly stood up. "Look at this ass, look at these titties, look at this gorgeous face… When I walk through the zoo, the animals get horny!"

Peaches did know how to respond because deep down she knew Molly was telling the truth. Molly *was* the baddest bitch she had ever seen and she knew it the first time she saw her that day at the car wash. Nevertheless, Peaches still had reservations about being with a woman.

Even though women fucking with women had become commonplace, Peaches still felt like dyke activity was beneath her. She believed pussy sucking was for freak bitches like Dasha, not for top notches like she considered herself to be. Yet and still Peaches couldn't deny that Molly was stirring her sexual pot.

Molly knew she had Peaches right where she wanted her and now all she had to do was sit back and let nature take its course. Molly had fucked half of the women in Atlanta, so she considered herself a master at bringing the dyke out of a bitch. "Well I ain't gon hold you up," she said as she reached into her wool Prada handbag. "I'm sure I'll be hearing from you soon." Molly handed Peaches a business card then got up from the table and walked away, leaving Peaches sitting there with confused thoughts and a wet pussy.

———————

Officer Strawberry would be the first to admit that Maria secretly recording him was a stroke of genius on her part, but that didn't mean he was going to stop being who he was. In fact, it made him worse.

Maria and Ace may have been off limits for Officer Strawberry, but everybody else Up The Way was fair game and Officer Strawberry made sure they caught hell. Besides his increased shakedowns of neighborhood drug dealers, he had, in a fit of drunken rage, brutally raped Jackie leaving her with a black eye and a busted lip.

Officer Strawberry felt powerless and didn't know how to handle it, but at the same time he was conscious enough to realize that the path he was on would lead to total self-destruction, so he needed to change course sooner rather than later.

Officer Strawberry's first move was to stop drinking. Getting drunk everyday wasn't going to change the fact that he had been outsmarted by a stripper. Furthermore, it was going to take a sober mind to come up with a sensible solution to his problem.

Then Officer Strawberry did something he hadn't done in a long time; he started thinking like a cop again.

After so many years of breaking the law Officer Strawberry had started believing that he was a street nigga, but in reality he was a cop and if he wanted to turn the tables on Ace and Maria he needed to do what cops specialize in; investigation and surveillance.

Officer Strawberry knew he couldn't keep with both Ace and Maria at the same time, so he decided to concentrate on Ace while enlisting Jackie's services to keep an eye on Maria.

Jackie had been missing in action since Officer Strawberry attacked her, so he decided to pay her a home visit. Jackie stayed with her grandparents on Clear View, a quiet residential street off of Lee Road, in a small colonial style home with a well-manicured lawn. The house reflected the fact that Jackie was in essence a good girl gone bad.

Officer Strawberry knocked on the front door and was greeted by a silver haired elderly black woman, who reminded him of the women who sit in the front row at Baptist churches.

"Good morning ma'am. I was wondering was Jackie home?" Officer Strawberry asked.

"Who are you?" the woman eyed Officer Strawberry suspiciously.

Officer Strawberry pulled out his badge, "My name is Officer Strawberry."

"Well I hope you tryna find the bastard that jumped on my grandbaby," the woman said, more relaxed now that she knew she was talking to a cop.

"Ma'am, I am doing all I can."

Jackie's grandmother turned around, "Jackie! Somebody here to see you." A few seconds later Jackie appeared. She paused halfway down the steps when she saw Officer Strawberry at the door.

"Hi Jackie, I was wondering if I could have a few words with you?" Officer Strawberry asked.

"Yeah sure," Jackie replied. Her lip had healed, but her eye was still bruised.

Jackie followed Officer Strawberry to his car which was parked on the street.

"First of all, I wanna apologize for what happened," Officer Strawberry began. "Jackie you know how I feel about you."

"What did I do wrong?" Jackie asked, still confused by Officer Strawberry's malicious treatment of her.

"You didn't do anything, I was drunk and I just lost it, but I promise I'll make it up to you… here I brought you something," Officer Strawberry pulled out a small baggie of cocaine and handed it to Jackie whose face lit up like a Christmas tree.

"Baby, I need you to do something," Officer Strawberry continued, "I need to keep an eye on Maria for me."

"Keep an eye on her how?"

"I wanna know everything she's doing, when's she's doing it, and who's she doing it with."

"No problem," Jackie said. "She sells me coke, do you want me to wear a wire?"

"Nah, just keep up with her movements."

Maria had always tried to be a friend to Jackie, but none of that mattered because of the mental condition Jackie was in. She was a full-fledge drug addict and as long as Officer Strawberry fed her addiction, she was willing to double-cross whoever he wanted her to.

Now with Jackie on board, Officer Strawberry could focus on what was really important; finding Ace's Achilles heel.

.

Chapter 15

Let's Make a Deal

As soon as Lil' Billy touched down in Atlanta there was a chauffeur driven black Maybach waiting for him at the airport.

"Sir, I have instructions to take you to Sincere," the chauffeur said to Lil' Billy as he grabbed his Louis Vuitton luggage and put it in the trunk of the Maybach.

While Lil' Billy got in the backseat, he took note of the fact that this was his first time riding in a car that had curtains. *Every time I come down here I experience something new*, Lil' Billy thought while reflecting on his previous visits to Atlanta. Meanwhile, he entertained himself with the amenities that come in a quarter of million dollar car.

Sincere's mansion was in the Belair Estates, a gated community in Lithonia, a suburb about twenty miles outside of Atlanta. Once they arrived, Lil' Billy followed the chauffeur to the front door. The door opened and a middle aged Hispanic woman, who based on her attire, was obviously the housekeeper stood there. "Come in, Boss expecting you," she said in a thick Spanish accent. "Follow me, Boss back here," she added.

The housekeeper led Lil' Billy to the pool area where Sincere was talking to a dark complexioned Hispanic man with a ponytail. "Well the man I've been waiting to see!" Sincere said with a big smile upon seeing Lil' Billy.

"Everything cool, ain't it?" Lil' Billy asked, wondering why Sincere needed to see him A.S.A.P.

"Everything's great and I'm hoping it can get greater, but we'll talk about all that later." Sincere turned to the Hispanic man, "Pedro this is Lil' Billy. Lil' Billy, this is Pedro."

Pedro was Angel Salazar's second-in-command. Since Angel couldn't set foot in America because of federal warrants, it was Pedro's responsibility to make sure the American operation ran smoothly. Pedro also lived in the Belair Estates, so all communication between Sincere and Angel went through him.

Lil' Billy extended his hand in an attempt to shake Pedro's hand, but Pedro ignored him. He simply nodded to Lil' Billy then turned to Sincere and said, "We finish talk later," and walked away.

Once Pedro was out of earshot, Sincere looked at Lil' Billy and shook his head, "You'll have to excuse my Columbian friend. Them muthafuckas ain't got manners where he come from, but anyway let's go to my office and talk."

While following Sincere to his office Lil' Billy couldn't help but wonder if Sandy was around. Ironically, no sooner than the thought crossed Lil' Billy's mind Sincere answered his unasked question, "My fiancé's out of town, so I figured you might as well stay here, if that's alright with you," he said.

"Yeah, that's cool," Lil' Billy replied.

What Sincere called an office felt more like a museum to Lil' Billy. On one wall was a ceiling high bookshelf with the most books Lil' Billy ever seen outside of a library. On another wall a large painting by Jean Michel Basquiat served as a center piece. The painting was surrounded by authentic African warrior masks. In keeping with the African theme, in one corner was a life size Egyptian mummy case.

"Come here, let me show ya something," Sincere led Lil' Billy to a lattice front mahogany china cabinet. Inside were various time pieces, ranging from watches to clocks.

"You know what that is?" Sincere pointed to a gold watch.

"That's a Rolex," Lil' Billy answered.

"Right, but that's more than just a typical Rolex. That's a 1964 Rolex," Sincere continued, "It's worth over a $100,000... Now see this clock right here, this is a 1920 Cartier desk clock made of gold, rock crystal, and onyx. I could get $500,000 for it easy."

Sincere paused while Lil' Billy stood there visibly impressed. "Now this one right here is my baby," Sincere pointed to a 1900 Tiffany chronograph. The elaborately engraved gold case was studded with diamonds, sapphires and rubies.

"How much is that one worth?" Lil' Billy asked.

"If I told you, I would have to kill ya," Sincere smiled. "Come have a seat." Sincere led Lil' Billy to a large English mahogany desk which oddly enough had nothing on it besides an open Bible. When Lil' Billy sat down he noticed the bible was open to the book of Ecclesiastes.

"You hunt?" Lil' Billy asked, acknowledging the rhino heads that were hanging on the wall behind the desk.

"Yeah, but not rhinos," Sincere laughed. "Those were a gift from a friend of mine."

This nigga is deep! Lil' Billy thought.

"Well, I'm sure you're wondering why I sent for you," Sincere began, "I wanna talk to you about your future… You making good money right now ain't you?"

"Yeah, I'm doing alright."

"Shit! You doing better than alright, but yet and still there's a whole lotta niggas doing just as good or better than you."

Lil' Billy nodded in agreement.

"But you know what you have that them other niggas don't have?"

"What's that?"

"A chance at real power," Sincere continued, "see Lil' Billy, Black kingpins been following the same routine for years. They spend all their money on gaudy jewelry, clothes, and cars. Then, because of all of the attention that bullshit brought em they usually end up dead or doing a football number in the Feds. Meanwhile, the white man sit back and laugh at the black man for spending all his money on shit that decreases in value. You know what the white man wants?"

"What?"

"He wants shit that *increases* in value. He wants my Basquiat hanging on *his* wall. He wants my time pieces in *his* china cabinet. He wants my 1955 Aston Martin parked in *his* garage. He even wants these rhino heads….Lil' Billy that's what real power is, having something the white man wants, but having the means to hold on to it. Our ancestors in Africa had something the white man wanted, but they didn't have the means to hold on to it, so they ended up powerless."

Lil' Billy sat there mind blown by what he was hearing. Sincere had presented him a perspective on the game that he had never heard before, but he instantly saw the truth in it. Every big time drug dealer Lil' Billy knew had followed the same routine Sincere had just described. Lil' Billy had met a lot of hustlers who said they were winning, but he had yet to meet one who could say he had *won*. Lil' Billy wanted the key to victory and it was obvious that Sincere had it.

"Okay, I understand what you saying," Lil' Billy said, "but my question is how do I get the means to hold on to this power you talking about?"

"I'm going to give you the means," Sincere replied. "We're going to do what's called a peaceful transition of power."

Lil' Billy looked confused, so Sincere put it in street terms, "I'm giving you my plug…that's if you want it."

Lil' Billy's mouth went dry. Sincere was so far up the totem pole, the thought had never crossed Lil' Billy's mind that there was someone above him. *That's why he told me to expand my market.* Lil' Billy had the feeling that Sincere had planned on offering him the plug a long time ago, but his question was why him, instead of somebody in the Black Cartel?

"Okay, I got a few questions," Lil' Billy began, "I know you got niggas you been dealing with a lot longer than me, so why not give them the plug? Also, I'm wondering are you gon give me your clientele along with the plug?"

"Well to answer your first question," Sincere replied, "I'm giving you the plug because I believe you're more mentally equipped to handle it than the guys I've been dealing with. And to answer your second question, no I'm not giving you my clientele because no body's going to ever know I gave you my plug. I'm dismantling my entire operation and going straight legit."

"Why go legit now?"

"Because my gut is telling me it's time. One day your gut gon tell you the same thing, just make sure you heed the call."

Lil' Billy mind was, for the most part, made up, but he still wanted to think things through. "Before I commit, I need a lil' time to think it over. You know to make sure my team is ready," he said.

"I understand," Sincere said, "but before you go back to Ohio, I want you to spend a few more days down here with me. You can keep me company while my lady out of town."

"That's cool. I ain't in no hurry to go back up there anyway."

Good, Sincere thought. He wanted to spend some more time molding Lil' Billy because they were approaching the most crucial point of the relay race; the passing of the baton.

———————

One of the reasons Premo had been so successful in the dope game was his ability to make lightening quick decisions. Once Big Mike exposed himself as a liability, Premo immediately called Peaches and informed her that he needed to see her and Fat Chad immediately. Premo had decided that it was time to solidify his relationship with Fat Chad.

Peaches asked Premo if there was a problem and he assured her that everything was cool. As a matter of fact, instead of staying at the Waldorf-Astoria, he wanted them to stay at his penthouse in the SoHo district of Manhattan.

Once they arrived and got settled in, Fat Chad and Peaches joined Premo in the living room of the penthouse to discuss why he needed to see them.

"Well first of all let me say that I'm glad we finally getting a chance to meet face to face," Premo said to Fat Chad. "Peaches said you were a earner and judging from the numbers you been doing, she was right."

"Thanks for giving me a shot," Fat Chad replied.

"You know when a woman that look as good as Peaches make a request, it's hard to say no," Premo smiled while Peaches blushed at the compliment. "But anyway," Premo continued, "I called y'all up here because I got some good news and some bad news. What you want first?"

"The bad news!" Fat Chad and Peaches said in unison.

"Well Big Mike seems to believe the two of y'all got something going on. I don't get involved in people's personal business, but Big Mike is tryna take things to a level that has forced me to get involved."

"What level is that?" Fat Chad asked.

"He tryna get you killed," Premo replied. "He tried to run the hit through me, but I denied him. Now he'll probably try to run the hit through different channels."

Fat Chad was stunned. First of all, he wondered how Big Mike even knew he was fucking with Peaches, but besides that he couldn't believe that Big Mike would try to take him out over some pussy. In Fat Chad's world, niggas fucking each other's bitches came with the territory. You didn't kill a nigga for fucking your bitch, you just went and fucked his bitch. Only a real live sucker would shed blood over pussy.

Meanwhile, Peaches sat there equally surprised, but not for the same reasons as Fat Chad. Peaches had known for a long time how weak Big Mike was, so she wasn't surprised that he was trying to get Fat Chad killed. What had Peaches in shock was that he even knew about her and Fat Chad and on top of that, that he hadn't said anything to her about it. Peaches was used to Big Mike telling her everything, so she figured that if he ever found out who she was fucking he would just call her and have an emotional meltdown. Big Mike had caught her slipping somehow and that made her uncomfortable.

"If you the nigga in yo city that I believe you to be," Premo continued, "Big Mike gon have trouble finding somebody to take the hit, so I wouldn't worry about that."

"Okay, so what's the good news?" Fat Chad asked.

Premo stood up, "Come on, let's talk in private…Peaches could you excuse us for a second?"

"No problem," Peaches replied, knowing she would find out later what they talked about anyway.

Premo led Fat Chad outside on the terrace. It was an unseasonably warm February day and the view of the Manhattan skyline was picturesque. Fat Chad stood there quietly looking at the skyscrapers and listening to the sounds of the city. This was his first time in New York, so he was in awe of the fast atmosphere.

"Check this out," Premo began, "I ain't gon bullshit around, it's like this, Big Mike is dead to me. He's too unstable and I can't trust a nigga like that. Now you on the other hand, you showing me that killa instinct that I like. I think it's time that we form a stronger alliance."

"Shit. I'm down for whatever," Fat Chad said. "Just show me the dotted line and I'll sign."

"I like that!" Premo laughed. "But all it take to seal this deal is a handshake. I don't know if you knew this or not but Big Mike was connected with a family, *my* family. From D.C. to Boston, we control the East Coast flow and once you're a part of the family, you get family love on all levels."

Fat Chad understood what Premo meant and his mind was made up. If Fat Chad didn't know anything else, he knew how to seize an opportunity. "Bruh I'm ready for the handshake," he said as he extended his hand.

"See, that's that killa instinct I was talkin bout!" Premo smiled as he shook Fat Chad's hand.

With that handshake on the terrace of his Manhattan penthouse, Premo believed he laid the foundation for his master plan; to break the Black Cartel's stranglehold on Midwest drug traffic once and for all.

———————

Once Rick concluded that him and Lil' Billy were on different pages, he didn't waste any time in relocating to Atlanta. Akron would always be his hometown, but Rick was ready for bigger and better things.

At the behest of Young Skrilla and Raw Breed, Rick moved into a Black Cartel-owned townhouse in the Bedford Pine section of Atlanta. Melissa wanted him to move in with her, but Rick didn't want to rush things. On top of that, Rick didn't know how well his up all night making music hours would mesh with Melissa's in bed early business woman hours.

Being way from all of the drama and intrigue of Akron was working wonders for Rick's creative juices. Atlanta was full of rappers, R&B singers, and producers from all over the country who were trying to make the connection that would bring them the fortune and fame they dreamed of. Coming in contact with so many different kinds of artists led Rick to experiment with a larger variety of sounds. He expanded his beat catalogue to include pop, R&B, and even some rock-influenced sounds.

Rick tried to turn Lil' Billy on to what he considered the next level, but Lil' Billy refused to rap over what he considered, "weirdo beats" and he informed Rick not to send him anything but street beats. Nevertheless, Rick continued on the path solo with one particular goal in mind; to develop his own R&B singer.

In the past, Rick had used R&B singers from the Akron and Cleveland area to sing hooks on Stay Solid songs, but none of them had the vocal range he was searching for.

One night Rick and Melissa were having a drink at a small jazz club in Bankhead when Rick came across the singer he was looking for.

Her name was Heaven Jones and she had recently moved to Atlanta from St. Louis in hopes of catching her big break. She was the typical unsigned artist; singing wherever she could just to survive.

After she finished her set, Rick introduced himself and gave Heaven his business card. Heaven noticed the Stay Solid logo and informed Rick that she wasn't interested in singing hooks for rap songs and he assured her that wasn't what he had in mind.

All it took was a few hours in the studio to convince Rick that Heaven had superstar potential. She had the vocal range of an opera singer and her exotic looks courtesy of her black and Filipino heritage would enable her to cross over.

Rick didn't think it would be wise to sign Heaven to

Stay Solid Records. Instead, he wanted to make her the flagship artist on a new label he planned on starting. The label would be called Sunrise Records and it would reflect Rick's eclectic musical tastes.

Heaven was one hundred percent on board with Rick's plan, so after signing the paperwork that made her officially Rick's artist they started recording the songs that would introduce her to the world.

Heaven and Rick agreed that her debut album would be called "New Day" because it was Sunrise Record's first release and for Rick the beginning of a career that didn't include Lil' Billy.

———————

Sandy returned from her trip out of town in good spirits. She felt like she was approaching the end of a long journey and would finally be able to enter a new phase of her life.

When Sandy arrived at Sincere's mansion she noticed the interior decorator's van parked outside. *I wonder how close they are to being done*, she thought as made her way inside the house.

When Sandy first moved in with Sincere he had given her the green light to redecorate the mansion as she saw fit and her first order of business was the bathrooms. All the bathrooms had mirrored walls which Sandy had replaced with slabs of crema delicato marble.

The decorators had finished working on the bathroom adjacent to the master bedroom and were now working on the other two full bathrooms simultaneously.

When Sandy stepped in the master bedroom she could hear the shower running in the bathroom. Sandy was horny so she quickly got undressed, figuring she would join Sincere in the shower for an impromptu lovemaking session.

Sandy didn't love Sincere by any stretch of the imagination, but she enjoyed having sex with him because he loved her and he was good at expressing that love physically when they had sex.

The steam from the walk-in shower made walking though the bathroom like walking through a cloud. Sandy quietly opened the shower door hoping to surprise Sincere. Once she was inside the shower she walked up behind Sincere, placed her arms around him, and kissed him gently on the back.

The presence of someone else in the shower startled Lil' Billy and his entire body jerked as he turned to see what was going on.

Lil' Billy's eyes met with Sandy's eyes and they stared into each other's souls and saw a love that had been buried alive, a love that was starving for nourishment, but was alive nonetheless.

Sandy could count on one hand the times in her life when she had encountered a situation that she was totally unprepared for, but this was one of those times. "Where's Sincere?" she asked in an attempt to regain clarity.

"He went to North Carolina, he said he would be back later tonight," Lil' Billy answered, just as confused by the situation as Sandy was.

Lil' Billy's answer was all the encouragement Sandy needed to allow her feelings to flow. She pulled Lil' Billy close and kissed him with more enthusiasm than she had ever kissed a man with before. Lil' Billy was overwhelmed by the onslaught of fiery passion that Sandy had unleashed. As they held each other close their hearts communicated silently, expressing unspoken words of apology and regret, while their bodies spoke the language of lust.

Lil' Billy reached down and palmed Sandy's ass and her thickness set him even more ablaze. Sandy took hold of Lil' Billy's fully erect dick as she backed up to the shower wall. Then she raised one of her legs up around Lil' Billy's waist as she guided his dick to her wetness. Lil' Billy accepted Sandy's open invitation and lifted her up so he could enter her completely. Sandy wrapped both legs around Lil' Billy's waist, put her arms around his neck, and started bouncing up and down on his manhood.

The feeling of ecstasy was so intense that neither Lil' Billy nor Sandy could speak. They communicated through groans and moans. Sandy bounced on Lil' Billy's dick harder and faster. She was driven by the multiple orgasms she was having and a desire to remind Lil' Billy of the pussy he walked away from.

The combination of the hot shower water hitting his back and Sandy's hot pussy riding his dick, stimulated Lil' Billy beyond anything he had ever experienced before. Add that to the emotional euphoria that came from being reunited with the woman he loved and what was taking place in the shower was like a religious experience for Lil' Billy.

Lil' Billy pinned Sandy against the shower wall and began serving her violent pelvic thrusts. "Give it all to me Baby," Sandy screamed as she dug her nails into Lil' Billy's back. Lil' Billy honored Sandy's request and drove his dick into her pussy as deep as it would go. It was raining inside Sandy's pussy and Lil' Billy couldn't hold back any longer. He held Sandy in a bear hug as he stood up in her pussy and let go.

What Lil' Billy and Sandy felt at that moment was

nothing less than pure unadulterated joy. The world around them had ceased to exist. As they held each other tight in their brief moment of paradise the question on both of their minds was, *where do we go from here?*

Chapter 16

Grey Skies

Lil' Man felt like a million bucks. He had just bought his first new car, a 2005 black on black Dodge Magnum, and now that Fat Chad had him moving bricks, he had more money in his stash than ever before.

Lil' Man was in the beginning stages of putting the block world behind him. The money he used to make in a month, he was now making in a week. He no longer had time to hang out on the block shooting dice and smoking blunts. He was spending more time where the kilo shoppers roamed. The bars, car washes, and restaurants where big timers met to make brief case drug purchases.

The world Lil' Man used to control was now in Pookie's hands. From Delia to Copley, Wildwood to Storer, Pookie controlled the street level crack sales.

If there was one person in the world that Lil' Man trusted completely, it was his Aunt Pam. Being that his mama was a crack head Lil' Man grew up in a house that was usually devoid of food. Whenever the hunger pangs became too much for Lil' Man to bear he would go see Aunt

Pam and she would feed him all he could eat.

Aunt Pam was Lil' Man's moral compass as he grew older and slipped into the abyss of the street life. Even though in her heart she knew Lil' Man was past the point of no return, Aunt Pam stayed in his ear admonishing him to be careful in the streets and that he needed to go to church with her on Sunday.

Aunt Pam lived on Baughman, a side street between Wildwood and Madison. Since Lil' Man had to meet with Pookie, who was at a spot on Peckham, he figured he would park his car at Aunt Pam's house then walk around the corner to meet Pookie.

When Lil' Man turned off Madison onto Baughman, he cut the music down in his Magnum. Aunt Pam hated loud music and Lil' Man always showed her the utmost respect.

Lil' Man pulled into Aunt Pam's driveway and parked. He was near the back of the house where it was pitch black dark. When Lil' Man got out of his car and shut the door, he saw a glimmer of chrome out of the corner of his eye. In a split second he ducked and a bullet flew over his head. Lil' Man pulled out his .45 just in time because the shooter was now approaching the driver's side of the car firing shots. Lil' Man returned fire from his squatted position at the dark figure who was shooting from the shadows. Lil' Man thought he may have hit the shooter, but he wasn't sure, so he kept firing.

Once Lil' Man emptied the clip in his .45, he had no choice but to run and hope that whoever he was shooting at was dead or out of bullets also.

Lil' Man ran out into the street and was greeted by the screeching tires of a police car. "Drop your weapon and get on the ground!" the cop yelled with his gun pointed right at Lil' Man. Lil' Man ignored the cop and ran down Baughman towards Madison. By now he heard multiple police sirens coming from all directions.

Lil' Man ran behind a house on Grace and tossed his .45 as he hopped the fence. He crossed Bacon, ran through more backyards and made it to Noble before he was side swiped by a police car. As Lil' Man lay in the middle of the street with a broken leg, the police proceeded to break a few other bones in his body.

It was the most pain Lil' Man had ever felt in his life and by the time he was thrown in the backseat of a police car, he was unconscious.

––––––––––––

The trip to see Premo in New York was not just a turning point in Fat Chad's life, but a turning point in Peaches' life also because it marked the end of her relationship with Big Mike.

After much analysis, Peaches had concluded that Big Mike didn't have anything to offer her that she couldn't get from Fat Chad.

Big Mike's ship was sinking. He was cut off from the Syndicate and whenever he did touch the streets Fat Chad was going to kill him for attempting to have him killed.

Peaches was leaving her relationship with Big Mike with $100,000 cash, a Range Rover, a Beemer truck, and two three bedroom houses that she rented out. With Fat Chad, Peaches expected to acquire even more.

Fat Chad was now a made nigga within the syndicate, so Peaches knew if he stayed focused he would be approaching millionaire status in no time and Peaches planned on being the one who made sure Fat Chad stayed focused.

Peaches felt like she was the one responsible for Fat Chad's success, so it was only right that she reaped the benefits. When they first started fucking around Fat Chad was just a young goon, but Peaches had molded him into a boss.

With Peaches training him every step of the way, Fat Chad had graduated from throw back jerseys to button down Armani shirts. She had helped him see the bigger picture and that had made him a better hustler.

Peaches had considered going public with her and Fat Chad's relationship, but decided not to. She was beginning to enjoy being the power behind the scenes. On top of that, as long as the other ballers thought she was a free agent, they would continue to pursue her and she enjoyed that attention more than anything.

Peaches also believed that other niggas pursuing her would keep Fat Chad in check. He may have been pussy whipped, but Peaches knew she wasn't the only pretty bitch with good pussy around. Fat Chad wasn't a local nigga anymore so he would be crossing paths with a higher caliber of women, women who look for niggas like Fat Chad to take care of them.

Peaches mama had taught her a long time ago the importance of competition. *A man don't act right unless he thinks a nigga on a higher level than him wants you*, she used to say.

While they were in New York Premo had flirted with Peaches the entire time. He wasn't as open with it as he used to be when Peaches was with Big Mike, but he flirted nonetheless. Keeping the game she got from her mama in mind, Peaches made sure that Fat Chad was aware of the fact that Premo wanted her too. Fat Chad got the message and before they left New York, he gave Peaches $20,000 to blow on clothes.

With Fat Chad under her control and a bright future ahead of her, Peaches was ready to make a clean break from Big Mike, but there was one mystery that irked Peaches; how did Big Mike find out about her and Fat Chad?

Fat Chad hadn't said anything to anybody and Peaches had kept her mouth shut, so who else knew? Peaches asked Premo about it and he said the only thing Big Mike told him was that he got the info from a good source.

The fact that Big Mike had tried to out think her infuriated Peaches and even though she was already kicking him to the curb, her vindictive nature demanded that she punish him even more, so she made a phone call.

"Good morning, Mansfield Correctional Institution, how may I help you?" the receptionist asked.

"Yes, I would like to report an inmate who has cellphone," Peaches replied.

———————————

"What's wrong? You ain't even hard," Dasha said as she looked at Lil' Billy.

"Ain't nothing wrong, go 'head," Lil' Billy replied and pushed Dasha's head back down.

While Lil' Billy tried to take his mind off Sandy and stay focused, Dasha went back to doing what she had been doing for the past twenty minutes; trying to suck a nut out of Lil' Billy.

Dasha's dick sucking skills were legendary and she usually had no trouble satisfying Lil' Billy, or any other nigga for that matter, with her mouth. Lil' Billy's mind was obviously somewhere else, but Dasha was determined to get his dick's attention.

Dasha began licking the shaft up and down like a lollipop while she cupped Lil' Billy's balls. Dasha licked nice and slow while looking up at Lil' Billy the whole time. Dasha finally got the response she was looking for as Lil' Billy's dick began to harden up. Lil' Billy's whole body jerked when Dasha took all of his dick in her mouth. She placed her hands on his chest and began deep throating him using nothing but neck.

The feeling of a hard dick in her mouth always made Dasha horny and the more aroused she got, the faster she sucked. Dasha didn't have a gag reflex so there was nothing to slow her down as she sucked the dick all the way down to the balls. Dasha dug her fingernails into Lil' Billy chest and began bobbing her head up and down on the dick so fast that when Lil' Billy looked down at her all he saw was a blur.

It was more than Lil' Billy could take. He grabbed the back of Dasha's head and released his seed in her mouth. The feeling of the semen shooting down her throat made Dasha even hornier and she tried to continue sucking, but Lil' Billy held her head.

"Dasha … I can't … take no more." Lil' Billy said in an almost pleading tone. He needed time to recover from what was hands down the best head he had ever experienced.

Dasha took Lil' Billy's dick out of her mouth and rested her head on his thigh. "You on a pill?" Lil' Billy asked her.

"Naw, why you ask me that?"

"Cause you just went crazy on the dick."

"I just missed you, that's all," Dasha smiled. "You hungry?"

"Hell yeah," Lil' Billy replied.

"How steak and eggs sound?"

"That sound like a winner."

While Dasha got cleaned up and prepared to cook, Lil' Billy's thoughts returned to what had taken place in Atlanta with him and Sandy and the offer Sincere had made him.

Sincere's actions made perfectly good sense to Lil' Billy. The man was rich and was ready to get out of the dope game. Sandy's actions on the other hand had Lil' Billy completely confused.

After making passionate love to Lil' Billy in the shower, Sandy didn't say another word to Lil' Billy for the remainder of his stay in Atlanta. It even seemed like she went out of her way to be overly affectionate with Sincere in front of Lil' Billy.

Lil' Billy loved Sandy, but he didn't want any part of whatever game she was playing. If Sincere loved Sandy enough to marry her, he loved her enough to kill a nigga for fucking her and Lil' Billy didn't plan on being that nigga. Sincere had offered him the keys to the Kingdom and Lil' Billy wasn't about to let any woman, not even the one he loved, come in between them.

Lil' Billy heard a knock at the door and got up to answer it. He was expecting Ace to come by and that's who it was.

"What's good fam?" Ace said when Lil' Billy opened the door.

"Nothin much, just chillin," Lil' Billy replied. "You hungry?"

"Yeah, lightweight."

"Dasha, make sure you fix Ace a plate!"

"Okay Daddy!" Dasha yelled back from the kitchen.

"What's the deal though?" Lil' Billy asked Ace.

"Ain't shit, I just dropped Maria off at the airport," Ace replied.

"Where she headed?"

"Her and two other hoes she dance with going to Denver for the NBA all-star game."

"Yeah, Walt asked me did I wanna go, but I got too much going on right now."

"What's poppin down in Atlanta?"

"Shit fam, I don't know where to start," Lil' Billy went on to tell Ace about Sincere's offer and what went down with Sandy.

Ace sat there quietly trying to analyze everything Lil' Billy was telling him. To Ace the whole story sounded like something out of a movie that was part action and part love story.

"If I was you cuzz, I would stay away from ole girl," Ace said. "A nigga ain't tryna die over no pussy."

"Man, I'm cool on that bitch," Lil' Billy said. "Once dude give me the plug my dealings with him is over with, so I shouldn't have to worry about seeing her no more." Lil' Billy sounded sincere, but deep down there was a part of him that was yearning for Sandy. Nevertheless, he was determined not to let those feelings cloud his judgment.

"The most important thing right now is that we mentally ready for the next level," Lil' Billy said, changing the subject.

"No doubt," Ace added.

"When Walt get back from Denver we all gonna sit down and go over how things gon operate. Also, I got this lawyer in Akron that's real slick helping niggas clean up dirty money that I want y'all to meet."

"Yeah, that's right on time cause I can't bury all this

money I'm making in the backyard."

"Hell naw you can't, you gotta make that shit legit cause like Master P said, *legal money last longer than drug money*."

No sooner than Fat Chad was back in Akron, he had another issue to deal with.

Pookie had made a move on Lil' Man and it backfired. Now Pookie was dead and Lil' Man was in the county charged with his murder.

The whole hood was in an uproar about what happened because it was common knowledge that Lil' Man and Pookie were best friends, so everybody was caught off guard.

Fat Chad made his presence felt in the hood on a daily basis in order to maintain control of the situation. The last thing his needed was his Gorillaz taking sides and being at each other throats. Even though he was fully connected with the syndicate, Fat Chad knew his foundation was the Gorillaz and the Hill and he had to always make sure that foundation was solid.

Fat Chad stressed to the Gorillaz that whatever was going on between Lil' Man and Pookie was personal and didn't have anything to do with the Gorillaz, so nobody take sides. In keeping with that theme, Fat Chad paid for all of Pookie's funeral arrangements and also put a thousand dollars on Lil' Man's books at the county.

While Fat Chad promoted unity in public, in private his mind was full of division. He knew Lil' Man was far from slow, so there was a chance that Lil' Man might be able to connect the dots between Pookie spending a lot of time with Fat Chad, then all of the sudden trying to kill him. Then again, on the other hand, Fat Chad knew if he kept looking out for Lil' Man while he was locked up those thoughts would probably never get a chance to take root. Like most young niggas, Lil' Man equated financial love with real love.

Fat Chad came to the conclusion that while Lil' Man while was in jail he would do everything to make sure Lil' Man felt like he had his back. Fat Chad believed that the only way Lil' Man would start running his mouth about what happened to Cash was if he felt like Fat Chad was leaving him for dead, so he planned on doing everything in his power to make sure Lil' Man never felt like that.

With all the drama surrounding Lil' Man and Pookie, Fat Chad hadn't had a chance to savor the victory of his trip to New York. Now that he was a part of the Syndicate, Fat Chad had access to all of the cocaine he could handle.

Through Buddha and Meech, Fat Chad had started seeing Youngstown money, plus he had kilo customers in Canton. Now with the Syndicate love he would be receiving, he could lower his prices and really expand into those markets. He also planned on sending some of his Gorillaz down to West Virginia where it was really sweet.

The future was looking bright for Fat Chad, so he was in the mood to celebrate. He hadn't been Jack's strip club since the night of the Stripper Fest, but he had been hearing about how off the chain it was now that Molly was running it.

As soon as Fat Chad walked in the strip club, he could see what all the fuss was about. Not only were the strippers top of the line, but there were nothing but major players in attendance.

When Fat Chad saw Lucky and Molly sitting at the end of the bar, he headed in that direction. This was Fat Chad's first time seeing Lucky since he had beat his murder case, so he was hoping he might be able to get a read on where Lucky's head was at.

"Welcome home nigga!" Fat Chad said when he reached the bar.

"What's up with the untamed Gorilla?" Lucky smiled and gave Fat Chad a hug.

"Ah man I just been travelling and tryna stay out the way."

"I hear you doing good."

"I'm doing alright, but you know how the streets go, you can be up today and down tomorrow."

Lucky nodded in agreement as Fat Chad continued talking, "But anyway, I'm happy to see you out here. Don't too many niggas shake murder cases. The game blessed you."

"Well after what happened to Cash, the game owed me and my team a blessing."

The mention of Cash's name made Fat Chad slightly uncomfortable, but he kept the conversation moving, "Yeah, you right, I just hope the game got a blessing on deck for Lil' Man," he said.

"I heard that lil' nigga caught a body," Lucky said. "That's crazy 'cause I thought him and Pookie was tight."

"Man, I don't know what that shit was about," Fat Chad shook his head.

"Well my nigga, I'm gon tell you the same thing I tell myself every day when I think about Cash, what's done in the dark always come to the light."

Lucky's remark unsettled Fat Chad even more than the first mention of Cash had, so he quickly changed the subject, "Yo, what these hoes in here hittin for?" he asked.

"My nigga, you know this some of the best pussy in the country up in here," Lucky smiled, "I hear they get loose for a rack, five hundred if they think you cute."

Fat Chad laughed and pulled out a wad of money, "Well let me get a bottle of that Black Label before I see which one of these hoes think I'm sexy!"

Fat Chad paid for the bottle of champagne and headed towards the main stage.

Meanwhile, Lucky sat there watching and replaying in his mind everything Fat Chad had said.

Chapter 17

Revelations

As Angelo Pellini sat behind his desk in his downtown Akron office it felt like all the oxygen was being sucked out of the room.

Sitting across from him with a big smile on his face was Detective Bryant. Pellini and Detective Bryant had been at war for years, but now Detective Bryant was in possession of the atomic bomb that would blow Pellini's world to pieces.

"Cut it off," Pellini muttered.

"Pardon me...did you say something?" Detective Bryant leaned closer.

"I said cut it off!" Pellini snapped.

"Okay man, don't get your panties in a bunch!" Detective Bryant laughed as he cut off the tape recorder that he had placed on Pellini's desk, "Just so ya know," he added, "there's a lot more where that came from."

Detective Bryant had just played a tape of some of the secret recordings he had compiled from the bug in

Pellini's car. Pellini could be heard on the tape engaged in all manner of illegal activity with a variety of people. Detective Bryant had Pellini by the balls and Pellini knew it, but he also realized that Detective Bryant had come to him in an off the record manner, so he obviously wanted to make some type of deal and after hearing the tape Pellini knew he had no choice but to play ball.

"Okay, so where do we go from here? I'm prepared to fight whatever charges you put on me," Pellini said, trying to sound strong even he was at his weakest point.

"Don't try to bluff me!" Detective Bryant laughed. "Pellini stick a fork in yourself, you're done. You know it and I know it. Your days of being a lawyer are over with. The only hope you have left is that you don't spend the rest of your life in a federal prison."

"If my situation is that hopeless why are we having this conversation?"

"Cause I believe in redemption."

"Explain."

"I believe you're a good man who just got mixed up in the wrong crowd, but what you have to understand about that crowd is that they don't give a fuck about you. If they did we wouldn't be sitting here having this conversation."

Pellini understood exactly what Detective Bryant was saying. It was obvious that one of his clients had put the bug in his car and Pellini was almost for sure that L.A. was the culprit.

Pellini knew something was fishy when L.A. called him out of the clear blue sky, but it was too late to dwell on hindsight, the name of the game now was self-preservation.

"Alright, how can I stop the bleeding?" Pellini asked, ready to make a deal.

"I want every drug dealer you got in this city," Detective Bryant replied. "I want the entire set-up and structure of the underworld. I wanna know how the drugs are coming in and where all the money is going."

"And in return I get what?"

"No jail time and relocation out of state, plus like I told you before no more practicing law."

Detective Bryant had decided after discussing it with Agent Ryan not to go after any public officials. Detective Bryant figured he could get the glory he was looking for by wiping out Akron's underworld and hold onto the info he had on judges and cops and use it as leverage at a later date.

Pellini on the other hand didn't have any leverage. His reign as Akron's underworld power broker was over with. It was a hard pill to swallow, but in the end Detective Bryant, the man Pellini had made look like a fool so many times through the years, had defeated him. Game, set, match.

———————

Three days after dropping dime on Big Mike, Peaches received a letter from him that was both tragic and comic at the same time. Big Mike was having the expected emotional meltdown that came from not being able to communicate with the outside world like he was used to.

When Peaches didn't answer his letters, Big Mike had his mama try calling her, but Peaches had gotten her number changed. Peaches had considered writing Big Mike a Dear John letter, but she figured why bother. He would eventually get the message.

Peaches didn't realize how much of her day was

spent talking to Big Mike until they weren't talking anymore. Now with more idle time on her hands, Peaches became more fully engaged in her newest addiction; Myspace.

Peaches was nosy by nature and Myspace gave her another avenue to keep up with other people's business.

One of the hottest topics on Myspace was Jack's Strip Club and in particular Molly and her Atlanta strippers. Peaches had never been to the strip club, but through Myspace she was able to get a daily report on what was going on there and keep up with Molly, who was the real focus of Peaches' cyberstalking.

Despite all that had been going on with her, Fat Chad, and Big Mike, Molly had remained in the back of Peaches' mind ever since their encounter at the mall, Molly had mentally dominated her, but surprisingly Peaches enjoyed the feeling.

She never takes a bad picture, Peaches thought as she looked at the pictures on Molly's Myspace page. Peaches was at home drinking 1800 becoming overwhelmed by curiosity and desire while looking at some of Molly's more provocative photos.

Peaches sat down her laptop and pulled Molly's business card out of her purse. As bad as she wanted to, Peaches couldn't fight the feeling any longer. *Just one time won't make me a dyke*, she thought in an attempt to put her conscience at ease.

Peaches called Molly and invited her over for drinks and Molly said she would be there in an hour.

Meanwhile, Peaches drank another shot in order to calm her nerves. She was anticipating Molly's arrival like a kid anticipates Christmas.

An hour later, right on schedule, Molly knocked on the door. Peaches took a deep breath and got up to answer it. When she opened the door Molly was standing there in a black London Fog trench coat with thigh high black gator skin Prada boots. Molly walked in and shut the door behind her.

"Do you drink 1800?" Peaches asked.

Molly didn't answer, instead she proceeded to remove her trench coat revealing that she was completely naked underneath.

Peaches had to catch her breath as she stood here staring at Molly's body. What had begun for Peaches as simple desire had graduated to full blown lust.

"Come on," Peaches said seeing no need to beat around the bush as she led Molly to the bedroom. Once there they stood at the foot of the bed and Molly pulled the red silk chemise Peaches was wearing over her head. Molly turned Peaches around and started kissing her gently on her shoulder while she squeezed Peaches' titties. Peaches moaned her approval as Molly ran her hands all over Peaches' body.

"Lay down," Molly whispered in Peaches' ear. Peaches laid on her stomach spread eagle and closed her eyes. Molly began placing kisses all over Peaches' back moving lower with each kiss.

Molly grabbed Peaches' ass, spread her cheeks, and stuck her tongue in Peaches' asshole. The sensation was so intense that Peaches dug fingernails into the pillow. By now the sexual beast that resided inside Molly was completely loose and while she continued licking Peaches' ass, she finger fucked her at the same time.

"Turn over!" Molly instructed Peaches as she

smacked her across her ass. Molly wanted to introduce Peaches to the taste of pussy, so she stuck the two fingers she had been finger fucking Peaches with, in Peaches' mouth. Once Peaches had sucked all of the pussy juices off of Molly's fingers, Molly pinned Peaches' legs all the way back and began eating her pussy.

For Peaches, it was without question her ultimate sexual experience and it wasn't long before she was returning the favor and licking Molly's pussy. Peaches had so many orgasms that night that she lost count. When she finally fell asleep she held Molly tighter than she had ever held *anyone* before.

Sincere knew one of the rules of life was to always expect the unexpected, but there are some things in life that are impossible to see coming.

Sincere was reaching behind the nightstand in his bedroom trying to retrieve his diamond pinky ring that he had accidently dropped. In the process of looking for the ring, he found what he originally thought was a bank book, but turned out to be a passport.

Sandy's passport.

Sincere thought Sandy had just come back from visiting her family in Toledo, but the inside of the passport was stamped *Bogota, Columbia*.

Sincere had put the passport back behind the nightstand, then sat on the bed and tried to catch his breath.

The first question that came to Sincere's mind was what was the woman he planned on spending the rest of his life with doing in Columbia, the home of Angel Salazar? On top of that, Sincere noticed that the name in the passport didn't say Cassandra, it said Sandy. None of it made any sense to Sincere.

Nevertheless, one thing was obvious to Sincere; Cassandra was not who Sincere thought she was, but who was she and what was her connection to Angel?

Sincere needed answers and he needed them fast, so he contacted the man he always called when he needed answers; private investigator Eddie Fields.

Eddie was an ex-street nigga who had got his life together. Because he maintained a good name while he was in the streets he was still wired into Atlanta's underworld and that made him a good private eye.

When Sincere had first relocated to Atlanta from Detroit back in the early 90's, he was just one of many drug kingpins from all over the country that had descended on Atlanta. With so much competition, Sincere needed an advantage and Eddie provided him with one.

Eddie gathered information on all the other kingpins and passed it on to Sincere, who used it to divide and conquer Atlanta's drug market. By the time Sincere became connected with Angel he had already destabilized all his competitors, so there was nothing to impede his rise to the top.

Working for Sincere had made Eddie a wealthy man and besides a few minor situations he had for the most part retired from investigative work. When he got the call from Sincere he was in Florida on a fishing trip. Sincere told Eddie the matter was urgent, so Eddie cut his fishing trip short and high-tailed it back to Atlanta.

Eddie met with Sincere at Sincere's downtown Atlanta office. As soon as Eddie saw Sincere's face he could tell that he was under a lot of stress.

"I want you to find out who this woman really is," Sincere said as he slid a folder across the desk to Eddie who had just sat down.

Eddie opened the folder which contained all the info Sincere had on Sandy and a few pictures of her.

"Now this is one attractive lady," Eddie casually stated as he went through the contents of the folder. "She from Toledo, huh?"

"That's what I want you to find out," Sincere replied.

Eddie closed the folder and stood up, "Okay, I'll get right on this," he said as he turned to leave.

"Eddie, one more thing," Sincere said.

"What's that?" Eddie turned around.

"I wanna know *everything* about this woman."

"I understand," Eddie said as he turned and left Sincere's office somewhat disturbed by the look he had just seen in Sincere's eyes.

———————

One of the habits Dasha had picked up from Molly was being more involved in physical fitness. Dasha's body was her meal ticket and the longer she kept it in good shape the longer she would reap the benefits from it. With that in mind Dasha went to the gym at least three times a week and she was careful about what she ate.

When it came to food, Dasha allowed herself one cheat day a week on which she ate something she knew had absolutely no nutritional value. Every cheat day she would indulge in something different and on this particular cheat day Dasha was in the mood for some Church's Chicken.

When Dasha pulled into the parking lot of the

Church's Chicken on Copley Road, it was crowded like it always was on the first of the month. Dasha considered going somewhere that wasn't as crowded, but she figured the greasy chicken, fried okra, and strawberry pop was worth the wait.

When Dasha made it to the counter to place her order, she noticed a familiar face working the deep fryer.

"Hey Spank! What's up?" she said.

"Nothin much…Long time no see," Spank smiled.

"Yeah, I know."

"Hey check this out, I go on break in fifteen minutes. Grab a table, I need to holla at you anyway."

"Okay," Dasha said and took a seat at one of the tables.

Spank was an ex-crackhead from the Wildwood – Madison area. Before he fell victim to crack Spank was a pimp, so even while he was getting high he held on to his game and his swagger. Some of the richest niggas on the Hill, including Lil' Billy, got their start hustling rocks on the block under Spank's tutelage. Despite being a crackhead, Spank was respected by all and known for keeping the game fair.

"I would give you a hug, but I got all this damn flour on me," Spank said as she sat down at the table across from Dasha.

"Nigga, I see you looking good!" Dasha flashed a genuine smile. She had heard Spank wasn't getting high anymore and she was happy for him.

"Shit, if I was looking half as good as you, I might be back riding Cadillac!" Spank shot back.

"With all the game you got, it ain't gon be long…but anyway what you need to holla at me about?"

Spank paused and looked around before speaking, "I need to talk to Lil' Billy face to face," he said in a lowered tone.

"Spank you know with all the bullshit that done went on Lil' Billy real choosy about who he deal with. I ain't saying he ain't got love for you, he just keeping his dealings with people real tight right now."

"I understand that and that's why I need to see him."

"What is it about?"

Spank started talking and after fifteen seconds Dasha had heard enough. She went outside and called Lil' Billy who was at his apartment in Cleveland. Dasha didn't go into specifics over the phone, but the little bit she told Lil' Billy was enough for him to tell her to bring Spank to him immediately.

Spank told his manager he had a family emergency and was able to get off of work early. He wanted to change clothes, but Dasha told him there was no time for that. They left Church's Chicken, hopped onto Interstate 77, and made it to Lil' Billy's apartment in 30 minutes.

Lil' Billy didn't waste time with small talk. He told Spank to have a seat and immediately got down to the nitty gritty. "Okay Spank, talk to me," he said.

"I was on Peckham the night Cash got killed," Spank swallowed hard.

Lil' Billy leaned closer, "Alright, tell me what happened."

Spank talked non-stop for the next thirty minutes, pausing periodically to answer Lil' Billy's questions. On the night Cash was killed Spank had stopped by Lil' Man's spot earlier in the evening to buy some dope. When he walked on the porch he overheard bits and pieces of a conversation that was taking place inside the house between Lil' Man and Fat Chad. From what Spank heard, Fat Chad was telling Lil' Man to call somebody over to his spot. Their conversation broke off when Spank knocked on the door.

After Spank bought a couple of rocks from Lil' Man, he went behind a house down the street to hit the pipe. When he was done, he stood on the side of the front porch so he could regulate whatever drug activity was going on.

Cash was driving a rental car that night, so when he pulled up on Peckham, Spank didn't know it was him. Because of that, Spank stayed in the cut observing the car just in case it was a customer looking for drugs.

Spank saw the porch light at Lil' Man's spot cut on and off and the unfamiliar car back up. Then he watched the two men with ski masks on come out of the shadows and unload on the car. When the men stopped firing shots one of them grabbed something out of the car, but Spank couldn't see what it was.

When Spank finished telling the story, he and Dasha were both in tears, while Lil' Billy sat there silently with a blank look on his face.

Lil' Billy thought about how much love Cash had shown Lil' Man when Lil' Man was just a pup. For Lil' Man to cross Cash the way he had was beyond foul. Then he thought about how Fat Chad had approached him at Cash's funeral as if he was a comrade when in reality Cash's blood was on his hands. Lil' Billy was full of fury on the inside, but he maintained the same blank expression on his face.

Lil' Billy had always knew that he would eventually find out the truth about what happened to Cash and he had promised himself that no matter what came to light he wasn't going to lose his composure. Even Lucky, who was usually the hot head had said that when they learned what really happened to Cash, that they had to be shrewd in their retaliation.

Lil' Billy finally broke his silence, "Ain't Lil' Man in the county for a body?" he asked Dasha.

"Yeah, they say he killed his best friend Pookie," Dasha replied.

"Look him up on the Summit County website and see what his bond is," Lil' Billy said, then turned to Spank, "Spank I want you to know that you ain't got to worry about what you told me ever getting out, I promise you that."

"I been wanting to tell somebody what I saw, but I was scared," Spank said.

"I understand bruh, everything happens when it's meant to happen, by the way, if you want something to party with..._"

"No thanks, I'm clean. I ain't got high since the night Cash got killed."

"That's beautiful, I always knew you could bounce back," Lil' Billy gave Spank some dap.

Dasha who was on the laptop cut in, "His bond is a million dollars, ten percent."

That's a hundred thousand, Lil' Billy thought before saying, "Call Jack and tell him I'll be in Akron tomorrow to meet with him about some important business. Then call Lucky and T-Man and tell them I need to see them here tonight."

"Okay, what about Rick?" Dasha asked.

"I'll holla at him myself next time I'm in Atlanta," Lil' Billy didn't think it was necessary to tell Rick what was going on, because Rick was in his own world and Lil' Billy loved him enough to leave him there.

Lil' Billy, on the other hand, was in a different world. He was in a world where when the blood of a loved one is spilled, retaliation is a must.

Lil' Billy may not have known the intricate plot, but what he did know was that when Fat Chad and Lil' Man set Cash up to be killed, they had reserved their seats on a flight to the afterlife and now it was time to punch their ticket.

Chapter 18

Two Minute Warning

When the guards searched Big Mike's cell, they found the cell phone and a half an ounce of weed. Big Mike's cellie, who had to see the parole board, wasted no time in telling the guards that any and all contraband found in the cell belong to Big Mike. He did this despite the fact that Big Mike had been paying him to hold the cellphone when Big Mike had to leave the cell.

For Big Mike it seemed like everything was falling apart. Besides the fact that he was in the hole waiting to ride out to the maximum security prison in Lucasville, Peaches was missing in action. Big Mike had written her every day since he had been in the hole and she had yet to respond. His mother had even tried to track Peaches down, to no avail.

Adding insult to injury was the issue of Fat Chad fucking Peaches. Everything else in Big Mike's life paled in comparison to that situation. All day and night Big Mike's mind entertained what were for him nightmare scenarios concerning Fat Chad and Peaches. *I wonder if she be sucking his dick? What if that nigga done got her pregnant?* Big Mike was miserable to say the least.

The one bright spot in Big Mike's life was Peaches'

mama Gloria. She was going above and beyond the call of duty to prove her worth to Big Mike. She wrote him every day and she never missed a visit. Because Big Mike was in the hold, his visits were only an hour behind the glass, but Gloria still made the drive from Akron to Mansfield every week.

For Gloria, thanks to Peaches, things were working out better than she ever imagined they would. Big Mike was at a vulnerable point and Gloria being the seasoned veteran that she was knew how to seize the moment. Even though Big Mike hadn't just come out and said it, Gloria knew him and Peaches were having problems.

To cause problems was Gloria's intent when she told Big Mike about Peaches and Fat Chad. Nevertheless, she was still pleasantly surprised by how fast things were working in her favor. Gloria had come to the conclusion that if she continued to be Big Mike's emotional place of refuge he would learn to love her and finally in middle age her dream of being a baller's wife would become a reality.

Meanwhile, Big Mike had come to a conclusion of his own; he had to get out of prison by any means necessary.

Paying a lawyer to find a loophole had proven to be fruitless. There was no loophole.

Because of what was going on with Peaches and Fat Chad, Big Mike felt a sense of urgency about getting out. Being isolated in a cell all day because he was in the hole only intensified his feelings. Big Mike was going through an affliction that was common to mentally weak niggas when they were in the hole; the cell was squeezing him.

Big Mike's only possible way of getting out of the joint immediately would be to snitch and snitching on local drug dealers would not get the job done. He would have to snitch on Premo and The Syndicate.

By snitching on The Syndicate, Big Mike would not only be signing his own death certificate, but he would be putting his entire family in danger. Despite all this, he still considered snitching on The Syndicate a viable option.

Big Mike was operating in a warped mind state. The only thing he could think about was getting out, so he could get Peaches back. Nothing else mattered to him. He envisioned snitching on The Syndicate, having Peaches and his mama join him in the federal witness program, then living happily after.

Big Mike knew he would be getting transferred to Lucasville soon, so he needed to get the ball rolling while he was still at Mansfield. On his very next visit with Gloria. Big Mike instructed her to contact Pellini and tell him that he was ready to take the prosecutor's deal.

It didn't take a rocket scientist to figure out that Big Mike was about to snitch, but Gloria couldn't care less. As far as she was concerned this put her in an even stronger position with Big Mike because now she was the keeper of his secrets. Big Mike had to know that if he didn't treat Gloria right he risked being exposed as a rat and that was exactly what Gloria planned on doing if Big Mike didn't keep every promise he had made to her.

Therein lied the irony of Big Mike's situation; he was so consumed with the snake shit that Peaches was doing that he didn't realize that in dealing with Gloria, he was sleeping with an Anaconda.

Sleeping with Molly had opened up a door within Peaches that she didn't plan on closing anytime soon.

Beyond sexual satisfaction, Peaches felt like having sex with Molly had expanded her level of consciousness. She was beginning to look at everything differently.

Peaches was still going at it hot and heavy with Fat Chad, but when she had sex with him, it was thoughts of Molly that kept her pussy wet.

Fat Chad had noticed that Peaches' freak meter had gone up, but his ego told him he was the cause of it. Now every time Fat Chad was around Peaches they engaged in some type of sexual activity. Whether it was getting fucked in her ass or getting smacked and choked, Peaches had Fat Chad participating in the type of extreme sex that he had never experienced before. It was like being at a sexual amusement park and Fat Chad paid Peaches accordingly for the ride.

Fat Chad was moving so much cocaine that the five to ten thousand dollars he was giving Peaches on a weekly basis was like chump change to him.

Peaches in turn, used the money she got from Fat Chad to pay for Molly's company.

Molly knew the first night she fucked Peaches that Peaches was head over heels for her. Molly wasn't surprised because she knew it was Peaches' first sexual encounter with a woman and the first cut is always the deepest. What really surprised Molly was the intensity of Peaches' attraction to her. It bordered on obsession.

Peaches would beg Molly to spend time with her and then cry actual tears when Molly had to leave. Molly enjoyed having sex with Peaches, but because Peaches was displaying so much weakness, Molly had no choice but to treat her the same way she would treat a rich white man; like a trick.

Molly had Peaches' mind in such a chokehold that she considered turning Peaches all the way out and having her sell pussy, but when she ran the idea by Dasha, Dasha told her that was a no-go. Lil' Billy hated Peaches' guts and he didn't want her in his mix directly or indirectly, so Peaches could be Molly's personal play thing, but nothing more.

With that in mind, Molly's agenda for Peaches became simply to have sexual fun with her and charge her for all she could. Once Molly grew tired of Peaches, she would leave her where she had been leaving niggas and bitches since she was a teenager; on the trail of broken hearts.

By keeping Ace under almost non-stop surveillance Officer Strawberry was able to get a closer picture of who Ace was and what he was about.

At first, Officer Strawberry thought he might be dealing with the typical inner city drug dealer, but it didn't take long for him to realize that Ace was a major player in the dope game.

Ace didn't move in a reckless manner, so he wouldn't draw the attention of the average cop. Ace operated like a man who had a lot to lose and Officer Strawberry was able to pick up on that.

Throughout the day, Ace was usually behind the wheel of a carpet cleaning business van. He would stop by a bar on 143rd and Harvard and a bar on 116th and Buckeye about once a week. Officer Strawberry noticed that when Ace wasn't driving the van, it was parked at a house in University Heights. One thing Officer Strawberry thought was odd was the fact that Ace never stayed at the house in University Heights longer than 30 to 45 minutes and he was always alone when he came there.

The rest of Ace's routine consisted of visits to his mama's house on Abell, to Maria's spot on the Westside, and somebody's apartment at the Qua 55. The fact that Ace even knew anybody that lived at the Qua 55 was another indicator to Officer Strawberry that Ace was moving in big money circles.

According to Jackie, Maria had changed up her program somewhat. She wasn't stripping as often as she used to and when she did she made it an event. Word on the street was that Maria had started an escort service and was taking dates out of town. Straight up prostitution must have been treating Maria good because she had also stopped selling powder at the G.P., although Jackie believed she had just outsourced her business to another stripper.

Between what Jackie told him and what his eyes saw, Officer Strawberry had gathered all the pieces of Ace's life. Now the question became how could he use those pieces to take back control?

———————

Lil' Man had spent his first week in the county jail sleeping off and on. The combination of detoxing from drugs and the stress of having a murder case had left him mentally and physically fatigued. Even when he was awake, he would just lay on his bed trying to comprehend the illogical turn his life had taken.

The fact that Pookie had tried to kill him made absolutely no sense to Lil' Man. They had been best friends since they were seventh graders at Litchfield Middle School.

They had got pussy together, fought niggas together, and made money together. They didn't always see eye to eye, but they always let each other know if they didn't like something the other one had done.

Lil' Man couldn't think of anything he could have done that would have driven Pookie to wait in the bushes for him. Lately they hadn't even been around each other enough to fall out about anything. Lil' Man had been busy moving weight, while Pookie had been riding shotgun with Fat Chad.

I wonder if Fat Chad sent Pookie at me? Lil' Man thought. It was a random thought straight out of left field, but being in jail with nothing to do but think Lil' Man entertained it.

If Fat Chad had found out that Lil' Man was fucking Felicia there might have been an issue, but even then Lil' Man didn't believe it would have escalated to murder. Fat Chad took care of Felicia because she was his baby's mama, but he had a lot of women. If Fat Chad wanted to get back at Lil' Man for fucking Felicia, he would just fuck one of Lil' Man's bitches, not have him killed. On top of that, since Lil' Man had been in jail Fat Chad had shown him nothing but love. Besides putting money on his books, Fat Chad even hired an attorney to represent Lil' Man.

Lil' Man came to the conclusion that Pookie had made the move on him for his own unknown reasons and instead of wasting his mental energy trying to figure out what those reasons were, he needed to focus on the situation at hand.

Lil' Man's lawyer was an Angelo Pellini clone named Chuck Gordon who was becoming the go to lawyer for dope dealers and killers from the Hill. According to Gordon, Lil' Man had a good shot at beating his case on self-defense, but because his name was connected to so many other unsolved murders the prosecutor was going to drag the case out as long as he could so the police could work on pinning another case on Lil' Man. Because of that, Gordon told Lil' Man he would probably sit in the county jail for at least a year before the case was resolved.

The only person who could connect Lil' Man to a murder was Pookie, so additional murder charges wasn't something Lil' Man was worried about.

Knowing that there was no chance of the judge lowering his bond, Lil' Man settled into the mind-numbing monotony of county jail living. Besides the different females that came to visit him, Lil' Man spent most of his time on the phone talking to Felicia. It was too risky for her to come see him, so the phone was their only means to communicate.

Felicia had recently dropped a bomb shell on Lil' Man; she was pregnant and believed the baby was his. In fact, there was no doubt in Felicia's mind that she was carrying Lil' Man's baby because he was the only one fucking her. For the past few months, besides a quick blow job here and there Fat Chad hadn't been fucking Felicia.

Lil' Man told Felicia she should get an abortion, but she wasn't trying to hear any of that. Felicia was in love with Lil' Man and was dead set on having his baby.

Lil' Man was on the phone with Felicia when he heard the deputy call his name, "Johnson!" the deputy yelled.

"Yeah, what's up?"

"Pack your shit."

"Where I'm moving to?"

"The streets, your bonds been paid, now hurry up and pack your shit."

Lil' Man was stunned, "Baby, I gotta go, I'm getting out!" he said to Felicia, hanging up the phone before she could respond.

Lil' Man ran to his cell and grabbed the brown bag he kept his mail and his legal work in. Meanwhile, the rest of the pod watched in awe. None of them had ever seen a nigga bond out on a murder case.

The whole time Lil' Man was being processed out he halfway expected a call to come through saying there had been a mistake, but no call came through and before he knew it he was standing outside the county jail.

Dasha saw Lil' Man standing there looking dazed and confused, so she honked her horn and waved for him to come on.

Lil' Man, wanting to get away from the county jail as fast as possible, hurried up and jumped in the Beemer truck with Dasha.

"Nigga I been sitting out here for three hours waiting on yo ass," Dasha said as soon as Lil' Man got in the truck.

"You knew I was getting out?" Lil' Man asked still confused about what was going on.

"Yeah I knew. Lil' Billy was the one that paid yo bond."

"For real?"

"Hell yeah he paid it. Lil' Billy got a lot of love for you…shit we all got love for you. We on our way to Lil' Billy right now, he wanna see you."

While Dasha headed to Cash's old gambling house on Stadelman, Lil' Man sat silently in the passenger seat overwhelmed by guilt. He had betrayed the Stay Solid Boys and here it was when his back was against the wall they were the ones who came to his rescue. Lil' Man decided right then and there that his loyalty lied with the Stay Solid Boys. He was through with that Gorilla shit.

When Dasha arrived at the house on Stadelman, Lil' Billy T-Man, Lucky, Molly and two of her strippers from Atlanta were there waiting.

After everyone welcomed Lil' Man home with smiles and hugs, Lil' Billy told him to have a seat in the living room so they could talk.

"Well how it feel to be out?" Lil' Billy began.

"Like I'm in heaven," Lil' Man replied, "Bruh I owe you big time. If you need me to do anything just consider it handled."

"Don't worry bout none of that lil' bruh, I'm tryna pull you up out of that life. It's time for you to return to your roots and fuck with niggas you can really trust. You know why you got a murder case?"

"Yeah, cause Pookie tried to kill me."

Lil' Billy shook his head, "Naw lil' bruh, that was just the end result. The situation really began when you started fuckin with Uptown niggas. You grew up under Cash's wing, so even when he was gone you shoulda stayed solid."

Lil' Man was about to say something, but before he could speak Lucky cut in, "The bottom line is this," Lucky began, "somebody sent Pookie at you and until we know who did it you need to let us keep you in the cut."

"I got a spot in Columbus, so you can lay low down there," T-Man added.

Lil' Man sat there feeling like he was around the people who really loved him, but it was an all an illusion. He was really in the room with his executioners.

Even though Spank had provided him with enough

evidence to kill Lil' Man on the spot, Lil' Billy didn't want to jump the gun. He knew the only way to make sure that everyone involved in Cash's murder paid was to unearth the whole plot and that would take a little more time.

Thanks to Dasha, Lil' Billy had learned that Lil' Man was fucking Felicia. Dasha's cousin Rachelle was Felecia's hairdresser and like most women, Felicia shared her secrets with the woman who did her hair. Rachelle also told Dasha that Felicia thought she might be pregnant by Lil' Man.

Lil' Billy assumed that Fat Chad must have found out about Felicia and Lil' Man and sent Pookie to kill him. Even if he was wrong, that was the scenario Lil' Billy was going to feed Lil' Man, who would then turn against Fat Chad like Lil' Billy wanted him to.

In the meantime, Lil' Billy planned on keeping Lil' Man isolated within the Stay Solid cocoon and away from the hood where Fat Chad could possibly touch him.

"Here, fire this up," Lil' Billy handed Lil' Man a blunt. "We got a surprise for you upstairs… hey Dasha show the lil' homie the surprise we got for him."

Dasha led Lil' Man upstairs where the two Atlanta strippers were waiting for him. They had been instructed by Molly to blow Lil' Man's mind.

Because of their close proximity to each other, Detroit and Toledo's underworlds tend to intertwine. If a man is a factor in Detroit, more than likely his name will ring in Toledo also and vice versa. It was for that reason that when Eddie Field's search for info on Sandy turned up empty in Toledo, he made the short drive across the border to Detroit.

A lot of things in Detroit had changed, but a few of the old watering holes and gambling spots Eddie was familiar with were still around. Eddie flashed Sandy's picture around on the Eastside first, but it wasn't until he got to the Westside that he started making progress.

The woman Sincere knew as Cassandra from Toledo was really Sandy from Six Mile and Livornois. Nobody had seen her in a while, but everyone agreed that the one person who would know Sandy's whereabouts was Sugarman who owned a hand car wash on Seven Mile.

When Eddie arrived at Sugarman's car wash it was during the afternoon rush which was even more hectic than usual because of the unseasonably warm weather that day. As soon as Eddie got out of the Chevy Impala rental car he was driving he was approached by one of the workers. "Sir, would you like todays special?" asked the worker who looked like he was fresh out of high school.

"Not today, but I would like to talk to Sugarman," Eddie replied.

"He's in the office, who should I tell him wants to see him?"

"Eddie Fields, I'm a private investigator," Eddie handed the worker a business card.

The worker inspected the business card with a surprised look on his face, "You sho don't look no investigator," he said, "but come on, the office is this way."

Eddie followed the worker through the small customer waiting area to a door at the back that said *Office*. The worker knocked on the door.

"I'm busy!" a voice shouted from behind the door.

"Boss you have a visitor out here!" the worker

shouted back.

"So what, I said I'm busy!"

"It's a private investigator!"

At that, Eddie could hear what sounded like frantic whispers coming from behind the door. The worker looked at Eddie and shrugged. Thirty seconds later the door opened and a disheveled Sugarman stood there. A woman who looked young enough to be his daughter stepped out from behind him and walked past Eddie with a look of embarrassment on her face.

"Eddie Fields…private investigator," Eddie extended his hand, but Sugarman ignored the gesture.

"Come in and shut the door behind you," Sugarman said, visibly upset that his afternoon oral sex session had just been interrupted.

Sugarman sat down behind his desk and motioned for Eddie to sit down. "Okay, let's make this quick," he began.

"Well my name is Eddie -"

"You said that already," Sugarman interrupted. "Let's cut to the chase."

"Alright then," Eddie pulled out a picture of Sandy and put it on Sugarman's desk. Eddie instantly noticed the change in Sugarman's demeanor. "You know her?" he asked.

"Maybe, maybe not," Sugarman replied. "It depends."

"Depends on what?"

"Depends on why you asking."

Eddie cleared his throat, "Well I was hired by a wealthy distant relative of Sandy's who's close to dying. Sandy is my client's only surviving relative, so before my client passes, they need to know if it would be feasible for them to leave their immense fortune to a relative they've never met."

Sugarman could smell bullshit a mile away, but he decided to continue the song and dance with Eddie, "Okay, so what part do I play in all of this?" Sugarman asked.

"Survey says, if a person wants to know anything about Sandy, Sugarman is the person to ask," Eddie replied. "Look, my client is just trying to find out if Sandy is worthy of the fortune they're considering leaving her."

Sugarman had heard enough. "Well, I wish I could help you and your client, but I don't know any Sandy so if you'll excuse me, I have business to attend to," Sugarman stood up.

"Well that's too bad," Eddie sighed, "but hey, maybe something will jog your memory later. If so, here's my card. Just give me a call." Eddie got up and walked out the door, having concluded that he would have to hang around the Westside of Detroit a little while longer to get the answers to the questions Sincere had about Sandy.

Meanwhile, Sugarman sat there contemplating his next move. Whatever Sandy was doing in Atlanta had aroused someone's suspicions and Sugarman was willing to bet that someone was Sincere.

Sugarman knew if the private investigator had gathered enough information to connect Sugarman to Sandy, it wouldn't be long before he knew Sandy's entire background.

Damn it Sandy! I told you Sincere was a dangerous man, Sugarman thought as he went through his desk looking for the number Sandy gave him to use in case of emergency.

Chapter 19

Vengeance

"Baby I think it's time," Melissa said. Her and Rick were in the living room in Rick's townhouse relaxing on the couch. Melissa was watching a movie, while Rick was staring at his laptop.

"Time for what?" Rick asked, not takin his eyes off the computer screen.

"Time for you to meet my boss."

"I thought I was yo boss."

"Stop playing! You know what I mean!" Melissa playfully poked Rick in his side, "Baby seriously, D.C. really wants to meet you and I think you should hear what he has say."

Rick had been hesitant to meet with D.C. Walker because he knew it would force him to make a decision about his future that he wasn't sure he was ready to make yet.

When Rick started Sunrise Records it was his first step in moving in a different direction, but, nonetheless, he had managed stay on top of his Stay Solid Records business also. It was a testament to Rick's musical genius that he was able to move fluidly back and forth between Lil' Billy's hardcore street music and Heaven's organic neo-soul style. Because both record labels were independent Rick had the freedom to move like he wanted to. He could work with any artist he wanted to and he could release any music he wanted to. He was in total control.

Doing a deal with D.C. Walker would mean making a clean break from Stay Solid Records and also giving up some of the creative freedom that Rick cherished.

D.C. Walker's Big Time Records was part of a billion dollar worldwide media conglomerate. D.C. may have been the most powerful black man in the record industry, but there were still men he had to answer to, men with Jewish last names who considered D.C. an investment.

With so much money in play it was imperative that D.C. maintained his reputation as a star maker and that meant maintaining a steady stream of new talent.

In exchange for the for sure fame and fortune that D.C. could provide an artist, the artist had to give up some control, some more than others, depending on their value to D.C.

Rick knew enough about the music business to know that his skills as a producer made him extremely valuable, so it was in his best interest to at least see what D.C. was offering.

"Okay, I'll meet with him," Rick said finally.

"Good!" Melissa exclaimed.

"But hey, I ain't meeting him at no fancy restaurant or his shiny office. He wanna talk to me we can meet at the studio." Rick wanted to see how serious D.C. was cause if he was willing to meet with Rick at a hood studio where street niggas roamed that would indicate to Rick that D.C. was serious about making a deal.

"Alright baby, I'll talk to D.C. and hook it up," Melissa kissed Rick on the cheek, happy that she was finally completing the mission that D.C. had given her.

———————

Telling Lil' Man that Fat Chad knew he was fucking Felicia had the effect on Lil' Man that Lil' Billy thought it would; Lil' Man immediately drew the conclusion that Fat Chad had sent Pookie to kill him.

From there manipulating Lil' Man was like taking candy from a baby. He spilled his guts about everything he knew about Fat Chad, including all the murders Fat Chad had signed off on. Through insinuation he even suggested that Fat Chad may have had something to do with Cash's murder.

Listening to Lil' Man attempt to be crafty made Lucky want to kill him on the spot, but he restrained himself. Lil' Man would meet his maker in due time if everything went according to plan.

Phase one of the plan would begin in the North Hill section of Akron on a quiet side street called Avon.

Felicia's whole family was from the Northside, so as a way to pacify her Fat Chad had bought a house on Avon for her and the baby. When Fat Chad needed a break from all the tension on the Westside, the house on Avon was his place to relax. It was also the stash spot for most of his money.

Fat Chad had stressed to Felicia not to tell anybody from the Westside or anybody connected to the Westside where the house was located, but Felicia had grown tired of lonely nights at home alone and before long Lil' Man was coming to visit her in the midnight hour.

Lil' Man was preparing to visit Felicia again, but this time under completely different circumstances. He and Lucky were sitting in a parked car, down the street from Fat Chad and Felicia's house dressed in all black.

"When we get in, make sure you don't say shit," Lucky said, "I'm gon do all the talking."

Lil' Man nodded as Lucky continued, "Once the bitch tell us where the money at, you go get it and then we outta there. By the way I know you said Fat Chad probably ain't there, but if he is, shoot on sight, we ain't playing no games." Lucky sounded as serious as cancer.

"No doubt," Lil' Man replied he cocked as his .40 caliber.

Lucky reached up and unscrewed the interior light then said, "Alright, let's roll." Lucky and Lil' Man got out of the car and headed towards the house. Once they reached the driveway they headed around the back of the house where the kitchen door was located.

Lucky and Lil' Man pulled the ski masks down over their faces, then Lucky quietly opened the screen door. The kitchen door wasn't particularly sturdy, so with one swift kick from Lil' Man the door flew open.

Felicia was on the living room couch half asleep when she heard the loud noise. Before she could react Lucky had his .45 pressed against her forehead, "Where yo baby daddy at?" he growled.

"H-H-He's not here!" a shaken Felicia stammered.

"Alright, where the money at?"

"I don't know."

"Bitch, don't play with me!" Lucky smacked Felicia

across her face with the pistol.

"It's in the baby's bedroom in the closet! Please don't hurt my baby!" a hysterical Felicia pleaded.

Lucky looked at Lil' Man and on cue Lil' Man headed upstairs to retrieve the money.

The three minutes Lil' Man was gone felt like three hours, but he finally came down the steps with a black duffle bag in tow.

"Okay, now put yo face in the couch and count to a hundred," Lucky instructed Felicia, "If you look up before you get to a hundred, I'm gon have to shoot you."

Felicia did as she was told, pressed her face into the couch, and started counting. Meanwhile, Lucky followed Lil' Man through the dining room. As they went through the kitchen, Lucky raised his .45, aimed it at Lil' Man's head, and pulled the trigger. Blood and brains splattered across the refrigerator door like paint thrown on a blank canvas.

Lucky grabbed the duffle bag and disappeared into the night leaving Lil' Man lying in a puddle of blood on the kitchen floor while Felicia continued counting to a hundred.

———————

Angelo Pellini's brain contained a treasure trove of information about Akron's underworld. He was a man the streets trusted, but now with his back against the wall he was betraying that trust. Pellini gave Detective Bryant the chain of command of almost every criminal circle in the city, that he dealt with. He told who brought the drugs in from out of town and who distributed them within the city. He told who signed off on the hits and who carried the hits out. He told about everything but the Stay Solid Boys.

When Detective Bryant pressed Pellini for info

about Stay Solid. Pellini became evasive saying his dealings with Stay Solid were strictly professional.

Pellini had met Lil' Billy and the rest of the Stay Solid Boys through Sandy, so in his eyes crossing them would be like crossing Sandy and that was something Pellini wasn't going to do. He and Sandy had a bond that went back many years.

Detective Bryant didn't believe Pellini's description of his relationship with the Stay Solid Boys, so he kept up the pressure on Pellini.

Pellini eventually made a compromise within his own mind; he would give up Stan. Technically, Stan wasn't a Stay Solid Boy, but he was close enough to them that Detective Bryant wouldn't know the difference. By giving up Stan, Pellini figured he could get Detective Bryant off is ass and still be able to live with himself knowing he hadn't betrayed Sandy.

Pellini had been laundering money for drug dealers for years. The avenue he used depended on the circumstances and he never used the same operation with more than one drug dealer.

With Stan, Pellini was employing an elaborate scheme that involved funneling drug money through Catholic Church bingo games throughout Northeast Ohio. For $50,000 in dirty money Pellini gave Stan $40,000 back in clean currency.

Every two weeks Pellini would meet with Stan at the small apartment above the Baird Hill store which served as a money stash spot for Stan and the owner of the store Ahmed.

Stan would be the last person Pellini set up before Detective Bryant began making raids. Because Detective Bryant wanted to really stick it to Stan and Ahmed, he outfitted Pellini with a cellphone which was really a camera.

When Pellini arrived at the Baird Hill store it was close to midnight so the store was closed. He called Stan to let him know he was there, so by the time he reached the top of the stairs that were on the side of the store, the apartment door was open.

As soon as Pellini stepped in the apartment he could hear the hum of the money counting machines, "Stan my main man, how's it going?" he shook Stan's hand.

"Shit, I'm good, you want a beer?" Stan asked as he headed towards the small efficiency kitchen.

"No thanks…hey Ahmed what's up?"

Ahmed gave Pellini the peace sign, he was too busy counting money to respond verbally.

Remembering the instructions Detective Bryant had given him. Pellini turned at an angle, so the camera that was inside the cell phone that was clipped on his belt could see all the money that was on and around the table he was sitting at.

Stan walked back into the living room carrying a black briefcase, "Here go fifty racks." Stan popped open the briefcase before handing it to Pellini. "I brought that soft you asked about too." Stan went in his pocket and pulled out a sandwich bag containing an ounce of cocaine.

"Okay thanks, instead of forty. I'll have forty-one for ya in about two weeks," Pellini said.

"That's cool," Stan said. "Hey is everything alright? You seem kinda uptight, you know Trina and Monique right around the corner if you need to unwind."

"I'm alright, I just got a big case coming up that's all, but tell Trina and Monique I said hello."

With that Pellini left the apartment, having just put

Stan in the clutches of twenty years in federal prison. Stan was a guy that had always kept the game fair with Pellini and for that reason Pellini was overwhelmed by feelings of guilt. So much guilt that his level of self-worth plummeted to zero and for the first time in his life thoughts of suicide entered his mind.

———————

"I'll wait about a week, then I'll go get that bond money," Jack said, referring to the money Lil' Billy gave him to pay Lil' Man's bond. Word had just gotten out in the streets that Lil' Man was dead.

"Alright, just hold on to it until I get back from Atlanta," Lil' Billy said.

Lil' Billy had come to the strip club to talk to Jack before he left for Atlanta. It was still morning, so besides Lil' Billy and Jack, the club was empty.

Lil' Billy always came to Jack when he was entering the unknown because Jack was a street knowledge guru. After talking to Jack Lil' Billy always felt wiser and as he entered this new and crucial phase of his life Lil' Billy needed all the wisdom he could get.

Lil' Billy was about to go to Atlanta and meet Sincere's plug. Sincere had already told Lil' Billy that once he introduced him to the plug there was no turning back. After he met the plug, Lil' Billy's dealings with Sincere would be over and he would become the man responsible for boat loads of cocaine.

"So you say you about to go to the next level huh?" Jack asked, alluding to a remark Lil' Billy had made earlier.

"Yeah, I'm about to be on a level that I didn't even know existed a year ago. I just hope I can stay there," Lil'

Billy replied.

"For how long?"

"I don't understand what you mean."

"What's your endgame? You can't hustle forever."

"Shit, I don't have a endgame, at least not yet. Right now I just want all the money I can get my hands on."

Jack got up and walked behind the bar. He sat two glasses on the counter, grabbed a bottle of Hennessy, and poured him and Lil' Billy a drink. "You know what the game is?" Jack began, "the game is like a cruel mistress…she'll fuck and suck you in ways that will blow yo mind. She'll make you turn yo back on yo wife, yo kids, yo family, and yo friends. She'll tell you she only has eyes for you, but then when you least expect it, she leaves you for another nigga and nothing you do or say can bring her back…Lil' Billy the game is smiling at you right now, but one day circumstances will change and you don't wanna still be hanging around when it's time for the game to frown at you."

Lil' Billy sat there silently reflecting on what Jack was telling him. For Jack to tell Lil' Billy he needed to think about life outside the game, carried a lot of weight with Lil' Billy. Jack wasn't some square nigga preaching positivity. He was a real O.G.

There was a time when Lil' Billy thought rap would be his ticket out of the dope game, but everything had changed when he met Sincere. Now Lil' Billy believed he could play the game a little while longer and still walk away on top.

"I feel what you saying and believe me, I don't plan on selling dope forever, but right now I gotta keep riding this momentum I got," Lil' Billy said.

Jack sighed, "Well with that being said, just don't forget the lessons you learned when you was a lil' nigga hustlin on the block."

"I won't, I promise you that."

That's what they all say, Jack thought, realizing that nothing he could say would deter Lil' Billy from continuing on the road he was on. It was the same old familiar road that the cruel mistress led all her lovers down and now it was Lil' Billy's turn.

———————

Fat Chad had been in gang fights, shootouts, and dope house robberies, but the drama he was going through right now was much more intense than anything he ever experienced because it was all mental.

It began when Fat Chad found out that somebody had paid Lil' Man's bond, which really unsettled Fat Chad because by the time he found out, Lil' Man had already been out three days.

Fat Chad had immediately contacted Lil' Man's lawyer Chuck Gordon to see if he knew who bonded Lil' Man out, but whoever paid the bond went through a bail bondsman and they weren't releasing any information, not even to a lawyer.

Next, Fat Chad went to the hood, but nobody had seen or heard from Lil' Man, not even his Aunt Pam.

The whole situation worried Fat Chad, but the only option he had was to wait for Lil' Man's next court date and see if he showed up. Until then, Fat Chad planned to continue doing what he had been doing; selling kilos of cocaine.

Fat Chad was in bed with Peaches when he got the

frantic phone call from Felicia. She was so hysterical, he could barely understand what she was saying, but when he heard the word robbery he hung up the phone and ran red lights getting to the Northside.

When Fat Chad got to his house and found one of the robbers lying dead on the kitchen floor he was completely confused. He was familiar with robbers crossing each other, but for a robber to cross his partner so brutally at the scene of the robbery was strange to say the least.

After checking the house and seeing that the remaining robber had made off with $400,000, Fat Chad called the police and paramedics. When they arrived, what Fat Chad had considered a strange episode took a sharp turn for the bizarre.

When one of the homicide detectives pulled the ski-mask off the head of the dead body Fat Chad was speechless. *Lil' Man?* he thought as he stood there staring at Lil' Man's lifeless body. Fat Chad couldn't figure out what surprised him more. The fact that Lil' Man had kicked his door in or that Lil' Man even knew about this house.

Felicia walked up beside Fat Chad and upon seeing Lil' Man's face broke past the police and paramedics screaming, "Ooohh Nooo!" as she attempted to cradle Lil' Man in her arms. Fat Chad stood there stunned watching the police pull Felicia away from Lil' Man's body. Felicia was so distraught that she went into a seizure and had to be taken to the hospital.

Meanwhile, Fat Chad called Felicia's mama and had her come pick up their baby, while he waited on the police to finish their investigation of the crime scene.

Was Felicia fuckin Lil' Man? The question was pounding on Fat Chad's brain to the point that he had a migraine headache. After the police left, Fat Chad locked up the house, then drove out to Arlington Road and rented a hotel room.

Fat Chad cut his phone off and didn't leave the hotel for three days in an attempt to clear his head. When he did return to circulation, the streets had the answers to the questions he had about Felicia and Lil' Man.

According to street gossip, not only was Felicia fucking Lil' Man, but she was pregnant with his baby. With each passing day, the story got juicier, but every version had one thing in common; Fat Chad was made to look like a lame.

Success breeds envy, so for the haters this story was a dream come true. They wondered aloud how the baby mama of a supposed to be boss like Fat Chad could be getting her back blew out by a lil' nigga.

To Fat Chad it seemed like the whole city was having a good laugh at his expense and he knew if Felicia had the baby she was carrying it would only get worse, so he gave her an ultimatum; get an abortion or their relationship was over.

Without any hesitation, Felicia responded, "Well I guess our relationship is over," and proceeded to move all of her belongings to her mother's house.

As Fat Chad tried to make sense of it all, he realized that he had no one to blame but himself. When he met Felicia she was a good girl and through him she got exposed to the shine of the streets and now she was no different than Peaches.

In this period of inner turmoil Fat Chad was even growing tired of Peaches. It seemed like all she wanted was sex and money, so instead of spending time at her house Fat

Chad was spending time alone at him and Felicia's old apartment out in Fairlawn on Zahn.

Ever since buying the house on the Northside, Fat Chad had been using the old apartment as a place to cook up cocaine when necessary. It was also where he kept his Grand National parked.

Fat Chad was tired of ordering food, so he stopped at the grocery store and picked up a couple of steaks before heading out to Fairlawn.

Fat Chad pulled his Escalade into the garage, cut the engine off, then hit the button that controlled the garage door. He got out of the truck and was about to grab the grocery bags out of the backseat when he felt cold steel pressed up against the back of his head.

"Lucky?" Fat Chad sighed.

"Good guess," Lucky replied with a cheerfulness that was unsettling.

"You killed Lil' Man, didn't you?"

"Bingo!"

"Look man, I ain't got no money at this spot, but I swear if you let me make a call I can have whatever you want delivered."

"I didn't come for no money. I came for answers... I wanna know why Cash had to die?"

"Man, I didn't have -"

"Nigga don't lie!" Lucky snapped, "I know what happened. I just wanna know why?"

Fat Chad realized that in all probability he was about to die and the only card he had left to play was the truth. He figured by telling the truth Lucky might understand his position and have mercy on him, but if not he could at least die knowing that Big Mike and Peaches would be held accountable for their actions also.

"It was Big Mike's call," Fat Chad said.

"Big Mike? What issue did he have with Cash?" Lucky asked skeptical of what he was hearing.

"Peaches said y'all robbed her and took five bricks and a hundred racks."

"That bitch gave Lil' Billy them bricks!"

"Man all I know is what the bitch told me and Big Mike...I swear to God I didn't wanna go to war with y'all, but Big Mike had me boxed in."

My nigga died because of a lie! Lucky thought as he felt his eyes well up with tears. Throughout all the scenarios Lucky had ran through his mind trying to figure out who killed Cash, Peaches being involved had never crossed his mind. Lucky existed in the coldest of worlds, but it was still hard for him to fathom that Peaches would tell a lie that she knew would result in an innocent man's death. Nevertheless, that was exactly what Peaches had done and that meant Lucky's tour of vengeance would have to make at least one more stop.

Sensing that Lucky might be willing to give him a chance Fat Chad continued to plead his case, "Bruh, you gotta understand, I was following orders. I didn't know the bitch was lying."

Lucky didn't respond and for Fat Chad that silence spoke volumes. It meant he didn't have much longer to live. He was about to join the long and illustrious list of fallen ghetto stars.

So this is it, Fat Chad thought as he closed his eyes and waited for the unknown. As few seconds later Lucky pulled the trigger and Fat Chad was consumed by darkness.

Chapter 20

The Power of Choice

Big Mike had been filled with anticipation ever since Angelo Pellini had facilitated the snitch deal for him with the feds. Now as he rode in the back of the sheriff's van, anticipation gave way to outright excitement as the downtown Akron skyline came into view.

Big Mike only had one more night left in jail. In the morning he would go to court and the judge would suspend the remainder of his sentence and he would be a free man. It would be a precarious brand of freedom because it was predicated on his complete cooperation with federal agents, but Big Mike considered that a minor issue. He was a desperate man employing desperate measures.

Upon arriving at the county jail, Big Mike was placed in a holding cell with inmates who were on their way back from court. It was a younger crowd, so none of them recognized Big Mike. Noticing that Big Mike was wearing prison blues, one of the young niggas asked Big Mike what joint he had come from, but besides that they ignored him and continued conversating amongst themselves.

A trustee was outside the holding cell mopping the floor when he motioned for one of the young niggas in the holding cell to come to the door. Big Mike heard the young nigga say Fat Chad's name, so he tuned into the conversation.

"Hey y'all, that trustee said they found Fat Chad dead!" the young nigga said after stepping away from the door. Now the atmosphere in the holding cell was one of utter disbelief. The young niggas in the holding cell may have been from different sides of town, but Fat Chad was revered by them all.

Big Mike listened intently as different theories were tossed around about not only Fat Chad's murder, but Lil' Man's too. The prevailing theory in the holding cell was that the two incidents had to be connected.

For Big Mike, who killed Fat Chad was irrelevant. The only thing on his mind was that Fat Chad wouldn't be fucking Peaches anymore. With Fat Chad out of the way, Big Mike believed that getting Peaches back would be a whole lot easier.

The biggest dilemma Big Mike was facing was how to get rid of Gloria in a polished way. As a show of appreciation for what she had done for him, Big Mike planned on spending his first week out in a hotel with her, then he figured he would buy her a used Cadillac and send her on her way.

Big Mike assumed since Gloria was from the old school she would respect the game, but if not that was her problem not his. Big Mike's mind was on one thing and one thing only; getting back with Peaches.

Cellini

The first thing Sincere noticed when he arrived at his mansion were all the Hispanic gardeners lurking around that were involved in what looked like a major landscaping project. Sandy had green lighted so many different remodeling projects that Sincere couldn't keep up. Sandy had, for the most part, made the mansion her own.

As soon as Sincere got out of his blue Bentley Continental his phone rang. Seeing that it was his private investigator Eddie Fields, Sincere answered the phone.

"Hey Eddie, tell me something good."

"Well, I found out everything you need to know," Eddie replied.

"Good, let's get together this weekend."

"I think we need to meet up a lot sooner than that."

"How soon you talking?"

"Like, right now."

Sincere knew right then that whatever Eddie had uncovered demanded his immediate attention, "Alright, give me an hour and we'll meet at our spot," he said.

"I'll be there," Eddie replied and hung up.

Despite finding the passport, Sincere had maintained his game face when dealing with Sandy. Part of it had to do with the fact that he loved her, so he was compelled to give her the benefit of the doubt. On top of that, making an emotional move wasn't his style. Sincere did everything with prior calculation and design.

Sincere planned to analyze whatever info Eddie had gathered, then deal with the situation accordingly regardless of what that entailed.

Once Sincere was in the house he headed upstairs to

the master bedroom in order to change clothes before he went to meet with Eddie.

Sandy was sitting on the bed organizing some type of paperwork when Sincere walked into the bedroom.

"Hey baby, what you up to?" Sincere gave Sandy a quick kiss.

"Just getting this paperwork together," Sandy replied.

While Sincere went through the process of changing clothes he tried to engage Sandy in a little bit of small talk, but she wasn't very talkative. The paperwork in front of her had her complete attention.

"Baby, I gotta make a run, I'll stop and pick up dinner on the way back if you want me to," Sincere said while grabbing his wallet and car keys off the dresser.

"That's cool, but before you leave I need you to sign this," Sandy handed Sincere a stack of papers.

"What is it?"

"Just some paperwork that gives me control of your entire empire."

"Excuse me?" Sincere was confused and startled.

"You're about to sign everything over to me," Sandy replied without a trace of emotion in her voice.

"Is this some type of joke?" Sincere threw the paperwork on the bed.

"Pedro! Es el momento!" Sandy shouted and right on cue Pedro busted through the bedroom door followed by the Hispanic gardeners Sincere had seen earlier. Sincere made a move for the nine millimeter he kept in the nightstand, but when he opened the drawer it was gone.

The gardeners all had pistols pointed at Sincere, who threw his hands up in surrender, "Would somebody please tell me what the fuck is going on?" he asked.

"I already told you what's going on," Sandy replied. "Now if you wanna live to see the sunrise in the morning you need to sign those papers."

"Cassandra baby look, I don't know what this is about, but baby let's talk about this."

"First of all my name ain't Cassandra and furthermore, I ain't in the mood for talking."

"Are you serious? I come home to the woman I love, the woman I'm about to marry and without any explanation she shoves paperwork and pistols in my face…I trusted you, why are you doing this?"

Sandy laughed, "Sincere miss me with all the melodrama. You didn't trust me, that's why you got the private eye digging into my background. To be honest I'm disappointed in you, cause the Sincere I know would have checked my background a lot earlier."

"What do you mean, the Sincere you know?"

"I mean the Sincere that killed his own brother in cold blood."

"W..W..What are you talking about?" Sincere felt like the room was spinning.

"You know what the fuck I'm talking about!" Sandy snapped, her emotions starting to rise. "I'm talking bout yo brother Cedric, the one you murdered in Minnesota for money. Money that you used to build your empire. An empire that belongs to my son, Cedric Junior."

Sincere dropped to his knees as it all hit him like a ton of bricks; karma had arrived.

Sincere had tried for many years to evade karma, but the laws of the universe dictated that he answer for his treachery. When it's justice there is no karma, but there was no noble cause behind what Sincere had done many years ago in a dingy motel room in Minnesota. He had spilled his brother's blood for money. Period, point blank.

"Nigga stand up!" Sandy barked, having no compassion for whatever spiritual awakening Sincere was having.

Sincere struggled to his feet and stood there like a defeated man. Without saying a word, he picked up the paperwork. Reading his mind, Sandy tossed Sincere an ink pen and he walked over to the dresser and began signing on the dotted lines. When he was finished he handed the paperwork to Sandy.

"Okay, I signed the papers, now what?" Sincere asked, but Sandy ignored him. She was too busy making sure the paperwork was signed properly. Once she was finished, she turned to Pedro and said, "Deshazte de él!"

"Llevarselo!" Pedro said to his Columbian henchman and two of them proceeded to grab Sincere by his arms and lead him out of the bedroom at gunpoint.

Sincere went back and forth between Sandy and Pedro begging and pleading for mercy to no avail. It was endgame, he was in check and checkmate would come shortly.

Meanwhile, Sandy felt the sense of relief that accompanies closure. After all these years Sandy had finally avenged Cedric's death, but despite the satisfaction she felt from defeating Sincere there also existed within Sandy a sense of unease. The source of this unease was a premonition that Sandy was having that was telling her that in her pursuit of destroying Sincere she had sold her soul to the devil. A devil named Angel Salazar.

D.C. Walker always travelled in style and in accordance with that, when he arrived at High Powered Studios to meet with Rick he was in the backseat of a chauffeur driven Maybach.

With briefcase in hand, D.C. walked inside the studio and approached the receptionist's desk.

The receptionist was sitting there popping gum with her nose in a magazine. She didn't look up to acknowledge D.C.'s presence, so he cleared his throat to get her attention.

"What time is yo studio session?" the receptionist asked dryly still not taking her nose out of the magazine.

"My name is D.C. Walker. I'm here to meet Rick from Stay Solid Records," D.C. replied, somewhat irritated with how unprofessional the receptionist was.

Upon hearing the name D.C. Walker, the receptionist's whole demeanor changed, "Excuse me sir, I'm so sorry…uh, I mean Rick is expecting you. If you give me a second I'll let him know you're here," the receptionist said as she stood up wearing a skirt that was too short and too tight. D.C. nodded as she scurried down the hall.

Less than minute later the receptionist returned and led D.C. down the hall to the room that Rick was in.

When D.C. entered the room, Rick was seated in front of the sound board next to Heaven, while Melissa was sitting on the leather sofa bobbing her head to the R&B track that was playing.

Rick stood up to greet D.C., "Hey, how's it going?" he said as he shook D.C.'s hand.

"I'm glad we are finally getting to meet each other," D.C. replied, "by the way, I'm loving this track I'm hearing."

"Yeah, that's a new track me and Heaven are working on. She's the flagship artist on Sunrise Records."

After Rick introduced D.C. to Heaven, D.C. was ready to talk business, "Shall we discuss business here or in private?" he asked.

"We can talk here," Rick replied. "These are people I trust."

"Okay then, let me start off by saying that you are hands down the most exciting producer in music today."

"Thanks, that means a lot from coming you."

"With that being said," D.C. opened up his briefcase, "I'm ready to make you an offer that will provide you the financial reward that befits a man of your talent and at the same time allows you to maintain the creative freedom that you cherish," D.C. handed Rick a contract and continued, "now I want you to read the fine print, but these are the basics, I'm giving you a million dollars just for signing. Big Time Records will be the exclusive distributer of Sunrise Records. In exchange for the marketing muscle that I'll be putting behind Sunrise. I want thirty percent equity. Now when I say marketing muscle, I meant that every artist on Sunrise will get T.V., radio, and print exposure. Also you keep complete control of your masters."

As Rick looked over the contract, it seemed too good to be true. Besides the million dollar signing bonus, Rick would be paid $500,000 a year for the length of the contract which was five years. In addition, he would be paid a minimum of fifty thousand dollars for every track he produced for any artist on Big Time Records.

The only thing Rick needed clarity about was the part of the contract that talked about him giving up his half of Stay Solid Records, "Explain this part about buying out Stay

Solid," Rick said.

"Well Rick, Stay Solid is your past and I'm investing in your future," D.C. began. "There's a street element associated with Stay Solid Records that won't translate well in the world that I'm going to introduce you to," D.C. paused, looked Rick in his eyes, and said, "let's be real, being rich and black in America makes you a target and the powers that be are always looking for a way to take a rich black man down. Holding on to the streets will only make it easier for them."

Rick understood what D.C. was saying and he was in total agreement with him. Rick's whole purpose for moving to Atlanta was to put space between him and the street life.

"I feel what you saying about the streets, but what does giving up Stay Solid mean?" Rick asked.

"It means severing all business ties with that label," D.C. replied, "I have a corporate attorney on stand-by that can work out all the specifics."

I guess I'm at the fork in the road, Rick thought. He could no longer delay the inevitable. It was time for Rick to choose between the past and the future, a past he shared with a man that he considered his brother and a future that didn't include that man.

"You think you can give me a couple days to look over this contract and make a decision," Rick asked, stalling for more time.

D.C. shook his head, "Rick, I came here to make a deal…now if you need a few hours, I can wait, but when I walk out of this studio we either have a deal or we don't."

Now Rick realized there would be no more stalling, he had reached the moment of truth and had to make a choice.

Memories of Rick and Lil' Billy as teenagers making

music in Rick's basement flashed through Rick's mind. At the same time, he looked at Heaven and thought about the look of hope and anticipation that was on her face.

Rick was conflicted, but then he asked himself the question that would help him make a decision. *What would Lil' Billy do if he was in my shoes?*

———————

I gotta get serious about cleaning up this money, Ace thought as he headed out to the stash house in University Heights.

Ace was moving so much cocaine that he had garbage bags of money at four different locations. Ace had a problem that most niggas would love to have, but it was a problem nonetheless; he had too much dirty money.

Ace knew in the future his dilemma would only get worse, because once Lil' Billy got back from Atlanta they would be dealing with cocaine by the ton.

Lil' Billy was having trouble touching base with the lawyer he used for money laundering, so Ace was thinking about exploring an option Maria had presented to him.

Maria had a trick named Preacherman, who was the pastor of the largest black church in Cleveland. According to Maria, Preacherman had the ability to clean up large sums of money and his rates were reasonable. Ace came to the conclusion that it would be in his best interest to have Maria set up a meeting with Preacherman sooner rather than later.

When Ace arrived at his stash house, he parked in the back next to the carpet cleaning van, which wasn't visible from the street. He then checked his watch to make sure he was on schedule.

Ace had an hour to change into his work clothes, grab

twenty kilos, and drop them off over on Buckeye. When it came to business, Ace didn't believe in being even one minute late.

Ace entered the house through the kitchen door as usual. After locking the door behind him, he opened the fridge and grabbed a bottled water, which besides some old bologna, was the only thing in the fridge.

Ace took a swig of water, then walked in the dining room where he saw something that was totally out of order. *What the fuck!* Ace thought as he looked at eighty bricks of cocaine, which instead of being in the upstairs bedrooms where he kept them, were now neatly arranged on the dining room table.

Ace didn't have to wonder for long because sitting on the living room couch was Officer Strawberry who was grinning from ear to ear, "Well Ace, looks like you gon be working for me," he smiled.

The last time Lil' Billy was in Atlanta, Sincere had given him the time and place where he would meet the plug. It was to be a one-time thing. If Lil' Billy didn't show up, the deal was dead. There wouldn't be any make up dates.

Since the meeting was taking place at Sincere's office in the Bank of America Plaza, Lil' Billy thought it would be more appropriate if he dressed like a businessman instead of a rap star, so instead of the designer jeans and special edition sneakers he usually wore, he arrived at the Bank of America Plaza wearing an Armani suit and Salvatore Ferragamo dress shoes.

As Lil' Billy rode the elevator to the top floor of the building where Sincere's office was located, he reflected on how the elevator ride was like a metaphor for his life; he was rising to higher heights. Lil' Billy had come a long way from orchestrating coke deals at car washes and soul food restaurants.

When Lil' Billy stepped off the elevator, the first thing he saw was the Black Cartel logo emblazoned on the wall. He looked down the hall and saw a Hispanic woman sitting at what he assumed to be the receptionist's desk, so he headed in that direction.

As soon as Lil' Billy approached, Rosa looked up and smiled, "Good morning Lil' Billy, I'll let the boss know you're here," she said as she left the desk. Meanwhile, Lil' Billy stood there wondering how she even knew his name since he had never been to this office.

Rosa wasn't gone long. "Follow me," she said when she returned.

Rosa led Lil' Billy down the hall to Sincere's office. After opening the door, Rosa stepped to the side so Lil' Billy could walk in, then she left closing the door behind her.

The first person Lil' Billy saw was Pedro who was seated in front of the desk. *He must be the plug*, Lil' Billy thought as Pedro stood up to shake his hand. Lil' Billy noticed that Pedro's demeanor was a whole lot friendlier than it had been when they had crossed paths at Sincere's house.

Lil' Billy turned to say something to Sincere whose chair behind the desk was facing the window. Before Lil' Billy could get the words out, the chair spun around revealing that it was occupied by Sandy.

"Hi Lil' Billy," Sandy began, "I'm really glad that you kept your appointment."

"Where's Sincere?" Lil' Billy asked, visibly unsettled

by Sandy's presence.

"He couldn't make it, he had business to tend to out of town."

"So he sent you to meet with me?"

"I'm sitting here ain't I?"

Lil' Billy didn't know what was going on, but he knew enough about Sincere to know he wouldn't send Sandy in his place for a meeting as important as this one.

I'm getting the fuck outta here! Lil' Billy thought and stood up to leave, but Pedro grabbed his arm and shook his head in a manner that conveyed the message to Lil' Billy that it would be in his best interest to sit back down.

"Lil' Billy, don't be alarmed," Sandy stated calmly. "The deal you discussed with Sincere is still a go, that's why Pedro is here."

"I would be more comfortable closing this deal when Sincere got back," Lil' Billy countered, still not at ease.

Sandy looked at Pedro, who shrugged. Lil' Billy was making things harder than Sandy could afford them to be, so she took a more aggressive stance, "Okay look, you came here to make a deal and that's what's going to happen," she said, "Sincere won't be back anytime soon and this meeting isn't about to be rescheduled. Now the boat docks in Miami twice a year –."

"Hold up a minute!" Lil' Billy interrupted, "I don't know if you realize it or not, but I'm not the same lil' boy who came to you when he needed a ounce. I'm a grown ass man and I make my own decisions. Now like I said before, no Sincere, no deal." Lil' Billy stood up to leave.

"Lil' Billy…please don't walk out that door," Sandy pleaded. What Lil' Billy didn't know and what Sandy couldn't tell him was that if he walked out of that office, both him and Sandy would be dead by nightfall.

Sandy couldn't communicate with Lil' Billy verbally, but while he stood there staring at her, she did all she could through the look in her eyes to convey the message to him that the choice he was faced with had nothing to do with money and drugs, it was about life and death.

───────────

Lucky was always one to keep a promise, so when he promised to kill everybody involved in Cash's murder, that was exactly what he meant.

After disposing of Fat Chad, Lucky turned his focus to giving Peaches what her hand called for.

When Lucky told Lil' Billy that Peaches was the one behind all the drama, Lil' Billy just shook his head and said, "The bitch live in Timber Top." Lil' Billy also informed Lucky that Molly was fucking Peaches and then said nothing else concerning the matter.

Lucky breathed a sigh of relief because he knew the history Lil' Billy had with Peaches and even though on the surface it seemed like Lil' Billy had moved on, nobody knows for sure what lurks in the dark corners of another man's heart. The last thing Lucky wanted was to fall out with Lil' Billy about killing Peaches, but since this wasn't going to be an issue, Lucky moved full speed ahead with his plan.

The first step involved Molly making a way for Lucky to get inside Peaches' house. Lucky suggested to Molly that the next time she hooked up with Peaches, that she find a way to make a copy of Peaches' door key. In accordance with being the thoroughbred that she was, Molly didn't ask Lucky any questions, she just immediately went about fulfilling the task that Lucky had given her.

Once Lucky got the door key from Molly, he headed to Timber Top and waited on Peaches to leave, so he could enter the house and wait on her to come back.

It was around ten in the morning when Lucky saw Peaches leave her house and as soon as her BMW truck was out of sight, he got out of the car and casually walked up to her front door.

Lucky quickly entered the house, quietly shut the door behind him, then pulled out his .45 that was equipped with a beam and silencer.

Lucky was almost sure that Peaches had been home alone, but just in case she wasn't he was prepared to kill whoever else might be in the house.

Lucky quietly tip-toed around the house, searching every room. Once he was sure he was there alone, he went back to the living room and waited on Peaches to return.

Meanwhile, Peaches was a nervous wreck as she drove to Summit Mall. Too much was happening at once and Peaches' gut instinct was telling her that she needed to get out of town fast.

The day before Peaches had just found out about Fat Chad's murder, which had thrown her completely for a loop. Then when she tried to call Molly, hoping to get some comfort in her time of need, Molly's phone was cut off, which Peaches thought was strange to say the least.

To top it off, Peaches had just received a phone call that morning from her oldest sister Sonya informing her that, not only was Big Mike out of the joint, but he was somewhere with their mother Gloria.

After going online to the prison website and confirming that Big Mike had been released, Peaches got dressed and headed to Summit Mall to buy some luggage.

Peaches never thought that Big Mike would be strong enough to go at Fat Chad himself, but she also remembered how unstable Big Mike sounded in his letters. Besides that she found it to be too much of a coincidence that Big Mike gets out of jail then Fat Chad turns up dead.

Peaches had family out of town, but she figured it would be in her best interest not to go to them because they would more than likely contact Gloria and if Peaches didn't know anything else, she knew she couldn't trust her mother.

Peaches concluded that she needed to be in the company of someone who was strong enough to protect her from whatever danger she may or may not be in and that someone was Premo.

Premo had told Peaches on several occasions that whenever she got tired of being a big fish in a small pond, she could come to New York City and he would make her the queen of his kingdom. Peaches didn't know if Premo was just selling her dreams in order to hit the pussy, but she was sure about to find out.

After buying some cheap luggage, Peaches headed back home. She figured she could pack her clothes, grab the $100,000 she had put up, and be on her way to New York City within an hour.

When Lucky heard Peaches' truck pull up he peeked out the window to make sure it was her. Once Lucky, saw Peaches get out of her truck, his adrenaline started pumping like it always did when he knew he was about to take a life.

Lucky had to make a quick decision; whether to wait behind the front door or wait for Peaches in her bedroom. Lucky knew people tend to be more alert when they first enter a house so he decided it would be more feasible to wait in the bedroom, that way Peaches would be all the way in the house, less guarded, and taken completely by surprise when Lucky appeared.

While Lucky took up his position in her bedroom, Peaches grabbed the luggage out of the backseat of her truck and walked to the front door of her condo.

Peaches stuck the key in the lock and turned the door knob.

THE END

Coming Soon!

The Epic Conclusion to The Plug Trilogy

The Plug 3 (Karma) by Cellini

Upcoming books from Stand Up Media, LLC:

Die Hard (Life of a Jacka) by Cellini

Pretty Bosses by Cellini

The Invisible Chess Match, Vol. II (From a Pawn to a King) by Cellini

Please Visit us at Standupmedia.net

ORDER FORM

Order your copy of The Plug, The Plug 2: The Power of Choice, or both books from Stand Up Media, LLC for the following prices.

Also note that we only take payment in the form of United States Postal Service Money Orders or Credit Cards (Visa or Mastercard). Please do not send personal checks or cash. We will process your order within 5 days of receiving the order form.

_____The Plug by Cellini $14.99

_____The Plug 2: The Power of Choice   = $14.99

_____The Plug & The Plug 2: The Power of Choice $25.00

_____ Total – Shipping & Handling included

If paying with Credit Card please provide the following:

Card Number _____ Expiration Date _____

3 Digit Code on back _____

Billing Address Zip Code _____

Name: _____

Address: _____

City/State/Zip Code:_____

Mail To: Stand Up Media, LLC
            P.O. Box 2385
            Akron, Ohio 44301

Made in the USA
Columbia, SC
25 July 2021